About The Author

Russell Mardell is a playwright, scriptwriter and filmmaker based in the South West of England. He is the author of four novels and a collection of short stories.

www.russellmardell.co.uk

D0452334

COLD CALLING

Russell Mardell

For Mum

Because you asked me to try and write something a little bit nicer.
Here you go. Best I could do.

x

I'm a bowl of bruised fruit
Inside a chapel of shiny apples
Tear up the photograph!
'Cause it's a bright blue sky.

Chapel Song, Augustines

The First Call

RAY

'I've never understood chess,' I told him, before stopping abruptly.

When I'd started speaking I had known the point I was trying to make, I'd got the analogy square in my mind and felt pleased with myself about it, yet somehow, after those first four words, I had completely forgotten what it was.

It just went.

'I mean…'

What the hell did I mean? I had no idea.

It had sounded good, somewhere at the back of my mind. I ploughed on anyway. I decided that if I kept on talking then perhaps I wouldn't have to explain myself. My counsellor, Dr Phillip, was used to this behaviour and he never knowingly tried to stop me from making a fool of myself. Idiot or sage, he got paid regardless. Which certainly makes him more intelligent than I am.

'I mean…well…you see…there was a point when I was a kid when I had convinced myself that I got it, chess, but I never really did, I don't think. I feel I should have learned to play it by now. I'm thirty and I never learned to play chess. I learned to drive before I learned to play chess. It never seemed to matter back then, but it sort of does these days. It's like a basic failing. If I can't get the basics right, then what hope have I got for love, right?'

He shrugged at me, and I prattled on, trying to find the start of my point instead of the fumbled conclusion.

'Because that's where you keep leading me, Doc, that's what you keep dangling in front of me, isn't it? Love. This universal need, this great unfathomable mystery that we all have to try and work out. Well, if love is the meaning of life, if that's the great answer that we are all searching for, then I'm screwed, aren't I? I can't even play chess.'

He leaned forward to speak, but I blundered all over his efforts.

'And the Rubik's Cube, that was a bloody mystery to me as well. My school friends all got it, did it, but not me though. I never worked it out. So that's why I've messed up my relationships, isn't it? That's the real reason.'

'Because you can't do the Rubik's Cube?' he asked, eyes narrowed, forehead creased. 'Or play chess?'

'Not that exactly, but what those two things represent, right?'

'What do they represent?'

'You're the professional here, you tell me.'

'You're the one in therapy, Ray. You should tell me.' Dr Phillip sat back, nestled into his comfy chair, his fingers steepled under his neat little beard and just stared at me in that way that he always did. *Carry on*, that look said, *this is your time, Ray. Carry on. Carry on making a complete twat of yourself.*

So I did.

'You're a therapist, so you must think it's all about love, right? You do, don't you? Love is the answer. Love is the answer to everything, the great world cure-all?'

Dr Phillip shrugged and nodded me on again.

'It's not, though, Doc. It's a need. I will give you that. It's a need, yeah, but it's not an answer. Yet even though it is a need, it isn't a universal need, so how can it actually be anything other than selfish? And if it's selfish, then how can it actually be a need? It's a desire really, isn't it? Like a nice car, or a conservatory. Some people think they need it and some live a whole life without it and never think they are missing anything. It's a desire. It's a drug. Some people use it, some abuse it and some just let it pass them by.'

'And some let it consume them and kill them?'

'Quite.'

He was talking about me, of course, the sly little bugger, but I didn't pick up on it at the time. In the months since Danny had convinced me to start seeing him, everything Dr Phillip said or implied or made me think about always came back to my Katie and me in the end. He would turn everything around to that somehow, as if what had happened between us defined my very existence. He had no idea, and I was paying a hefty chunk of change for the privilege of experiencing his ignorance. One of us was in the wrong job. I should have stopped going after the first few weeks, but I've never been that decisive, I've never been that proactive. That was pretty much the only thing he got right about me.

'Do you need it, Ray, this drug?'

'I need faith,' I told him, getting my thoughts back on track.

'Religion?'

'No. Faith in people. I need to invest in something with answers. My perpetual confusion is the only thing that really makes sense any more.'

'You have all the answers. We all do. Deep down.' His fingers moved off his chin and then crossed together in his lap, and still he stared at me with that same expression, his compact facial fuzz twitching slightly as he briefly considered a smile. 'Does that surprise you?'

'If that's the case, what am I doing paying you an hourly rate?'

'I'm a conduit, maybe. A sounding board. I'm what you need me to be to enable you to find your own answers.'

'You religious?' He looked the sort – neat beard, knitwear and sturdy shoes.

'I believe in people.'

'That always sounded like a decent concept.'

'Try it. You might be surprised.'

'People break things, Doc.'

'Sometimes.'

'It's what we do best.'

'What have you broken recently, Ray?'

I had thought at the time that he was referring to Anya Belmont and the phone call we'd had, because he had been going on about that just before the wonderful chess analogy came and went. As it was, he was actually talking about my Katie. I should have realised. Of course he was talking about Katie, because he always was talking about Katie – everything was about her, and me, and what happened, so why should then have been any different? The man was fixated on it, on us, my Katie and me. Maybe he had slept with her as well. She always did like a beard.

'Anya, you mean? You're talking about the phone call?' I asked, grabbing the wrong end of the metaphorical rope he was dangling in front of me, just so I could hang myself all over again. He shrugged, half-smiled, and nodded me on. 'It was just a phone call, just a conversation. It doesn't really mean anything.'

'Then why did you tell me about it?'

He had me there.

Anya Belmont came into my life as just another name on a long list of strangers in a database at work. She was merely another cherished customer (or friend, if I'm following the diatribe Mr Evans likes to lay down) of Babbidge Insurance in north London. Her husband had a policy with Babbidge, and was due a courtesy call, a little "how-the-hell-are-you?" from the firm that likes to say, 'Your family is our family!' Obviously once we had made them feel special, broken down their defences with our charm and disarming sense of humour, we were then to convince them that their policy was no good and that they needed a new one. Break them with charm, bombard them with words, baffle them with figures, or if all else fails, guilt usually managed to tilt the scales. That was my job. Us phone assassins at Babbidge aren't so far removed from those charity muggers you see in the high street with their clipboards and their earnest charitable concerns, cornering people with their youthful effervescence; five minutes of your time turning into half an hour's verbal barrage before relieving you of your bank details and a soul of repressed guilt you never knew you had. That was really what we were, too – but without the noble motives, though where those chuggers tend to have to look young and lithe to trap you, those of us behind the phones at Babbidge could get away with being as ugly as sin and as miserable as a bar room prophet catching sight of the sun. Which was just as well for Pat Bollard. It's a terrible job, there's no glossing over that particular weighty life turd, but rather ironically, considering my natural antipathy towards the human race, I found I was actually rather good at it. 'The coldest cold caller in north London,' Danny dubbed me. The little ginger tosspot.

Anya had answered my phone call without actually answering. I could hear her breathing, and that's all we ever really needed. Just one sign of life and we jump on in there with our diatribe: 'Good afternoon, my name is Ray English and I'm calling from Babbidge Insurance. I wonder if I could have a moment of your time?'

'Whatever,' she replied.

'Mrs Belmont? How are you this afternoon?'

'Indifferent.'

I found myself laughing at that. You get so used to people's responses when you make these calls, that when you get a new one it's hard not to admire it. There are usually only ever two sorts of responses we get from people – the hanger-uppers (or the Triple-Nos, as we call them, as invariably they never hang up straight away, but first blast you with their excuses and justifications: not convenient, having tea, just leaving the house. We worked out once that on average their reasoning is repeated three times before they have the courage to hang up), and the other sort is the complete opposite: those that roll over for you immediately, those without the fortitude to blast through the cheery barrage of guff and just let you hammer them with your patter. They may not be taking it all in, they may well just be waiting for enough of a gap to jump, but that's not really a problem for us; we still get paid whether they bite or not. Our role is essentially tentative foreplay for another person's pleasure. Looking at it any other way would be to suggest that I cared. Three years into that job, and that sure as heck never happened.

It was fair to say that Anya Belmont had me at her indifference.

'Well, yes, Mrs Belmont, tell me about it!' I replied through a cheery voice and a laugh that I actually meant.

'Really?'

'Sure, why not?'

'You make a living either way, I suppose?' she asked.

'If you want to call it a living.'

'Hard to care enough to call it anything, Ray. What is it you're selling?'

'Nothing, no, nothing at all,' I lied. 'This is merely a courtesy call to make sure Mr Belmont and yourself are happy with everything.'

'Not so much. Life is shit.'

'Well, I actually—'

'Yes, I know, it wasn't really a general chitchat. You just want me to fall for your friendly patter and open my arms to whatever it is you're trying to push. I, for my part, have been brought up well enough not to hang up on people. So here is the impasse, Ray. Who will yield first?'

'I'm really not trying to sell you anything, Mrs Belmont.'

'Of course you are.'

'Honestly, I'm not.'

'So you really are just phoning to see how I am?'

'I have to…it's—'

'Your job? Well, tell me, Ray, what on earth are you hiding from in life to make this your job? Was this always the dream, or did you just fall away at some point? I do hope she was worth it.'

She had me tagged good and proper. To Anya Belmont I was an open book with big print and pictures, and she was idly thumbing through my story with all the disinterest of a mother reading a fairytale to their child for the thousandth time.

'That's a bit presumptuous, isn't it?' I asked with a tinge of fake hurt.

'Am I wrong?'

'No.'

'Look at us then, presumptuous and predictable. Quite the double act.'

'Sorry, Mrs Belmont, I was labouring under the impression I was unique.'

'Lucky me.' She chased the words with a little laugh, and it sounded good. You don't hear laughter much in this job – not genuine laughter, anyway. In office jobs you hold on to laughter as tightly as you do the comfiest chair. Though I must have been holding on too tightly because I couldn't think of what else to say from that point. Here was something new: Anya Belmont wasn't a Triple-No, nor was she likely to roll over anytime soon. She, rather incongruously as it seemed to me, actually wanted to have a conversation. 'Not thinking of hanging up on me are you, Ray?'

'Of course not, Mrs Belmont.'

'You've been brought up the right way too then, that's good to know. We have something in common. Look at that. From such sturdy foundations do worlds collide.'

Dr Phillip was still staring at me. I had forgotten what he had asked me. Had we been talking about Anya or Katie? Had he asked me a question?

'Yes?' I found myself saying to him, hoping that was some sort of answer.

'You still miss Bertie?'

I wanted to pull him up on that. No one called my granddad Bertie except me. It was our little thing he always told me, and I didn't like the doc jumping on that. Plus Bertie would have given him small change for being so familiar, and I felt I should make that known. I didn't though. Of course I didn't.

'Yeah. Course I do.'

'But you still go to the nursing home?'

I gave him an affirmative in a half-hearted shrug.

'Do you miss your parents, Ray?'

'They are only in Spain. Not exactly the other side of the world.'

'See them much?'

'No.'

Dr Phillip gave me another smile, another nod and then gently brought his slightly effeminate hands together. 'That's us for today. To be continued, I think. I want you to tell me about this mystery lady.'

'She's not mysterious. Her name is Anya. She's just a voice on the phone. End of story.'

'Okay. Did you bring the list of things I asked you to jot down?'

I had forgotten about that. That stupid bloody list. Pointless. He had asked me at our last session to list five reasons why I had loved Katie. He used the past tense too. I had done it, begrudgingly, just to shut him up, but still saw no reason for it. I had no idea why I loved her, and told him that such things shouldn't be understood. I said that the moment you realise why you love someone then the magic goes, and when the magic goes you are solely reliant on nothing more than your personalities, and that is far too dangerous in a relationship. I agreed to compromise and write a list of five things I liked about her instead. I took the list out of my coat pocket, along with my money and placed both on the table between us, tucked underneath the edge of the box of tissues that always seemed to be there.

'Does anyone ever use them?' I asked him.

'The tissues? Yes, sometimes, of course they do.' Those eyes were on me again, probing and searching. 'Did you cry when Katie left you?'

'No.' I was up and at the door before I realised he was following me out.

'Perhaps it's about time you did, Ray.'

'Make me a better person, would it?'

'It's part of the process of letting go.'

'Thanks, Doc.'

One weak handshake later and I turned out into the corridor that fed from his office, and began the all-too-familiar walk along the thick, horridly bland carpet, towards the staircase at the end, closed doors and faceless whispering on either side of me. Much to my surprise, Dr Phillip was matching me step for step.

'I say this as your friend, not as your counsellor,' he started, ushering the words in on a little cough. 'You and Katie, there's no plaster you can put on that, you know? You have to move past it. It's been five years.'

'I'm working on it.'

'She's not coming back, Ray.' He surely didn't mean the harsh snap in the words as he said them, but I replied in kind nonetheless.

'You think I don't know that?'

'Yes. I really think you don't.'

I moved out onto the stairwell, and he finally hung back, leaning against the large doorframe like the world's least intimidating bouncer, blocking entry to the world's worst party.

'You know something, Doc? You said to me weeks ago that I was grieving. Because of Katie. Do you remember?'

'You are, Ray. But I don't think it's for her any more. I think you are grieving for the person you used to be.'

'Nice guy, was he?'

'I don't know. Was he, Ray?'

Was I?

My mother always said I was such a happy baby; this fat little thing with a mop of dark hair, she said that I used to sit and smile at everyone all day long. She'd stick me in my high chair and put me in front of the window of our living room, and I would just smile and laugh and wave at all the people that walked past the house. I'd have been happy doing that all day long, she always said. I have to take her word for that. Can't see it myself. But even if what she says is true, it's not a state of being I'm hankering after. Besides, you smile or laugh or wave at people these days, you're liable to get a punch in the face. I don't want to be that sort of happy any more. That would be a different sort of unbearable. But if that was one extreme, and I'm now living the other, then surely finding a happy medium can't be so difficult?

I know I can be an intolerable little shit these days. Cynicism and self-indulgence aren't the most glorious of character traits, but I'm trying, really I am. I just can't get past it. I can't get past her. I can't get past losing that feeling in my gut, that little flutter of the heart at the beauty of the mundane, the absolute certainty of every emotion, the simple, unavoidable knowledge that, yeah, me and her, we were just so right. There were fumbles and snogs and shags before her, and there have been others since her, each more watered down and unmemorable as the last, yet nothing fitted together before her, and nothing fitted together after her. With Katie, everything snapped into place, all those little pieces of a life that makes it worth living; they all aligned with us and created something that was right. It was just so damn *right*. Inevitable. Meant to be. Why can't she see that?

'Seatbelts, Ray. Seatbelts,' Bertie once said to me. 'Relationships are like seatbelts. Some are too tight, some are too loose, and some just get jammed. Sometimes you try and tie the seatbelt into a knot, desperate to make it have any effect, but it never does. You're looking for the perfect fit: not too tight, not too loose, something that holds you safely in place in case you crash. Them…they are the keepers.'

I asked how come then, when Katie and I crashed, I ended up so battered and bruised? He merely raised an eyebrow that seemed to suggest I knew the answer.

But he was wrong. Even Bertie was wrong about that. He had to be.

I'd never looked for 'the one'; never considered marriage, or even living together (admittedly, I think Tara Hart and I might have got married on the school playing field when we were nine, but I don't think that counts), but with Katie it was all just obvious. We were young, but still older than my parents were when they got together – older even than Mum was when she had me – and at a time when my mates were all carefree and single and going out with different people at a rate of what seemed to be every week, I was in perfect contentment with Katie. I certainly never felt I was missing anything.

'There's no rule book that tells you when you have to meet the right person,' Bertie once told me. 'They come along when they come along – it's just down to you to see it, and if you do see it, not to screw it up. See it, don't screw it up. That's the only two rules.'

He was the first person I told. He always seemed to have all the answers. I know he would be pissed at me for still being this way after five years. He would say all the right things, tell me everything I probably already knew, and just for the time we were together, he would make things better. But he would never be able to make the feeling go away.

That was solely down to me: the fat, laughing baby; the cynical, screwed-up gobshite.

And whoever the bloke was in between the two of them.

THINGS I LIKE ABOUT KATIE FENSHAW

1) Her eyes, obviously. Gorgeous eyes. Big and expressive. She also does this thing with them, a little flutter, and somehow she seems able to make them twinkle. She claims she has no idea that she's doing it, which makes it even lovelier.
2) She wears good shoes. Vital in any person, and certainly in a girlfriend. What shoes a person wears tells you everything you ever need to know about them. It was the shoe thing that got us together in a way. I inadvertently trod on her foot in our common room and then noticed we were both wearing grey Converse trainers. I made some stupid little comment about that and we got chatting.
3) Even more important than the shoes, Katie has perfect taste in music. I remember seeing her bedroom at her parents' house for the first time; the walls were covered floor to ceiling in posters – Bobbie Gentry,

Beth Orton, Aretha Franklin, Carole King and, rather peculiarly, Phil Spector. (This was her mother's fault – Katie adored Ronnie Spector, and her mother had misheard her and had cut out and laminated a full-page photo of Phil – the big hair years too – she had found in a magazine. Katie didn't have the heart to tell her she'd got it wrong and so put it on the wall.)

4)   She loves her mother.

5)   When I introduced her to Edward Hopper's art she got it straight away, totally understood why it was perfect.

6)   She rarely breaks wind in public and on the few occasions I have heard her, it was like a little mouse squeak and was almost tuneful.

7)   That thing we spoke about a couple of weeks ago. I'm not going to write that down here, and I don't think you would expect me to. But, that thing.

DANNY

The first year after Kate gave him the flick, Ray was intolerable to be around. He hadn't got to the morose stage in that first year – he's been perfecting that these last four since we've been living in London. (I don't think the two things are related.) No, that first year whilst we were still in Southport, he was worse; he was at the delusional, blind, pig-headed, refusing to accept it stage. He still believed he would woo her back. That she would see the huge error of her ways and knock on his door and then he would be there with open arms ready to whisk her up and carry on like nothing had ever happened. Yet it had happened. Another man had happened. Maybe a few men had happened, if Vera's venomous tittle-tattle could be trusted. Though of course Ray said he didn't care, it didn't matter, none of it mattered – but it did and it would and there was no getting away from that. It was an intense relief to all of us that cared about the little sod when he finally progressed to putting her on street corners rather than a pedestal.

By the time we both moved down to live the big city dream, he had managed to turn her into the devil incarnate. It was an act, of course, but those months of hatred and loathing were a blessing for the rest of us. Kate was barely mentioned, no longer the centre of every thought or the full stop to every anecdote. Ray's crippling hatred and fury gave us all a lot of peace and quiet.

Those months were good for us. We bummed around the fringes of north London, moving between overpriced crummy bedsits so awful even the rats shunned them, and overpriced shared houses, occupying space with the weird, the scary and the unhygienic, all of us financially violated by shit-bag landlords trying to build castles on desperation. But back then none of it seemed to matter, because we were out and about; drinking away money we didn't have but that always seemed to be there, turning up to parties we hadn't been invited to and then spending nights with women who mattered as little to you as you did to them. We saw people and went places and did things, as ravenous for that big city dream as any young kid let out of their suffocating small-town home.

Then the screw tightened. That good old screw of reality. And when it screws down in London, it takes a hell of a lot of loosening. The money we came down with had gone and the crap jobs we had stumbled between just weren't cutting it. We both bought ties and pimped embellished CVs to anyone and everyone, it didn't matter what and it didn't matter where. It just mattered that we didn't have to go back home to Southport. Our tails were up and we didn't want them between our legs anytime soon. Ray took the best-paid job he could get away with at a place called Babbidge Insurance, which was every bit as dreary as it sounds, and I began what would become a revolving door of bar work. Not what my mother had in mind when I started my psychology degree, I would imagine. Though through that first bar job I did manage to luck out on a flat for us. A friend of a regular knew a guy who knew someone else, who might know another, and thus the mythic splendour and unobtainable majesty of a two-bedroom maisonette flat on Muswell Hill Broadway found its way down the grapevine towards us. The flat should, in all honesty, have been condemned but we bit their hands off. We could just about afford it.

I can't remember when Ray's attitude changed again, when Kate stopped being the tramp and found herself becoming a picture of perfect beauty daubed in a rosy tint. Was it time, was it distance, or was it just because Ray would never have had the energy to be bothered keeping a wilful delusion going for long? Who knows? But sometime after we first moved into the flat on the Broadway, I heard Kate Fenshaw's name for the first time in months. Right about the same time Ray's life stalled again and I knew I didn't have it in me to help him jumpstart it any more. I let him have the misery he seemed so intent to feed off.

Now here we are, three years in Muswell Hill, four in London, five since Kate binned him off, and nearly twenty-five since Ray and I first became friends and I think we are stuck with each other. I'm not sure it is through free will and choice any more, him and me – I don't like him as much as I did, sometimes I don't like him at all, and I'm sure the feeling is mutual. But I do love him. He used to be a brother. Now he's more a wife. Our old friendship feels like a long marriage, and as with a lot of long marriages neither of us is getting much out of it any more.

'Hello, dear,' he called out, strolling in through the front door of the flat.

'All right, love?'

I was sat in the kitchen, the post scattered on the table next to me, along with the plate of mouldy toast neither of us was prepared to admit was ours (it was his), and I was turning an envelope over in my hands. Inside the envelope was the start of a conversation I was dreading having to have with him.

'If that's another bill I've moved the overflow to the drawer underneath the TV.'

'We've been invited to a wedding,' I said nonchalantly, as he set about filling the kettle and scraping something unidentifiable from a spoon. 'Isn't that nice?'

'Thrilling. Which poor unfortunate is it this time? Do we like them?'

'It's Tim.'

'Who?'

'Tim and Tamara.'

'Have you just made that up?'

'Tim from college?'

Ray's reaction had been much the same as mine had been when I first saw the invite. It had taken a good ten minutes before I twigged who Tim was, though, to be fair, it had taken two years at college to do the same. Tim was a decent guy, too decent to ever have been good friends with. Tim had been the swotty kid who envied the cool kids, who was always destined to become the rich man the penniless cool men all wished they were. He had also been Broken English's first, and I'm ashamed to say, only groupie. Our college band was no great shakes and our ability to ponce around on stage may have far outweighed our songwriting abilities, but it's a sad state of affairs when a gawky-looking pillock is more of a constant at your gigs than your drummer.

'He wants us to play at the wedding,' I said.

'Play what?' Ray replied.

'Broken English, you dickhead, what do you think? Our one and only fan wants the band to get together again and play at his wedding.'

Ray snorted his disdain and continued making his cup of tea.

'You remember the band, don't you, Ray? The little four-piece you had the humility to name after yourself during the difficult God complex stage of your frontman development?'

'It was a good name.'

'We had a good name.'

'How far do you think we would have got with a name like Climax?'

'Guess we will never find out.'

'Anyway, it's pointless, no way will he get Clive to do it.'

'But you would? If I could get Clive and Dave to agree?'

'Why would I?'

'Why wouldn't you?'

'What is this, the third wedding invite in this past year? We never went to any of the others, why this one?'

'You never went to any of the others. I did. But this is about the band, man – wouldn't it be cool to get the band together for one last dust-off? I miss it, don't you?'

'Shit, no.' Ray had turned to me and now seemed to be scrutinising the envelope, working something over in his mind. 'Hang on, that's just one envelope. Where's my invite?'

'Oh, yeah, this is…there's just this…just the one invite.'

'We're on the same invite?'

'Yeah.'

'Like a couple?'

'Yeah, seems so, love.'

Ray spun away in disgust. 'Good God, what have we become?'

'Also, it's…erm…it's back home. The do. The wedding.' There was a loud clunk and then a smash as Ray's mug slipped out of his hand, struck the edge of the sink and then shattered. 'But so what, right? Doesn't mean she will be there. Why do you care anyway, right? The band, Ray, wouldn't it be fun? Your shrink recommends fun, doesn't he?'

'Counsellor!' he snapped back at me. 'I'm seeing a counsellor, I'm not seeing a shrink! I don't need a shrink!'

'Either way, he's not doing you much good is he? Only thing going to sort you out is a mental enema.'

'And there speaks the psychology student. Good to see that year before you flunked wasn't wasted.'

'It wasn't.'

'You work in a pub, Danny.'

'I'm resting.'

'Gonna be a hell of a culture shock when you wake up.'

'C'mon, Ray – the band, the four of us again, what do you reckon?'

'I reckon Tom can enter marital life slow-dancing to third-rate tunes from a second-rate mobile disco like everyone else.'

'Tim.'

'Him too.'

'Tim says there's liable to be a talent scout there. Tamara's cousin. Bit of a big shot, he reckons. Gotta be worth a go, right?'

'You do it. You can sing.' Ray gathered up the broken bits of his mug and dumped them in the bin. 'Give them full Hucknall.'

'You know Clive will never allow himself to be Hucknalled*, Ray.'

'Sod Clive.' Discarding the idea of a cuppa in favour of a dramatic exit, he yanked his tie loose and flounced from the kitchen.

'One of your women called again.'

'Don't call them that.'

'Okay, one of the old loves in the nursing home called. Again. Love. A Mabel or a Maureen, or something. Wondering why you hadn't been in.'

'I was in yesterday.'

Ray's dramatic flounce had been ruined and now he hung in the doorway of the kitchen, moving from foot to foot, looking like he needed to pee.

'It's a big place, you know? Our old hometown.'

He didn't seem to hear me. For a moment he just stared at the wall above my head, lost in thought. 'You know, I spoke to this woman at work today, on the phone, and she…'

'She what?'

He looked blank, suddenly confused by his own words. A quick shrug and then he was off again, recommencing the flounce.

'Doesn't matter. Doesn't mean anything.'

*Hucknalled

The embarrassing of a music snob.

The hipster was Hucknalled by the quality of the singer's voice.

A dislike of a collective based on a hatred of an individual.

He accepted his refusal to like them was because he was Hucknalled.

Synonyms: *Bonoed, Chris-Martined*.

Look, I like Mick Hucknall's voice, okay? I will fight you, if not to death, then certainly to extreme tiredness, to defend that. It may be the ginger thing; some part of me has no doubt developed a light bias, as it tends to do towards my redheaded brothers, but the man also has a hell of a set of pipes on him. It can't be denied. Sure, the achingly trendy twats who base their music collection on the results of the cool barometer in some self-styled this-is-what-to-like rag will never admit it. But bollocks to them. I like what I like and I like soul, and Mick's got a great soul voice. No Sam Cooke, of course, but then no one is. Except for Sam Cooke. Trend killed music. It really did. Trend and music snobs. We were never trendy, never successful either; we sang soul and blues covers – despite the other three all being shoe-gazing, *NME*-reading indie kids – and looked like we had just fallen out of the student debating society, but we held on to our principals. We were trend tramps and that suited us fine.

Except for Clive, of course. Clive and his correct shoes, his correct record collection, and his correct haircut. When we started at college there were still a few fumes left over from the fag end of Britpop, even though the Cool Britannia bubble had long since been pricked by just too many pricks, and at that time (and I have no reason to doubt, still) Clive, like so many other men, was living by the Paul Weller cut-and-paste image code. If you didn't have the right look, the right clothes, and certainly the right sort of hair, you were shunned. Particularly if, as Clive so succinctly put it, 'you like a singer with a head that looks like it should be on the end of a child's pencil'. I imagine it was not too dissimilar an attitude in the Nazi Party.

I'm an okay singer and before Ray joined us, there was talk about me fronting the band, but it was never likely to happen. Not with our lineup. Not with Clive. Not with his bigotry and bullshit. I think the world has moved past its ginger bigotry nowadays, at least in music, but back then, when he asked me to name three good ginger singers, I was struggling. (Axl Rose, Art Garfunkel and Mick were all I could come up with.) Maybe if I had mentioned Axl instead of Mick, we may never have had this longstanding battle. Maybe he would have just accepted it and shut up. Who knows? But that argument lasted so long, longer than the band did, and neither of us was ever going to back down. I doubted that time would have mellowed Clive's prejudice. And certainly not his record collection.

EVA

Anya had dragged me out of my writer pit and forced me to join her at her coffee shop in town for our weekly caffeine and cake catch-up, a stupid little ritual she makes me indulge in when I'm between books. She's always had a bee in her bonnet about getting me out of the house in my downtime, convinced as she is that I'm liable to turn ever so slightly vampiric if I don't get aired now and again. The conversation usually goes the same way every time – she pisses and moans about Len, I piss and moan about my latest novel and then we both talk about people we haven't seen in ages and tell each other what a shame that is, without ever acknowledging the glaring truth that the reason we haven't seen them is because we don't like them.

Anya's coffee shop is, by and large, an extension of what my dearest friend has become – achingly bohemian. Not that it's a bad thing, but I could certainly never pull off the billowing skirts, tatty vests and those ghastly beads in my hair, and no one alive could get me into flip-flops. Feet should be kept safe and securely hidden at all times. Like plutonium. But all that looked good on Anya, and she wears it well and it's certainly an improvement on the dress suits and heels that her job in the city used to require of her. She was never cut out for that sort of life.

The coffee house seems to have been around since day dot, and wears its history proud – all Tudor beams, rickety stairs and wonky walls – it's the sort of place all the arty types in Salisbury gravitate to and is laid-back and welcoming, with a warm heart, just like my mate, and if your coffee shop has a warm heart you can forgive a lot of things. Except their unisex toilet; I haven't ever been able to forgive that.

'Shakespeare came here once,' Anya told me the first time I visited, just after she had taken it over, pointing out a sign proudly proclaiming the fact above our heads. 'And Pepys. He stopped in once too. Lot of history in this building.'

I told her it was a pointless thing to say after so many years. 'Unless they have whittled their signature into the tables, I really don't see the point. How does this make the coffee shop a better coffee shop?'

'It's culturally inspiring. Having such great writers pass through here should serve as inspiration to you at least. I think if I were a writer this place would empower me and make me want to create.'

'Not with a unisex toilet.'

It was a grotty, winter's end morning and the coffee shop was packed. We were up on the top floor at our usual table, looking out over Salisbury's rain-drizzled high street, and had already got through two mugs of coffee and a plate of nutty, ethically sourced something-or-other, whilst verbally tearing Mary Conroy's pitiful life a new one. We'd been at it for at least an hour and we still weren't done with her. Mary bloody Conroy, honestly, what a smug bitch.

Anya was on a roll: 'Seriously, what happened to her? Mary was such a rebel at school. She was such a laugh. She was so cool. We all wanted to be like Mary. Well, I did. Started reading Bukowski because of her, and Vonnegut. I took my first drink of alcohol with Mary, had the first spliff. We even got arrested for flyposting for that punk band she was in. The amount of trouble I got into with her, she was crazy. But she was intelligent too. She was clued up. Wasn't she the one who twatted Mr Maple with the chalkboard rubber?'

'No, she was the one who stuck it down her granny flannels to see if she could dye her pubic hair.'

'Oh, yeah. That's right.'

'I was the one who lobbed the rubber at Maple.'

Anya laughed and slapped me on the arm. 'Course you were, darling. Now I remember. Well thank God you haven't changed at least. You see that thing she posted on Facebook last week?'

'The hundreds of identical photos of her cut-and-paste kid, or the one of the turd?'

'Oh, the turd, please, what else?'

Turd-gate. It had become quite the conversation piece between the few of us in our social group on Facebook that hadn't succumbed to the sort of inane, beige-tinted drivel Mary bloody Conroy had devoted her life to spouting. She had become one of those people so empty at their core that they let all their originality dribble out of them the moment they drop a new life into the world, every action captured in a parade of endlessly tedious photos, every word tinged in faux-baby gobbledygook. Our group have lost a few interesting, once original, sometimes ferocious women to motherhood over the years, but Mary bloody Conroy is by far the worst. Why she is even a friend of ours, neither of us could say. (Anya claims I accepted her repeated friend requests first and that she felt it only right to join me for moral support, the bloody liar.) A few years back, Alice Wilson cross-invited as many of us from our year as she could find, to some ghastly 80s-themed school reunion – roller-skates, legwarmers, backcombing, Bonnie Tyler (because, yeah, those were things we were all missing from our lives) – and as such all the little homogenous, homemaking Hollies that we used to know suddenly found us and started getting in touch. 'Hey, I've got a beautiful baby, a handsome husband and a very big house, what about you?' they all might as well have said. Anya said they were probably only sending me friend requests because I was a bit famous. I'd like to believe it was that. Be horrible to think it was because we had anything in common.

So, anyway, last week Mary bloody Conroy posted about a hundred photos of one of her kids, as usual, and then, a little bit later she posted a picture of a small turd in a potty and put next to it – *Little chubby-cheeks did this tiny poop but it looks a bit green to me. What do you think?*

Seriously. That happened. That was a thing. The Rubicon has been crossed. The shark has been jumped. Mary Conroy, the coolest girl at St Ed's, the bass-playing punk who once broke James Pickles' nose for groping her arse and decided to touch up her pubes with a chalkboard rubber, is now calling her child chubby-cheeks and posting pictures of his shit online. End times.

'It breaks me a little,' Anya was saying as we both stared down at the market-day shoppers trudging through the rain in their garish macs and even more colourful umbrellas, 'to see people change like that. I got married, but I'm the same. You got successful but you're the same. We are, aren't we? We haven't changed that much, have we?'

'We just got better, darling.' A group of school children were walking along, hand in hand in a crocodile, underneath the window, their excited gibber-jabber cutting through the air like nails down a blackboard. 'Bloody kids.'

'Probably shouldn't have become a children's author then, eh?'

She had a point.

Anya delighted in beating me with that stick; she found the idea hilarious, though the trap I had sprung for myself in my working life was, I should imagine, infinitely more bearable than the one she had found herself living. She always claimed the kid thing was no big deal for her any more. There was a time where she yearned for it, she said, but after all that had gone on, all that business with *him*, she claimed her priorities had changed long ago. I think she probably believed it too. I didn't, but I never pushed. She wasn't likely to talk to me about her biological clock anyway. Mine stopped ticking long ago, if it had ever even started. I knew it was the anniversary of that day today though, the day Henry Gage died, and I wondered if that was why she had invited me out.

'It's today isn't it?' I asked quietly, testing the waters. 'The anniversary?'

She didn't turn around from the window, but shook her head slowly. 'Yesterday. Though, yesterday, today, what difference does it make?'

'Need to talk about it?'

'No. Of course not.'

I turned back to the table, giving her space to change her mind.

'I got this call yesterday though, from this guy, a cold caller.' Anya stopped and then looked back to me, seemingly unsure of what she was saying and why.

'I hope you gave him short shrift and told him to get a proper job.'

'Not so much, no. We got chatting.'

'Oh, Anya, when will you learn? Why do you even give them the time of day? You know they aren't real people, don't you?'

'Guess I was brought up better than you, darling.'

'No good can come of talking to these people.'

'He was just a poor little lost lamb, maybe I felt sorry for him?' she said with a wistful smile. 'I don't know. He's a screw-up, but I kind of liked that.'

'Screw-up?'

'Oh, sure, but nothing original – just your typical spurned male, unable to get over the ex, unable to get over himself. Self-pity, self-flagellation, very little self-respect.'

'Sounds like a riot.'

Still she smiled. Then she shrugged and the smile went with an absent whip of the hand. 'He phoned about an old insurance policy Len has, I dunno, it was something like that. We never actually got to the point of the call. Still, yeah, whatever…just a phone call. Meaningless. Don't even know why I told you.'

'Yet you did.'

'I liked talking to him, that's all. Nothing wrong with that is there?'

'You tell me.' I swirled the dregs of my coffee around the cup and swallowed them in one large gulp. 'And how is dear Len?'

'Is that an accusation, Eva?'

'No, not at all.' It was, of course. 'Just a question.'

'It was just a phone conversation. That's all.'

'Yes. Meaningless. You said.'

'Yeah. Exactly.'

She turned back to the window, and I turned to my phone and the conversation disappeared into the idle chatter in the huge room at the top of the café. We had more important things to talk about anyway. Mary bloody Conroy had just posted 125 photos of one of her children eating a sandwich and, it seemed, was due a little further character assassination.

ANYA

It truly was just a phone call. It was just an impersonal conversation between two strangers and it meant nothing. Len wouldn't have even batted an eyelid if he knew. Though Len never does bat an eyelid about anything except his work and his health. Maybe I just had to tell Eva simply to reassure myself. Perhaps, subconsciously, I told her because of the ridicule and scorn I knew she would pour on it.

When it comes to cold callers or door-stepping salesmen, my dear friend has a history. Not for simply walking away is my girl Eva Cunningham. No. No way. A polite "no thanks" or a "sorry, I'm busy" is nowhere near enough for my force-of-nature friend. This is the woman who, when some poor little man came knocking asking if she wanted her drive tarmacking, told him that the uneven surface was due not to tree roots but more because of the butchered corpses of her husband and his two lovers that she had buried there. Twins they were, and Swedish, and did he know how to mend a chainsaw? This friend of mine was also the same woman that, when confronted by a canvassing politician on her doorstep, said she could never vote for him because it was a local council controlled by his party that had granted planning permission to that old busybody at number forty-two so he could fashion a giant bronze phallus in his back garden. It was blocking out the light and messing with her phone reception, and what about the children? Hadn't they considered the children? She had heard he danced around it at night in his pants as well. Shameful. It used to be such a nice neighbourhood…

Only the other month I was at her house when she took a call from her building society asking if she had five minutes to take a questionnaire. She told them she did, but would they mind awfully waiting a moment because she was just herding in the last of the goats? She then put the receiver down on the hall table and made us both a cup of coffee. It was still there when I left. I don't know whether it is boredom or just sheer devilment with Eva, but she just doesn't seem to be able to help herself.

Even though they both seemed to share a certain cynical sensibility, Eva would have torn poor Ray apart.

The day he phoned I had spent the morning sorting through the offices, and tidying the living room (Christ, even writing that makes me feel ten years older). The birthday cards were still up in the living room, the big sparkly *40*s on the front somehow even more glittery and garish then than when I had opened them. The giant balloon with the equally giant *4* and *0* plastered in the centre that was tied to the mantelpiece had started to shrivel and droop. The watercolour set that Len had presented to me with such happiness sat unopened on the table, the ribbon he had stuck to the wrapping, hanging over one end. Limp. Pathetic. By the time I had cleared everything away I could feel tears and I had no idea why.

It had been a great day. A nice lunch out in a restaurant in the Woodford Valley, then back into Salisbury for a little bit of retail splurging and the cinema, then a small party at the house. By small I really do mean small – Len and I, Eva, Mum and Dad, our neighbours Jackie and Dennis, and some guy that Len knew and said I did too, but I really didn't. Mum and Dad had spent the day cooking up a storm and it really was lovely. It was all so very, very lovely, but it was all so very, very small.

I had been sitting there on the sofa with Eva, listening to her wittering on about her new book and moaning about her agent, and was just looking around the room, staring at each person there in turn and then the cards on the mantelpiece, all five of them, when suddenly a cold chill ran through me and I knew I had to get out of there. I had to get far away from that room and those people. My insides churned, my head buzzed, and pins and needles prickled through me. I cut Eva off mid-rant with a wave of my empty wine glass and then bolted through the door.

I got to the kitchen but that wasn't far enough. Suddenly I couldn't breathe properly, my chest felt tight and my head was swimming away from me. I hadn't had a panic attack in almost five years, so long ago that I had almost forgotten what they were like. I was out on the front drive, steadying myself between two parked cars before my head came back to me and the tight grip of fear relented. By then Len was there behind me, his sweet smile and twinkly eyes making me feel guilty and stupid and pathetic. Wordlessly he handed me a glass of wine, kissed me on the cheek and wandered back into the house. I wanted to bawl my eyes out there and then, and I knew they would have been childish tears; uncontrollable snotty wails, and that terrified me because I didn't know why. I knocked the wine back and then went into the kitchen and refilled my glass. By the time I rejoined everyone else my childish impulses had been well and truly subdued by the good old reliable adult suppressant.

When the phone started ringing I must have been staring at the kitchen wall for a good half an hour. Tears had dried under my eyes and my cup of coffee was stone cold. His cheesy, well-rehearsed patter was delivered with such a grating cheeriness that it gave me a headache.

'Good afternoon, my name is Ray English and I'm calling from Babbidge Insurance. I wonder if I could have a moment of your time?'

'Whatever,' was all I could muster, all I could think to say, stirring out of my fug of self-pity.

'How are you this afternoon?'

'Indifferent.'

'Well, yes, Mrs Belmont, tell me about it!'

'Really?'

'Sure, why not?'

'You make a living either way, I suppose?'

It was a strange sensation, those first few exchanges with him: I felt detached from the conversation, as if I were a ventriloquist's dummy and someone else was doing the talking for me. Probably Eva. I was aware that I was talking to him, even knew that for some reason I wanted to, yet at the start of the conversation I had no real idea what I was saying. I should have made my excuses and hung up, but something kept me there. Something kept me talking. I suppose, right at that moment, I needed someone. Fate sent me him.

'This is merely a courtesy call to make sure you are happy with everything.'

'Not so much. Life is pretty shit.'

'Well, I actually—'

'Yes, I know, it wasn't really a general chitchat. You don't really want to talk to me, you just want me to fall for your friendly patter and open my arms to whatever it is you're trying to push. I, for my part, have been brought up well enough not to hang up on people.'

'I'm really not trying to sell you anything, Mrs Belmont.'

'So you really are just phoning to see how I am?'

'I have to…it's—'

'Your job? Well, tell me, Ray, what on earth are you hiding from in life to make this your job? Was this always the dream, or did you just fall away at some point? Did life kick you in the face, Ray? I do hope she was worth it.'

Silence swallowed us up. I was staring into my cold coffee, and there were those sodding tears in my eyes again, and I felt dirty, dirty with disgust. What the hell was I saying to him? *Henry Gage.* It was probably Henry Gage that was making me say those things. It was the anniversary of that day, the day I watched him die, and despite the sharp edges of that horrid nightmare blunting year on year, there was still enough in it to cut me. Even recalling it I could still smell that dreary old pub that we called home for a year, and feel the stickiness of the blood between my fingers. That memory is a scar on my soul that all the kindness in the world can't heal. Even Len couldn't, and damn if he hasn't tried. Maybe this would be the year I told him about it. That was what I always said to myself when the anniversary of that day rolled by. *Maybe I could tell him now.* I never had, and I knew I probably never would. I knew I was too scared.

I waited for the phone line to go dead. But it didn't. I don't know what made me assume Ray would have any dignity. For several seconds he said nothing at all, and then he gave a small laugh and it was a nice laugh, and it felt like he was there in the room with me.

'I'm sorry, Ray.'

'No need to apologise, Mrs Belmont.'

'So, am I wrong?'

'No.'

'Look at us then, presumptuous and predictable. Quite the double act.'

'I was labouring under the impression I was unique.'

'Lucky me.' I found myself laughing along with him then, and hoped he didn't think I was laughing at him. I didn't know what else to say, only that I had to say something. 'Not thinking of hanging up on me are you, Ray?'

'Of course not, Mrs Belmont.'

'You've been brought up the right way too then, that's good to know. We have something in common, Ray. Look at that. From such sturdy foundations do worlds collide.'

It could have ended there. It should have done. I should have turned him back to the point and then gone back to my cold coffee and self-pity. But I didn't. I don't know why I carried on talking to him, why I pushed the conversation, why I still needed him. The truth was probably there somewhere, back in that old pub and that bastard Henry Gage, or maybe bound up in garish birthday cards and that ugly, lifeless balloon, hanging off the mantelpiece. Maybe I didn't see the truth because it was too close to my eyes. Maybe I just had my eyes closed.

'Want to talk about it?' I asked him.

'You first, Mrs Belmont.'

'Oh no, Ray. Most definitely you first. Go on.'

'I've done nothing but talk about it. I've said it all.'

'Not to me you haven't.'

'And who are you?'

'A stranger. Much easier to talk to a stranger about these things, wouldn't you say? Come on, what was her name? What did you do wrong?'

'You think it was me that messed it up?'

'If I was a betting women, yes, I reckon it was.'

'Go on then, let me hear it. Tell me all about my predictable life, Mrs Belmont.'

I stood and crossed to the sink. I had started to try and picture his face in my mind. Dark or blonde? Tall or short? Short, I figured, almost definitely, probably weighed down by that chip on his shoulder. I had a fleeting notion of a Kirk Douglas type. Not too tall, but chiselled, tough, and with a roughish smile and a twinkle in his eye. By the time I started rinsing out the cup and refilling the kettle he had become a young Paul Newman, the spit of Fast Eddie Felson.

'Mrs Belmont?'

'You hate all women now, of course,' I said, jumping over his words. 'Your natural self-loathing is shared out evenly these days because you finally have someone to blame for how crap your life is.' I poured a spoonful of coffee into the cup and wiped the teaspoon clean on my sleeve. 'Yeah? Something like that?'

'That's a bit forward isn't it?' he said through another, warmer, laugh.

'You phoned me, Ray. I was perfectly content staring at the wall. Come on, fess up, who was she? I'm guessing she was a college sweetheart, is that right?'

'She was. Well done. Top marks, Mrs Belmont.'

'Well there's your first mistake, Ray. You should never settle for the first sweet from the sweet shop. Get a sugar rush from the pick and mix before you suck on your last lolly.' Eva had said that to me the day I first got married, to the bastard Henry Gage, but Ray didn't need to know that. It had always sounded good and I had always wanted to use it. Eva wouldn't care that I stole it from her. She never did mind when she knew she was right. Besides, it had made Ray laugh again, and that seemed to matter right at that moment. 'You took the same courses, I suppose? Sociology and politics, I'm thinking. Two wide-eyed optimists that wanted to change the world until you saw the hours. Am I right, Ray?'

He was sniggering like a child by this point. 'Actually, no. You're not. She sang backing vocals in my college band. That was how we were going to change the world, Mrs Belmont.'

'Any good, this band of yours?'

'Could have been great.'

'What happened?'

'Turned out we were shit.'

And then we were both laughing, and it was easy, so very easy, this stranger and I, laughing with the freedom of irrelevance.

'So?' he asked through his laughter, rather coyly, it seemed to me.

'So what?' I replied.

'So that's me. I went first. What about you, Mrs Belmont?'

'Really nothing to say, Ray. Nothing to say.'

'I think I should be the judge of that.'

'I tell you what, Ray. I will make you a deal. I will tell you my story the day you get back in the game. How about that? You get a date. Get back out there and I will tell you. Once you get over yourself and under a woman, we will have a deal. Deal?'

He paused for what seemed an eternity. 'Deal.'

I honestly believed I would never speak to him again.

The Second Call

RAY

Mabel stared at my iPhone as if it had just fallen off the mothership. It probably didn't help that I had *Starman* as my ringtone. It was the third call from Danny since I had arrived at the nursing home, so I assumed it must actually be important. I excused myself to Mabel, left the room and answered the incessant call just before Bowie went in for the chorus.

It couldn't have been less important.

'So, guess what I see in the window of the newsagents?' Danny spluttered between gasps of barely suppressed laughter.

'Surprise me.'

'You won't guess, man, seriously. You wouldn't believe it.'

'You know me, dear, I'd pretty much believe anything.'

'Mickey P's is holding a speed dating night, tonight!'

Silence was the only response to such a statement.

'Yeah, okay, I don't believe it,' I said, eventually.

'What time are you done with your women? Obviously we've gotta go, right? Starts at seven, you be there?'

'Look, I don't mind going along for a drink but—'

Danny, still far too amused to pay me any attention, broke into peals of laughter and then seemed to drop the phone; his squeaky, mirthful voice sounding like it was now locked inside a cupboard. 'Oh man, that's too much, too much…never heard anything so funny…' His words were hijacked by a coughing fit, and when he tried to speak again there was nothing but a *nu… nu…nu…nu…* noise backed by a chesty wheeze. Then there was nothing at all.

'Was it something important?' Mabel asked as I returned to the sofa next to her, and she set about offering me the plate of cakes she had only just waved under my nose five minutes previously.

'I hope not. I don't think so. It's possible my friend just died laughing.'

'Well, if you've got to go. There are worse ways.'

'Can't argue with that, Mabel.'

'Like getting chewed up in a combine harvester. That would be worse.'

'Yeah, that's not ideal.'

'Knew someone went that way once.'

'Death by combine harvester?'

'No, sausage, they died laughing. Quick it was, and they went with a smile on their face. Not so bad. They did foul themselves though. That wasn't so good. Best trousers they were, an' all. Matron had to burn them after. We all watched.'

'Okay.'

Good old Mabel Brockley. She's ace. When she first arrived at the home she was so apologetic about moving into my Granddad Bertie's room. And it was

HIS room, everyone knew it, and those that hadn't been foretold were soon aware of the fact. Granddad had all but taken a piss on the carpet to mark it – Room 18, the big one, overlooking the lawn, the one with the sink with the big taps. That was how he always described it whenever asked. It was the best damn room in the place and it was his, so there. It was always curious to me how it took him leaving a plush semi-detached home in one of the poshest parts of Buckinghamshire, and moving into a shared cell in this glorified plaid prison, for him to become materialistic and proud. I always assumed it was probably because of Liz. I saw no other reason for it.

Mum always hated Liz. Despite there being a good twenty years between Gran passing away and Elizabeth Margaret Gilston entering his life, she always made Granddad Bertie feel like he was betraying her mother's memory somehow. Ridiculously unfair, of course, but he always took it with a calm acceptance and never bit back. 'She's still grieving,' he told me once. 'She always will be, let her have it. She's protecting herself. It's a way of deflecting her need to understand what she can't.' I didn't understand that. I still don't. But Bertie was a wise old sage so I had no reason to doubt that he knew what he was talking about.

I always suspected that Mum would have been a lot easier about it all if Bertie and Liz hadn't moved away to Buckinghamshire. That was what really hurt her: the fact that they chose to be nearer her family than his. Though she never said as much. 'Listen to what people don't say, kid. That's where the truth is, yeah?' he often said to me. That I understood.

I don't half miss him. He always had such a knack of grabbing the point of a situation, and busting through all the flannel and the crap and getting to what mattered, summing everything up in some sort of wise-old-man-of-the-woods fashion that you just knew was right. He would make light of it, but that was just his way. 'It's just cracker wisdom, kid. Honestly, it is. You just believe it because it's coming from an old voice. You instinctively assume age brings wisdom and great truths. Does it bollocks, kid. We are just as confused as everyone else.'

'Dear old Albert.' Olive Machem's voice startled me. 'Such a lovely man, he was. Dead though now, of course.' There she was, as she always was, sat astride her mobility scooter, staring wistfully through the open doors of other people's rooms, talking about people that she had outlived. Arnie Baxter told me once that she had a little notebook in her room where she was keeping a corpse tally. 'Old crone isn't gonna be happy until she's the last one standing. If she could stand. Which she can't. So I guess she's never gonna be satisfied.'

'Hello, Olive. How are you?'

She sighed heavily and then stared across at Mabel, who seemed to have dozed off. 'Hello, Ray.' With one quick movement she had turned her scooter through the door and was pulling up alongside the sofa, narrowly missing my foot. 'You are a lovely boy, why has no nice girl snapped you up yet?' Olive gathered up two pieces of Battenberg from Mabel's plate of cakes and squirreled them away in her cardigan. 'All the months you've been coming here and I've never seen you with a lady friend.'

'I'm working on it, Olive.'

'No you're not. Your friend says you are living in the past.'

'Olive…'

'Where is there to go if you keep going backwards? You're just as likely to fall over as get anywhere at all.'

'Olive, you really shouldn't phone me at home.'

'I didn't. Mabel did. You did give us the number. Why would you do that if we weren't to phone?'

'Because…well, in case anything…' I motioned towards the bed and the little, crumpled shape lying there. 'If you needed to phone and tell me anything important. You know what they are like here. I would be the last to know anything.'

'Well, what's more important than matters of the heart? Your Albert would have agreed with that, and you know he would.' Olive had such an air of melancholy about her, but whenever she spoke about Granddad, and she did a lot, always recounting the same thing, the same story I knew she was about to tell me again now, she seemed to develop a little mischievous twinkle. 'He knew about great love affairs, did Albert. Some of us spend a lifetime searching for one, and there was Albert with two to boast of. Not that he did. No, he always appreciated his fortune, did Albert.'

'He loved my Gran. Even though I was a kid when she died, I knew he loved her.'

'He mourned her every day of those twenty years he was alone. He told me that, and oh, what a sweet thing to say, the dear old man. He never thought he would meet anyone else. I don't think he ever even considered it would be a possibility. He said once that meeting and falling in love with someone else again at his age was one crazy thing, but meeting and falling in love with a Tory was just too absurd to believe. Still, as he was so fond of saying…'

Love can conquer all evils, my mind repeated with her. I smiled as if hearing this for the first time. Mabel snored lightly next to me, and outside the window, across the beautifully kept lawn, Dick Oakley was flying a toy plane with his grandson. The all-too-familiar stuffy smell of steamed vegetables was now wafting through the open doorway to the room, and I knew that one of the nurses, probably Abigail, would be along any moment to announce that tea was ready. I had already lived this moment a hundred times and I was so calm, so peaceful, I could have fallen asleep.

'Moving in here together, watching her fade like that, so sad for dear Albert. So sad.' Olive's voice had dropped to whisper, and were it not for the sponge fingers she was snaffling away into the seemingly endless deep of her cardie, I would have said she was about to cry. 'The body is one thing – the body betrays us all in this place, look at me on this cumbersome contraption – but the mind, oh, that was so sad. So sad. So alive she was. So bright. But then bit by bit, day by day, going, going, going…dimmer and dimmer.' Olive shoved a sponge finger into her mouth and chewed noisily, somewhat ruining the emotional nuances of her story. 'And then for her to finally fall away so far, to look at the man she had found to love and to not even remember his name. So sad. And then for dear Albert to give up the ghost the way he did and slip away the very next day. So sad, and yet somehow so romantic. Natural causes, they said. These people that know these things. And I suppose they are right. Is there anything more natural than a broken heart?'

I leaned back on the sofa as Olive continued to ramble, and stretched my hand out, feeling for the small, bony fingers that hung over the edge of the bed. I held her hand, that strange, tiny little thing that used to be Elizabeth Margaret Gilston, and felt the brush of the wedding ring, and then squeezed thumb and index finger gently against tissue-paper skin, feeling nothing but bone. She didn't reciprocate. She never did. But I always tried.

DANNY

Mickey P's bar, a ten-minute walk from our flat, positioned pretty much evenly between Muswell Hill and Crouch End, was a decaying watering hole with a dangerously low, corkboard ceiling that had been putting drunks on their backside since the early 90s. Mickey was a lethargic, plump waster with no idea about personal hygiene who had got lost somewhere at the end of the 70s, and his pub was very much an aesthetic representation of the man, with its processed ham sandwiches, bowls of dried nuts and a jukebox stuffed to the glass with prog rock. They were just about kept afloat by a few old barflies drinking themselves slowly to oblivion, and the weekly game of poker run by Mickey's son Tobaccofinger (no idea what he's really called, but he's got a Bond villain vibe and has an obscenely fat index finger that looks like a lemon popsicle). I had done some shifts for Mickey a couple of years back, and even managed to sweet-talk him into letting me play a few acoustic shows now and then. It wasn't the same without Ray warbling along next to me, but I did enjoy it.

It was fair to say I was gobsmacked when I first saw the advert for Mickey P's inaugural speed dating night, and then after that I couldn't stop laughing. But there it was, bold as brass, this giant poster shoved in the window of our local newsagent in an explosion of primary colours and big fonts. There may be some places in north London less conducive to matters of sexual attraction, but I've certainly yet to find them. So it was, curiosity getting the better of my flatmate and I, that we rolled up at Mickey P's bar and found ourselves amongst a scantily clad scrum of N10's singletons.

'You've got to be kidding me?' Ray mumbled to himself as we signed up. Already on a downer after visiting the nursing home, just as he always was, he was taking the whole thing with his usual bad grace. 'I don't want anything to do with this charade. I'll be at the bar.'

Mickey had made what for him passed as an effort; he'd put new bar mats out and cleaned the floor. He even wore a clean shirt. Tobaccofinger stood to one side of the bar area in a snug-fitting tux, holding a small bell, his beady eyes lecherously roaming over the passing women.

The turnout was impressive. Tables had been placed in a wide square around the floor with high-backed chairs either side, and a large crushed red velvet curtain had been rigged up at the far end of the bar to block out the view of the bins. People flitted around the bar itself imbibing Dutch courage, nervously talking to friends and eagerly eyeing strangers.

Mickey was in his element. 'Sex!' he growled at Ray as we squeezed ourselves to the bar. 'That was what we were missing here. That's where the money is. You got to cater to the promise of sex.' Mickey slipped a hand up his shirt and scratched at his navel. 'People either drink to numb the pain or they drink to loosen the inhibitions. Right? We've catered too much for the former, not enough for the latter. Like you, Ray. You still pining after that little northern strumpet that broke your heart?'

I could feel Ray straighten up next to me. 'Course I'm not. That was years ago, Mickey. What do you take me for?'

Mickey flashed me a quick look, a look that told Ray that we had been discussing the barren wasteland of his love life. 'Just that we don't ever see you here with anyone, thought perhaps you were still, you know…' Mickey made the sound of a cuckoo.

'Still what?' Ray snapped at Mickey, before rounding on me. 'What have you been saying?'

'Well, Danny tells us she messed you up good,' Mickey went on. 'I know how it goes, I've been married. But you gotta keep moving forward, lad, otherwise…'

'I'm here, aren't I?' Ray snatched his pint from Mickey and took an over-dramatic gulp, spilling some down his shirt. Turning to the crowd gathering around the tables, he wiped his lips on the back of his hand and belched. 'Right. Who's first then? Line 'em up.'

With participants outnumbering chairs by at least four to one (who would have thought?), I sat out the first round. I could feel Mickey's face looming close, his breath announcing its proximity, and when I turned to face him he had a bunched-up wad of notes in a fist.

'Fifty quid he gets no match. What do you say?'

'Are you seriously trying to make money on the back of my best friend's social inadequacies?'

'Well, yeah.'

I rummaged in my wallet. 'Yeah, okay then. But can we make it twenty?'

We watched Ray from the bar and I felt a queer mixture of guilt and pride. He didn't want to be here, he didn't want to be anywhere; certainly not conversing with the opposite sex. It was all a token gesture on his part, a pretence born from my insistence and Mickey's jibes, but it was something, and after years of nothing, I was proud to see him doing anything.

He sat there stony-faced, his lips barely moving. Occasionally he would flash contemptuous looks in our direction, and we would return them with a smile and a raised thumb.

'I feel like a parent watching their kid on sports day,' Mickey chuckled before pulling away to serve a customer. 'Call it a ton if one of them chins him?'

As Tobaccofinger rang his small bell for the third time and everyone shuffled on to the next table, a very attractive blonde stood to greet Ray and they shook hands. I saw her pointing to his name badge – she was telling him it was upside down. Instead of fixing it he merely shrugged, and then I began to wonder if he was doing it on purpose or if he genuinely just didn't have a clue. Had he ever? At the very least, this time he actually seemed to be talking. He even seemed relatively animated.

I swivelled back around on my stool and waved my empty glass at Mickey. 'You can take that off my twenty.'

Mickey filled my pint and then peered suspiciously over my shoulder. Slowly a wet, wide grin spread across his face, and at the same time I heard the raised voice of a very pissed-off woman coming from the other side of the pub. The tedious, crushing inevitability wasn't far behind.

'Easy money, Dan. Easy money.'

'Remind me again how you talked me into this?'

Ray was stood under the hand dryer in the gents', the warm air directed between his legs and the large beer stain that was covering his crotch. I was handing him wads of toilet paper and trying hard not to laugh.

'I told you, this is what you need. Get yourself back out there again. Mix it up a bit with members of the opposite sex.'

'How's that great idea working out, do you think?'

'What the hell did you say to her?'

'Nothing!'

'You sure about that?'

'Well, she just told me that I wasn't going to be having sex with her. Straight up, that's the first thing out of her gob. How bloody presumptuous! "You're not getting sex off me," she says, just like that. So I told her that I didn't even want to be here, that she was wasting her time even telling me that. So then she asks me why I came, if I didn't want to be here

– all suspicious she was, like I was devaluing it or something. "You sound defensive. Clearly you must only have come along looking for meaningless sex." So I laughed because I thought she must have been joking. But she wasn't. She gets pissy and then she says, "I know your sort, some sad case looking for a quick and meaningless bang against a cubicle door because some woman laughed at your winkie and your masculinity dribbled down your leg. I've met your type before." Then she says it again: "You're not getting sex off me.'"

'And?'

'So I told her, "I don't want sex off you, on you, or around you." I hoped she would talk about something else then, but that just seemed to make her angry. "Oh you don't?" she starts at me. "Why not? I suppose I repulse you, do I? Is that it? I repulse *you*!"

'I tell her I didn't mean that. I try and say that she's very nice. I think I say she's lovely, and then I get worried that she will think I'm trying it on with her, and I get confused and don't know what else to say, so I just sort of stumble and mumble, and I end up saying, "I'm sure that many men would…"'

'Oh dear.'

'She didn't even let me finish speaking. "I'm not easy, you know," she screams at me. "*Many* men?" Then she launches my drink at me, just as I'm standing to leave.'

I was trying hard to stifle my amusement. 'Well, yeah, just…well, you know, when people say you should always be yourself, I suppose sometimes that's not the best plan. Learn and adapt. I think that's the secret. Don't you?'

'Stop talking to me like I care.'

'Play it right and you might actually get your leg over.'

Ray started dabbing at his wet crotch with the bunched-up toilet paper. 'That's something to aim for, is it? You've seen what's out there, haven't you?'

'Table three?'

'Yeah, table three! I couldn't get my leg over that with a stepladder and a compass.'

'Well, Raymond, what can I say? It's surely better than another night at home, moping around in your pants, isn't it?'

'Oh, almost definitely. I honestly don't think I've been this excited since I quit smoking.' Ray nodded down to his crotch. 'How do I look?'

'You really want me to answer that?'

'Piss off.'

'Eye of the whippet, kid. Eye of the whippet. Get back out there and get on with it.'

Next in line for the Ray English charm offensive was an irrepressibly happy woman with a case of the verbals, by the name of Beth Garrett. This time Ray didn't need to recount the encounter to me as Beth's table was right by my seat at the bar. I tried to move, but by the time Beth greeted Ray with a piano-key smile and shook his hand like she was pumping water, my best friend's withering glare found me and ordered me back to my seat.

Ray and Beth were an impossible fit. These two were oil and water, chalk and cheese, glass half-full and glass shattered in the sink. Thankfully she did the talking. And a lot of it.

'Hello there,' Beth chirped, finally releasing Ray's hand. 'Hey, Ray! I'm Beth. Beth Garrett. I'm a fitness instructor. Not that I'm one of those lunatic fit freaks, all pecs and abs and walnut-cracking butt cheeks. Hahaha! No, I had an ex got me into it a few years back. He was on steroids though. I never liked going to the gym before that, I was always a bit lazy really, but I love it now. Not that it's an addiction. No, I wouldn't say that. I do feel great though, lots of energy. And then there's skiing, I go skiing again now. We used to go to Switzerland every winter when I was a girl. I used to love that. I'm going to run the London marathon next year. My sister wants to do it dressed as a rabbit but really that's just daft. I told her but she's got no shame. Have you got any family? I've got a sister and two brothers. Ryan and Bryan, they are called. Hahaha! We reckon Mum and Dad were having a laugh with that. Poor old Bryan. We call him Ryan B. You know, like he's the less-loved son. He's Bryan with a Y, that's why. Ryan with a B in front! Hahaha! They are very protective. Ryan's in the army and Ryan B is a chef. Can you cook? I was a vegetarian for five years. I'm not much of a cook but I dabble. I can knock something up. My family is from the southwest. By the coast. They have a boat. I can't sail much. Don't much care for the water. But I like swimming, that's strange isn't it? Isn't that odd? Well, listen to me, rabbit, rabbit, rabbit… maybe I should do the marathon dressed as a rabbit? Hahaha! I must stop talking so much. So anyway…'

'Anyway?' Ray repeated, dazed by her bombardment.

'What about you?' Beth replied.

'What about me what?'

'What do you do?'

'I work in a call centre.'

'Really? Wow. What do you sell?'

'Misery.'

'What?'

Ray leaned forward and rested his elbows on the table. 'That's strange. Very odd. That statement usually ends conversations. You did hear me right, didn't you? I work in a call centre.'

'Yeah, I heard. That's wonderful. I'd love to work in a call centre. I love talking to people. I like people.'

'Never mind.'

Beth shuffled forward, propping her elbows on the table and resting her chin on interlocked fingers. 'So, tell me some more about yourself.'

'Like what?'

'I don't know…what do you like? What do you dislike? What's your favourite colour?'

'I like singing,' Ray said flatly.

'Excellent! Give us a song then!'

'No.'

'Are you any good?'

'No. I dislike drummers and tall men. Men with beards. Tall men with beards. Tall women. Women with beards. Country music. Rap music. Dance music. Reality shows. Talent shows. Sausages, rugby, horse racing. Society girls. Politicians. Theme pubs. Mobile phone shops. Racism, bigotry, liars, corduroy, pipe smokers, journalists. Teenagers, hot air balloons, religious salesmen, people called Steve, and the incessant bleakness of the world.'

'Oh. Okay. You got any fish to go with that chip?'

'My favourite colour is black.'

Yeah, Ray English and Beth Garrett: two more opposite people you probably could never meet.

Naturally she ended up staying the night. So what the heck do I know?

RAY

Beth Garrett can talk. She could break records. She talked all the way back to the flat. She talked Danny into an early night, and talked two cups of tea cold. I suppose it would stand to reason that she would also talk during sex. And talk in her sleep. I had known from the moment we got home that another night of staring at the ceiling beckoned, and not in a good way; my insomnia had been getting more and more predictable throughout the past few weeks, and not even Beth's promise to 'see if we can do something about that' was going to do anything about that. My body clock set its own time, and no amount of verbiage or audio descriptive sex was going to turn the hands. The final irony was that talking about it with Beth actually sent her to sleep.

'Oh, I had a friend who was an insomniac – she once went a week without sleeping,' she told me. 'Drove her slightly cuckoo, I think. Lovely girl. Think she's okay now.' Beth stifled a yawn and slung an arm over my waist. 'Think she got some pills or something or other. How long have you been an insomniac? I suppose you are always susceptible to it, aren't you? Insomnia. Is it a mind thing? Maybe you need to see a shrink. Perhaps that's what my friend did, I should ask her for you. Yeah? Shall I do that? She might be able to recommend someone. How long is it since you last slept?'

'Four…five…I dunno, four or five years,' I told the ceiling.

Beth was snoring into the side of my face five seconds later.

Danny had pinned the wedding invite from Tim at the base of the small noticeboard in the kitchen so it would be directly next to anyone that sat at the table. In the three weeks since it had turned up neither one of us had mentioned it again, so instead it just hung there threateningly like an unpaid bill, and we played the game of seeing who would blink first. I know he had spoken to Dave the previous week, because I earwigged in on the conversation, and I was pretty sure he was up for getting the band back together – he would be, though, that was no real surprise – but I knew Clive was going to be a tougher prospect. By all accounts Clive had slipped so far into suburbia that he was all but lost to those of us without a hatchback or a shed. Plus he had married a notoriously volatile, social-climbing baby factory by the name of Anna Mann. She and Clive were both twenty when they got spliced, and now, four kids and a garage conversion later, she not only wore the trousers, she wouldn't even let him wear the dress. Clive was going to be the saving grace. Or rather, his wife was.

Sitting there in the kitchen, toying with the plate of mouldy toast (nothing to do with me) and listening to

Beth's incoherent sleep rambling and snores coming from my bedroom next door, I found myself starting to think about Anya Belmont again. She'd been there at the back of my mind, on and off, in the weeks since we spoke, an encounter I couldn't quite put to bed. She intrigued me. I started hearing her voice again, and the strangest thing was, I could recall it perfectly. Not that she had any definite accent – her voice was deceptively soft, with a tiny twinge of Wiltshire, a little smattering of posh London, and a light playfulness in her insults. I found it strange that I could hear her so crystal-clear. For all the years I have had to listen to strangers on the phone – a tuneless cacophony that has long since morphed into one grating whine, so easily dismissed – that this woman's voice was so easy to bring to mind was something I couldn't ignore.

I thought about what she had said, those three long weeks ago on the phone – 'I will tell you my story the day you get back in the game,' she had promised me. Despite the laugh that seemed to hide behind most of her words, that had felt real. It hadn't felt like a brush-off. Perhaps she had genuinely meant it. I liked to think, doing the job I did, that I was pretty good at spotting the bullshit in strangers. Anya Belmont had meant it, I was sure of it. She'd want to know about the speed date, about Beth, she surely would. She'd said as much. And I wanted to know about her as well.

Okay, she'd also hurt my male pride and I needed her to know that I wasn't yet a lost cause. There was that as well.

I had written her number down on a creased Post-it note and stuck it in my jacket pocket, then transferred it to my phone when I got home. Just for safekeeping. It wasn't some kind of statement. I had felt a bit like a stalker searching for her on Facebook that night, but I needed to try and put a face to the voice, more to see if I had guessed her right than anything else. I don't think that's particularly weird. (I didn't find her, anyway.) Though I should probably have drawn the line at searching out her house on Google Maps (detached, three storeys and a long back garden with what looked like an apple tree at the bottom). It looked really nice, as did Salisbury as a whole, but I had the suspicion that there was a vague absence of chins about the place, so I wasn't planning on booking in a visit anytime soon.

A lot of things make sense in the midnight hour that probably wouldn't in the light of day. Even phoning up a complete stranger at half past midnight seemed an acceptable thing right then (though in my defence I hadn't noticed the time until after I had dialled, and by then, well, if I was going to wake her up I would have done already. That was how I saw it, anyway). The phone rang three times before switching to the answerphone. A man, obviously her husband, he of the insurance policy, spoke soft words I didn't hear, and then the phone beeped at me like it was annoyed.

I hung up.

'Shit.'

I was still sat at the kitchen table, scolding my stupidity, when Danny wandered out of his bedroom in a beanie hat and a loose-fitting dressing gown.

'All right, love?'

I grunted something he seemed to understand and he nodded towards my half-open bedroom door and raised an eyebrow that asked more than enough questions. I gave him a shrug, which was all the answer he needed.

'We should have got some champagne. Ray English, back in the real world, with a real woman – they will surely write books. We still got any Babycham?'

'We polished that off celebrating when you learned how to rewire a plug. You want to talk of momentous days, that's going to take some beating.'

Danny gave me the finger and set about making a cup of tea. 'I know you've been out the loop a while but I believe it's commonly accepted to be good etiquette to stay in the room with your one-night stand. At least for five minutes.'

'One-night stand, is it?'

'Is it? I dunno. You tell me, what is it?'

'Why's it got to be anything?'

'She's a bit too…what's the word?'

'Chatty?'

'Nice. She seems a bit too nice for you. Don't you think? She doesn't strike me as someone looking for a raincloud to darken her sunny disposition.'

'Nice people like me. Katie was nice.'

Danny's shoulders sagged at the mention of her name. 'Yeah. Yeah, Ray. She was. But you weren't who you are now back then, that's kinda the point, wouldn't you say? You let Kate turn you into…this.'

'This?'

'Seriously, Ray, you need me to draw you a picture?'

Talking about Katie to Danny was a sure-fire way to piss him off. I know he thinks I go on about her too much, and I probably do, but such things are part of the best friend contract, the way I see it. It's what you do. The months I spent listening to him fretting and flapping about the fearsome Vera Franks, trying to decide how he could leave her and still retain his balls – well, that was pretty tedious, but I let him prattle on and helped him the best I could. It's what friends do. Not that he listened to me. Danny was such a coward when it came to Vera that his grand plan was simply to move to London and not tell her. Never mind the friends and family that knew where we were going. I kept telling him not to, that it wouldn't work and that not even Vera deserved to be treated so badly. I even thought about telling her myself (I didn't, so maybe I'm a coward too – seriously though, if you'd met her…) but in the end, that was just what Danny did. My relationship had just imploded, all that I knew going with it, so in truth he'd have been better off asking anyone else but me for an opinion. Finally though, as I told him would happen, all it had taken was a visit to Mr and Mrs Radleigh from Vera and five minutes later the am-dram queen of Southport had our address and a bag of laundry that Danny had left. Four days later, Danny had a split lip and a bag of ripped-up, sweet-smelling clothes.

'Can't sleep again?' Danny asked, clearly trying to change the subject.

'Is that really a question?'

'How was Liz? I didn't ask earlier.'

I'm never sure what the correct answer to that question is. Bless him for asking, he usually did, but what the heck was I supposed to say? Thankfully, as so often happened, our shorthand saved us and articulated all that was unsaid: I shrugged, he nodded, and we moved on.

'Who you phoning?'

'No one.' I put my mobile phone down and shoved it across the table as if to reiterate the point. 'Just…just having a…nothing. No one.'

Instantly the damn phone began to vibrate as a call lit up the screen.

Anya Belmont's timing was impeccable.

EVA

It is impossible to fully do justice to how ghastly, slippery and preening my literary agent is. Truly, it is. It would need a better writer than I to do it sufficient justice. Certainly compared to my first agent, dear old Mervin Dobbs, the contrast couldn't be greater. Gruff, grizzled and gregarious, Mervin had been an old friend of my creative writing tutor and had come to do a couple of talks to the group. Decked out in tweed and stinking of cherry tobacco and mothballs, Mervin was certainly old-school, but had also clearly sneaked a peek at the new syllabus, as his instincts about the way the literary world would turn were always on the money. He was a wonderful agent. A good friend. But also, rather inconveniently, dead.

Jim St James was one of the underlings at Mervin's agency, a strutting mannequin of a man who conducted most of his business from a bistro in the West End. He had taken over the bulk of Mervin's list and he made his pitch for me over a three-hour lunch; a smorgasbord of platitudes, a side order of ripe cheese and a dessert of skirt-blowing hot air. I didn't like him, but then I decided that wasn't really the point. It was all about the books. My babies. Like many marriages of convenience, you really just have to learn to tolerate each other when you are only together for the sake of the kids. And as far as that went, Jim talked a good game. Plus, I reasoned that in a business built around knocking down doors, it would be useful to have an agent that also had the option of oozing through the keyhole instead, should it come to it.

I only had two titles in print at that point, a couple of modestly successful, cosy crime novels that hadn't exactly pulled up any trees, and I was stumbling over the why'd-he-do-it of a potential third, when Jim St James came to me with the notion of reworking *The Warlocks of Wolverhampton*. At that stage it was little more than a novella, a story for kids (so Mervin had convinced me) that was born from the creative writing course. Mervin had liked it a great deal but had taken against all the ritualistic slaughter and F-bombs. 'Write about what you know, I told you, Eva. My dear, is there something I should know about you?' It was a nothing story. A story for children that could never be read by children, written by an angry woman with a long list of people in Wolverhampton that I wanted killed. It was cheap therapy to me, and nothing more. Jim St James saw it differently.

'There's something there, Eva. At its core it is a quite wonderful story. Mervin always spoke about how much he liked it. Believable characters, for the most part...'

'Warlocks, monsters and zombies?'

He talked over that. 'Exciting plot. Witty dialogue. Huge potential, I think. There's a series here. If we can just reshape it.'

'It's a kids' book. Or it was supposed to be.'

'Yes, I do suggest there is slightly too much… aggression. If we could just hint at the trailing intestines, and have a few more darns and blasts rather than the fucks and motherfuckers, then we can go somewhere with it, I think. Honestly, I think this is a special book. What do you think?'

'I don't want to write for children.'

'It is a very lucrative market, Eva.'

'I don't understand children.'

'*Au contraire, mon ami*, I think you have quite an empathy with them. It is merely how you express it.'

'Don't speak French to me. You're from Berkshire.'

That little dance went on for quite a while. Jim St James is not a man to give up on an idea once he has convinced himself it is a winner. Or rather, when he has got pound signs burnt onto his corneas. In the end he got his way, of course. My publisher wasn't showing much interest in any more Earl Grey and arsenic novels from me, and, if truth be told, there weren't that many readers holding out for them either. Terrified that I would have to go back into some sort of real world that required social etiquette to earn a living, and yet faced with a bone-dry well of creative inspiration, I tossed in my old coin and turned out a treatment for *Warlocks of Wolverhampton*.

Now here I am, book two in a series I never wanted to write, and I'm sitting on a four-book deal and a nice bank balance. I'm the most exciting thing to happen to children's literature in a decade and I have no idea how I got here. What a farce.

Of course, if it were just the words it would be so much easier. If it were just the books, it would be fine. It's all a sham, but so what? Aren't most jobs? When I was working in that stationery shop, or the florist's whilst I was at uni, or even when I was a waitress, all of that was a sham too. Most people's jobs mean they have to learn a pretence. I'm no different. No, the problem is that hideous word that Jim St James likes to toss around like it's going out of fashion – *brand* – because it's not enough to be a good writer apparently, nor is it always enough to shift a load of units; nowadays Jim decrees that writers also need to sell themselves. In this global village, in these days of social media, the author needs to be a brand. The author needs to blog, to do talks and offer opinion, to discuss and entertain. Worse than all those things, they actually have to meet their readers. What a ghastly notion. Jim will tell you we have no choice. Jim says writers aren't allowed to be an enigmatic, hermitical scribe these days. You can't be mysterious. You have to be accessible. I always remember a writer from the agency telling me in terror before he had to do a signing, 'I don't want to meet the sort of person that would read my books.' I couldn't agree more. Even worse, now that means meeting children. As Anya so succinctly put it once, 'It's like a vegan visiting a slaughterhouse.' I'm not sure who was supposed to be the vegan in that analogy, but I got her point.

A whole carnival of publicity had been lined up for the launch of *The Demons in Dudley* (a shit title), a launch that seemed to be stretching for months and months if Jim was to have his way. Jim was in his element, and when I got his call to say he was coming to Salisbury to see me I should have known what to expect. He only ever comes to me when he knows I'm not going to be happy. So it was that he presented a provisional list of book-signing sessions to me over coffee at Anya's coffee house, with all the salesman charm he could muster.

'Pepys came here once, and Shakespeare,' he mumbled through a gob full of éclair, waving a hand around at all the boho wonk of the café. 'I saw a sign on the wall. Mighty fine company has supped here before us. There's inspiration if you ever needed it.'

'They have a unisex toilet.'

The book signings were to be taking me up and down the country. On top of that there were radio stations and TV shows champing at the bit to interview me. He even had me speaking at a children's literary festival. He mentioned talk of a film option, producers wanting to wine and dine me, all of them oh so very excited, and oh so very, very keen to bring my story to life on the big screen. Jim talked at me, pontificated and preened and made all manner of grand promises, and all the while I sat there imaging how, if he were a character in one of my books, I would kill him.

I decided that either zombies would eat him alive, or he would be bludgeoned by a frozen foot-long éclair.

ANYA

Eva had spent the evening moaning, which wasn't uncommon. It was one of my dear friend's greatest and most oft-flaunted talents. My offer of supper had been gratefully received, as had two bottles of cheap red wine. Len called it a night earlier than usual, and after his nighttime ritual of checking his heart rate, his testicles, and then drowning himself in vitamin pills, went to bed with a mug of green tea and a weary expression. Len finds Eva's self-indulgent whining intolerable. 'What is she pissing and moaning about?' he said to me at one point. 'The fame, the great career success or the wealth?' It was hard to argue with him. I've spent years listening to Eva's often nonsensical drunken tangents, her rages and her rants, but even I was finding it hard to keep the look of feigned interest from slipping off my face this time.

'I'm a fraud. That is what I am! A twenty-four carat fraud.'

'No you're not, Eva.'

'I am, I bloody well am! I'm a fraud. You hear me? A fraud!'

'Yes, Eva, okay, you're a fraud.'

'"I've not met a writer yet that doesn't feel that way at one time or another." That was what Jim said to me.' Eva was leaning drunkenly on me at this point as I led her up the stairs to my office. '"Even a writer that achieves such success as you," Jim says to me, "they still feel frauds. Honestly they do, Eva. They all feel that way from time to time. In fact, in my experience, it is often great success that brings those feelings to the fore. Trust me, I've seen it many times before.'"

'Well, there you go…'

Eva grabbed my arm in the office doorway and stared at me with panicked, watering eyes. 'They dress up, you know?'

'Who do?'

'At book signings. My readers. Sometimes the parents do too. They dress up. As characters from the book. They think it amuses me. They want to make me happy.'

'So? That's a good thing isn't it?'

'But I don't know what to say to them. I don't want them to try and please me. I don't want them to touch me. Dirty hands. Always dirty hands. I just want them to buy the books, but then how long will that last? Children are fickle, easily distracted – how am I supposed to build a career on the back of children's whims?'

'Eva…'

'Some better author comes along with something sparklier and more interesting and then they will fuck off over to them and leave me. Then those that stay with me will grow up and just want sex and violence and I won't be allowed to write sex and violence because now I'm a children's author and once you're in that box they won't let you out again. You know that? They won't let you out of the box!'

'Eva, darling…'

'Oh, sure, Jim tells me that children are more loyal readers than adults, but what does he know? He's from Berkshire and smells of Old Spice, what can he possibly know?'

I took the empty glass from her hand and let her fall face first onto the sofa in the office. 'Eva?'

She mumbled something into the cushions and then, finally, fell silent. I took off her shoes and got a blanket from the cupboard and slipped it over her. I was just about to leave when she grabbed me by the arm again.

'They dress up, you know?' Eva's face was still buried in the cushions, making her words blur together even more.

'Yes, Eva. I know. You said.'

I had only been in bed five minutes when the phone rang. Tiredness had found me, and I let the answerphone have it. Len continued his light snoring next to me, blissfully undisturbed. That was the way with my husband: nothing disturbed him once his head touched the pillow. He could sleep through anything. Though with the amount of life-preserving pills he necked, perhaps it wasn't a surprise. I often wondered whether he'd even notice if I wasn't there next to him. God forbid the house ever got broken into because it was patently obvious which of us would be getting out of bed to check. Mind you, with all his pills he would be no use anyway, he would likely rattle all the way down the stairs.

My husband the hypochondriac. Just what every girl wants in her life. For the last few years, at least since the great five-zero started looming on the horizon, Len had convinced himself he was dying of one thing or another almost every month. Every scare story in the paper, every colleague that got ill, every new disease or illness that he read about, a new pot of pills would appear, some new food would be bought at the supermarket, or some pamphlet would be found. Quite why he wanted to achieve immortality I don't know. Life wasn't that wonderful. Of course the great irony of it was that Len was in better shape than anyone else I knew. He worked longer hours than he needed, never knew how to relax, was always stressed about something, and yet Len Belmont would be there at the end with the cockroaches.

I kept the bedside light on and watched him sleep for a few minutes, something I did from time to time. Something that would no doubt have made him unbearably paranoid if he knew. The small tuft of a fringe, that island separated from the rest of his hair, that he was forever trying to flatten down, was sticking up at a slant. I lightly pushed my palm against it and it immediately sprung up again. He rolled onto his back and let an arm flop down onto my leg. Watching him in that weak glow of light, I found myself smiling, smiling at the snoring, the stupid tufty fringe, the tired and lined fifty-year-old face, and even the greying clump of hair in his ears. His newspaper lay open on the bed next to him, and I gently folded it up and put it on the bedside table next to a cluttered mound of pill packets and potion bottles.

I'm glad I found him. The stupid old fool.

I was about to turn the bedside light off when I heard a hefty thud coming from my office. I quickly swung the duvet back, slipped on my dressing gown and crossed the landing to find Eva face down on the floor, one leg hooked over an arm of the sofa and the blanket tied around her like a cocoon. She was happily snoring away too.

The phone on my table was flashing.

There was no answerphone message, and when I retrieved the number – a mobile – I didn't recognise it. I should probably have left it until the morning. Or just left it, full stop. But I didn't. I pressed redial like it was the most obvious thing in the world to do.

'Hello? Anya Belmont here, you just called me?'

'Oh, yeah, hi Anya. Mrs Belmont…erm…'

'Yes?'

He carried on stumbling over his words. I should have guessed it was him, but despite how much he had hung around my mind those first few days after we had initially spoken, right then, at that moment, Ray English couldn't have been further away from me.

'It's Ray,' he spluttered, 'Ray English. We…I don't know if you remember, we spoke…'

'Ray?' Our previous conversation started to drift back to me, words and laughter piecing themselves together as if they had always been there. 'Oh, okay.'

'Yes.'

'Yes. Now there's a late-night caller I wasn't expecting.'

'Yes, sorry about—'

'I didn't say you had to apologise.'

'It's late, I know…I didn't realise the time until I had dialled.'

'Right.' I wandered out of the office and tiptoed down the stairs to the living room. 'Don't worry about it, I wasn't asleep.'

'Me neither.'

'You don't say?'

'Oh, yeah. Okay. Obviously.'

He was nervous. Ridiculously so, it seemed, and he didn't really know why he had phoned me, that much was patently obvious. Why had he phoned me? What had I said to him last time, apart from deconstructing his relationship failings? Nothing, I don't think; I hadn't given him any reason to be phoning me again, and yet here he was calling me, and there I was, listening to him. I was surely the bigger fool.

'I haven't been sleeping much,' he started.

'So?'

'Yeah.' Nervous laughter. A cough. He was probably blushing too. Ray was coming across as a stumbling, bumbling adolescent standing on the doorstep of his school crush with a bunch of wilting garage flowers. I couldn't pretend that a part of me didn't start to enjoy it. It's been a while since I tongue-tied a man. 'I got a date,' he blurted out, before falling silent. 'You…I don't know if you remember but you said that…'

I will tell you my story the day you get back in the game. Shit…

'I know what I said, Ray.'

'So, there you go. I'm not the lost cause you thought I was, Mrs Belmont.'

'I never said you were a lost cause.' *Did I? Had I?*

'Ray…'

'I know…stupid, isn't it? I shouldn't have phoned you. You're a customer. Or at least your husband is. Sorry. This is wrong. I shouldn't have phoned.'

'Why did you?'

'I don't know. I shouldn't have, should I?'

'I don't know.'

'Is this wrong?'

'I don't know what this is.'

'It's nothing. It's just a phone conversation.'

No way did he look like a young Paul Newman. A young Paul Newman surely wouldn't have been this unsure of himself. He didn't look like Kirk Douglas either. No chance. I went into the kitchen and started to make a cup of coffee and an awkward silence followed me.

'What do you look like, Ray?'

'Why?'

'I want to put a face to the voice. I'm intrigued, I want to know, and I wouldn't leave that up to my imagination if I were you – you surely wouldn't come off too well. Or maybe I should just look you up on Facebook like some weirdo? Isn't that the way it works now? Isn't that the thing people do these days? Should I do that?'

'I'm…I'm a…nothing special…'

'Sell yourself, Ray, for crying out loud! Put some effort into it. Come on. I'm just some strange voice on the phone. You could be anything to me and it wouldn't matter. If you can't embellish with me, then what hope for you when you meet a real woman? Use your imagination a bit. Honestly, no wonder she dumped you.'

'I wasn't…I was different then.'

'Oh please, Ray, please don't use that line!'

'What line?'

'You were going to say that she made you someone, weren't you?'

'No.'

'What were you going to say, then?'

His silence confirmed my suspicions. He was an easy read. I was at the kitchen table, mug of coffee in hand before he said anything again.

'My profile picture…it's not a picture of me. On Facebook…so you wouldn't…'

'Yeah, I was only joking. I'm not in the habit of searching for younger men online. I haven't quite reached that stage yet.'

'How do you know how old I am?'

'It's in your words, Ray, dear. It's in everything you say.'

That hurt him. The silence that followed then was longer. Once again I had the perfect opportunity to end the call. If I had hung up on him then, there was no way I would have heard anything from him again. But of course, I didn't. I was enjoying myself too much.

'I'm on Facebook under my maiden name. In case you had been looking for me,' I said, rather pompously. In truth the aching silence on the end of the line was starting to make me feel guilty. I could have just apologised for what I'd said, I realise that, but then that would have handed him the initiative in the conversation. If I had conceded that then the whole thing might have started to mean something.

'Why would I do that?' he said, rather too quickly.

'Well, quite. So, Ray English, tell me about this date of yours then.'

'You really want to know, do you?'

'You might as well tell me. Don't you think? I've got a cup of coffee now. It is why you phoned after all, isn't it? Would hate for you to have a wasted phone call. So, go on. Tell all.'

'This is your phone call, Mrs Belmont.'

'Good point. Best get a move on then, Ray.'

'I met her on a speed dating night.'

'How modern. Never been on a speed date. Was it everything you hoped it would be?'

'I only got one match.'

'One is all you need. Sometimes.'

'I think my social skills are a tad rusty.'

'You've been out of the loop too long. It's a different world out there now.'

'Says the married woman. How would you know?'

It was my turn to stumble over my words and fall into silence. 'Yes, well…I watch a lot of daytime TV. So, one match, that's not great, is it? What did you talk about with these potential future Mrs Englishes? I'm quite curious as to what passes for a chat-up line with you. What did you say, Ray?'

'Not sure I can remember. What should I have said? "Hello, I'm Ray and I work in a call centre"? That seems just a little too—'

'Oh heavens above, yes, I certainly wouldn't tell them the truth. What did you say to hook this sweet little dear that matched with you?'

'I forget. She did most of the talking.'

'And what about…what is the name of this girl that broke you, Ray? I don't think you ever did tell me, and I never did ask. That was remiss of me, I'm sorry.'

'Katie,' he said defensively.

'Well, what about Katie then? What did you say to the love of your life when you first met her?'

'"Sorry," I think. I trod on her foot.'

'Needs work, Ray.'

'I know.'

'You're welcome to try on me, if it helps. Perhaps if we can get you conversing like a human being we might get lucky and life will align with you.'

'You want me to chat you up?'

'But you wouldn't be, really, though, would you?'

'I can't chat you up. That's…that would be a bit weird, wouldn't it?'

'And phoning a stranger up at half-twelve to tell them you have a date is…what? That's normal behaviour for you? I certainly hope not, Ray. A girl could get her feelings hurt.'

To that he gave a laugh, another warm and friendly laugh that made him sound like he was there in the kitchen with me. And that was just as well. 'Well, thank you for your most gracious offer, stranger, but I think I will pass on that.'

'Why? It doesn't mean anything.'

'No. I know.'

'No, right, so? There you go then.'

'Right.'

I had no real idea where I was leading the conversation, but thankfully I didn't have to find out. A squeaky floorboard and then the sound of footsteps on the stairs snapped me back to the real world.

'I've got to go,' I gabbled. 'Bye, Ray.'

'Hang on, what about what you said?'

I hung up on him. Ten minutes and two phone calls too late.

Eva stood in the kitchen doorway, the blanket wrapped around her tightly, from knees to head, a befuddled face poking out and fixing me with big eyes. She tottered over to the kitchen table and took a seat opposite me.

'One time,' she started in a croaky voice, 'this boy comes to a signing dressed up as a zombie, and he asks me, in this put-on Black Country accent, if I could sign one of the flaps of skin on his costume.'

I stood up, patted Eva on the blanketed head like she were a child, and put the kettle back on.

The Third Call

RAY

Our office liked to use the word "team" a lot. As if we are all part of some crack unit fighting the good fight for the great and the worthy, led into battle on a daily basis by our valiant team leader, some heroic sort who arms us with stirring, passionate words. At the head of our merry band of brothers and sisters, bound together by a mutual love of insurance policies, Mr Evans cut an imposing father-figure style – a tall man, broad-shouldered, with a hair flick that could open envelopes, this oft-decorated survivor of the insurance world was a sage and confidant to those of us held in thrall by his wisdom. He was the captain of this ship, and we his oarsmen, diligently cutting a path through choppy waters to a green and pleasant land.

At least that was the idea.

The truth was, none of us gave a shit.

Pat Bollard and Wendy French were the only two to actually notice when Mr Evans was sacked, and even then it was assumed by most that dear old Dad had got caught with his hands where they shouldn't be. No one suspected that redundancies were on the cards. Of course, some little man in a posh suit came along and used words like "reshaping" and "efficiency" and made it sound like our dismissals were actually noble sacrifices. We all cheered when Pat Bollard threw her miniature cactus in his face as she stormed out.

So it was that those three years at Babbidge Insurance dwindled away and became nothing more to me than a few lines on a new CV, and that CV was pimped and pushed and shouted everywhere I thought would listen. I needed a job, and fast. Danny was already working lunchtime and evening shifts at two different pubs, seven days a week, and we were barely scraping the rent together as it was. Thankfully, a fortnight of daily scours of the *Ham & High* later and what seemed to be the job I was born to do – at that moment at least – presented itself. It would combine both my wealth of experience in the world of insurance offices, and my faithful old friend, insomnia.

Galton Insurance, deep down in good old London town, needed a night security guard.

The building was everything you would expect from an insurance company office and less: a dreary, grey, rectangular slab of suffocating anonymity, sat nestled amongst other buildings that looked equally empty and soulless. Suited people strode the pavements, eyes turned down, hurrying for cabs, tubes and buses, hurrying away to anywhere that wasn't there. On the corner of the street was the obligatory coffee shop, and inside people were lost on their phones and their laptops. I ordered a tea and stood outside in the greying evening watching lights come on in the buildings across the street. It was an alien world, and each orange square of light was an eye watching me, unnerving me, judging me. Without much hesitation

I joined everyone else and turned my attention to my phone. I didn't want anyone thinking I was some sort of weirdo.

There were two missed calls from Beth, and a text message too. She was wishing me luck for the interview. Something she had already done, copiously. The cheeriness in her messages made me feel loathsome. It would have been so much easier when we broke up if she had despised me rather than become my friend. But Beth had been fine with it, she'd even preempted me when I took her to one side and asked to "talk". (Rough translation into coward: "you're dumped".)

'You're not ready,' she told me. 'Like I didn't know that when we first met? Please, Ray, you're so easy to read. And I've read that story before, you know?'

She had surprised my well-rehearsed words away. 'But…then…'

'What? Why did I go out with you, knowing that you were still hung up over someone else and it was never going to go anywhere?'

'Well, yeah, kinda…'

'I wasn't looking for the great romance, Ray, sorry to shatter any illusions you had there. I never needed you to sweep me off my feet, you know?'

'Oh.'

'Women can use men just as easily as the other way around. I would think we've both done okay out of it, haven't we?'

'I guess.'

'Oh, Ray, you've got so much to learn about women, haven't you?'

'Have I?'

'Uh-huh. Perhaps if you let this ex go you might surprise yourself. She'd be horrified if she knew what she'd done to you. Really, she would. Move on.'

'How do you know? You know nothing about her.'

'Don't I?'

I arrived early for my interview with Mr Galton and he was a quarter of an hour late, strutting out into the reception with a swagger but no apologies. Older than I had expected, but every bit the suited and booted boss at the big chair that I had imagined. He gave me his hand, moist and well-manicured, and led me into a small office, ushering me into a seat and picking up a clipboard.

'I'm having sex with a twenty-one-year-old tonight,' Galton said as he sat. He didn't look up at me, and didn't seem to want a response. 'Six-foot lingerie model she is, Danish on her mother's side. I know it's just because I have money, but should I care? What is wealth if not the chance to shift the balance of opportunity?'

'Well, quite.' If first impressions were anything to go by, I sure as hell didn't want a second interview.

Galton tossed the clipboard down and leant back in his chair, gazing at me properly for the first time. 'I don't hold much with CVs, Ray, if I'm honest. Not for this sort of job. Most times our security are ex-plod, ex-forces, or some old chap who likes a bit of power and isn't getting his trip off the neighbourhood watch. Why on earth would a young guy like you want it? Sitting on your arse all alone, living through the night. I couldn't do it. Left alone with your thoughts? What a horrible idea. That's why I do the job I do. Luckily I'm rich enough so I don't have to think. A man mustn't think too much, I don't think.'

'I enjoy solitude.' It was all I could think to say. 'Plus, I'm an insomniac. It sort of makes sense to me, as much as anything really does, Mr Galton.'

'Well, shit, don't explain yourself. It wasn't really a question. I don't want to talk you out of it. We're not exactly flush with applicants. The last incumbent was convinced the place was haunted. Maybe word got around.' Galton stood and laughed, ushering me out of the room.

'Haunted?' I could understand the need to be some sort of corpse to work there, but that was taking it a bit far.

'I know, ridiculous, isn't it? Though I suppose if a grown man is left alone long enough he starts to talk to himself. Talk to yourself enough and, well, I guess you can convince yourself of anything. I'm sure you get my drift. Bring a good book, that's my advice.'

The next evening Galton led me through the dreary maze of corridors and identical rooms that was Galton Insurance. The security guard uniform was a little too snug and itched in all the important places. The torch Galton had supplied was useless and would have to be replaced. The keys jangled and clanked from my belt, banging against my right hip with every footstep I took. The air conditioning whirred and buzzed above our heads, and the rooms held a delicate tang of the recently departed. It reminded me of being in detention at school: that hollow warmth, of shadows of people that should be there but have left you alone. Like school, Galton Insurance was the sort of nondescript place where a man could forget himself with half a mind.

Galton strode on, waving his hand into open doorways, pointing at signs on the wall and then led me out again onto the main stairwell. As we got back to reception he ushered me behind a long, semi-circular desk and shoved me down into a swivel chair. In front of me on the desk was a small CCTV monitor showing the view from just above the main doors, and on and around it were myriad papers, bound and fastened, folders and pens and all manner of disorganised clutter. A phone system with lines upon lines of buttons sat to one side, a greasy sheen on its black plastic house. Across from us an old man was mopping the floors, whistling a recognisable tune and staring at me from the corner of his eye. He was bent and haggard, wispy grey hair on his head, and darker, rougher patches in his ears. He was edging slowly down the corridor directly in front of the table, the whistling echoing away into the walls and then dribbling to nothing. He cast one final look in our direction then hobbled away.

'That's Morrison, our janitor,' Galton said dismissively, jabbing a finger in his direction and then twirling it quickly around the side of his head to signify his opinion of the old man with the mop. 'He knocks off at eight. Knocked off years ago, if you ask me. You're getting no conversation from him. Not that you'd want it. Man's got nothing to say. If he said anything at all.' Galton perched himself on the desk and then swivelled my chair around with one foot so I was staring directly up at him. 'Any questions, Ray?'

I hadn't decided whether Galton was just bluster and posture, a man too wrapped up in his own importance to bother to really listen to anyone else, or whether he was still too distracted by the twenty-one-year-old half-Dane that was chewing on his wallet with a gob full of promises. Either way, I didn't want to extend my conversation with him longer than I had to.

'No, Mr Galton. I don't think so.'

Galton smiled, patted me on the shoulder in a way that couldn't have been more patronising if he'd offered me a lollipop, and then leaned in close; a stupid, wet, smile breaking across his stupid, pointy face.

'Good. Welcome to the team, Ray.'

The job was dull and obvious and I loved it. I hadn't been lying to Galton; I truly did enjoy the solitude. There were no old man Evanses in this job, no passive-aggressive Pat Bollards and most importantly no tedious, whiny phone calls to people who would rather be anywhere else, conversing with anyone other than you, and would make no attempt to hide it. It was just me and my radio and a slow parade of crappy crime novels. Perfect. Except, of course, Galton was right about one thing: sometimes being left alone with your mind is not an ideal place to be.

The third shift, it began.

The graveyard shift radio DJ, who seemed to be trying to channel Tom Waits (fair enough, I suppose – I mean, if the nighttime did have a voice, it would be Tom Waits, right?) decided to give my memory a quick one-two by playing Augustines and Bobbie Gentry back to back. A pretty perfect double-header in anyone's book, but as far as I was concerned those two tunes (*Cruel City* and *Mississippi Delta*) floored me, and then there I was thinking about her again. Not that I ever really stopped, but certain things would always intensify the thoughts and the memories, and blow at the flame. And music was a pretty sure way to bring her back to me in an instant.

We'd discovered Augustines together, five months before she left me, when they were supporting one of our favourite bands, The Boxer Rebellion, at The Ruby Lounge in Manchester (one of the only bands I would ever go to Manchester for). She'd already heard *Chapel Song* online somewhere and gone a bit gaga over it, replaying the video time and again, singing it everywhere we went, and then she proceeded to scour the net for anything and everything else, developing in the process a rather unhealthy infatuation with the lead singer. Initially I put it down to another case of her beard preoccupation (it was quite extreme towards the end of our relationship), but truth is, that voice could have snapped the lock off a nun's wrought-iron chastity belt. Augustines and The Boxers tore that venue apart. It was a perfect gig and a perfect evening. It's the last perfect time that really stands out in our relationship for me. Five months later it was all Caesar salads and bus-stop goodbyes. I don't remember the in-between.

Then there was Bobbie Gentry and *Mississippi Delta*, and the nagging feeling that this gravelly-voiced DJ was somehow soundtracking my failed relationship.

Katie had loved *Mississippi Delta* and would sing it during rehearsals; she did a decent passing impression of Bobbie Gentry, but she was never arrogant enough to think she could ever come close to her. I liked that about her. Katie could have made a career as a singer if she'd really wanted to. She was certainly more than good enough. The year before she dumped me I had mocked up a CD cover with her face on it for a birthday present and she said she loved it. I think she genuinely did. Inside I had burned a CD of her singing with Broken English, pretty shitty quality but that didn't matter; she thought it was a cool present.

I had been trying not to think about the birthday I knew she had coming up. But during that third shift I could think of nothing else. In the years since we hadn't been together I still sent her a birthday card to her parents' house. Even once they had moved away from Southport, I carried on sending one, guessing that they would pass it on to her. I thought it was pretty harmless. It's polite, isn't it? Well, Danny didn't think so. He would say to me that I was only tormenting myself, that I was making myself look desperate and that nothing was less attractive than a desperate man. He said that I was pathetically clinging to the deluded hope that she would reciprocate one year and then I would grab that, misread it and then go back to how I was. I saw his point and I knew deep down he was probably right, even if I wouldn't give him the satisfaction of admitting it. I had vowed to myself, and to Dr Phillip, that I wouldn't send her one again. But this year was her thirtieth. That's a milestone, isn't it? I had to get her a card. Just one last time. How could I send one all those other years and then neglect to send one on her thirtieth? That would just seem like I was trying to make a point. Like I was suggesting that I was over her now and didn't care. I couldn't do that. Just one more card, I needn't send any more after that. I was pretty confident that I should be over her by the time she hit forty.

Beth helped me choose the card.

'No hearts or flowers or teddy bears, no pink, no ribbons, no sparkly tat that sticks to your hands. Nothing too big, something simple and plain,' she started.

'Like me?'

'Exactly.' I don't think she meant it the way I took it, but she didn't pause to let me find out.

'Nothing too humorous either. That can too easily be misunderstood. Did she have a sense of humour? No, scratch that, it doesn't matter, let's play it safe. Something with an animal on. Not a cute piglet or rabbit – no, certainly not a rabbit, and no duckling either, nothing like that. Maybe a horse? Though that could be misinterpreted. A dog. Maybe not. No. Actually, not an animal. Play it safer. Just something that says *Happy Birthday* on it. Not too big or colourful, though.'

'Something with *30* on it?'

'Certainly not. Here, this one, I think. Or this… pick one of these.' She handed me a few dull-looking cards with a simple *Happy Birthday* on each. I bought the most expensive one in case Katie ever saw it in a shop and decided to check.

Danny was right: I knew I would be sitting by, waiting in the vain hope that, come my birthday, I would find one from her sat on the doormat. Even though she didn't send one for my thirtieth, there was still a chance she would on my thirty-first. She might have been away at the time of my thirtieth, in some far-flung place without a postbox or a Clinton's Cards, or someone might have died and she could have been bereft and not thinking straight at the time. That would be understandable. She wouldn't have forgotten the date, I knew that much at least. It was the day we first kissed, my birthday, and she wouldn't have forgotten that.

As ever, Dr Phillip was siding with Danny on the matter of the birthday card; I could see it in him even if he wasn't going to say it. Dr Phillip rarely said anything. He just looked at me from his comfy chair.

That's a good job he's got. I should be doing that sort of job. I spent years listening to people whining at me on the phone and I never had a comfy chair or a decent pay packet. I'm not sure I could grow a neat little beard though, and Danny says that's a prerequisite.

'It's just a birthday card, why has it got to mean anything?' I asked Dr Phillip.

'If it doesn't mean anything, then why send it?' His fingers were steepled under his chin again in that poncy way of his. 'Why waste your time on meaningless things?'

'It's what you do, isn't it, with people's birthdays: you send cards?'

'To people you care about.'

'Of course I care about her.'

'Then it does mean something?'

'Stop twisting my words,' I snapped, immediately regretting the tone. I held a hand up in apology and gazed from the window, losing myself in the jagged edge of the north London skyline. When I looked back his expression hadn't changed one iota; still the steepled fingers, still the half-smile and still the eyes boring into me, waiting for me to splutter and blather more crap.

'I want her out of here,' I said, tapping my head. 'She's never going to leave, is she? This is how it's always going to be, isn't it? I'm fucked.' I don't know where those words came from. My honesty surprised me, even if it didn't surprise my counsellor. Dr Phillip's face remained as it ever was. 'Please, I want her gone.'

'I can do that?' he asked quietly.

'You're the quack in this relationship. Do something, will you? I just need her plucked out, cut off, anything. Whatever's easiest.'

Dr Phillip shuffled in his chair, hands resting on his knees, and gently leaned forward as if he were about to plant a kiss on my head. 'Perhaps we should look at what's stopping you from doing it, Ray?'

'I knew this was a waste of time.'

'What is?'

'This – all of this, you and me. Mostly me, but also you. This…it's all cobblers, really, isn't it? It's a racket.'

'What made you come to me?'

'My flatmate kinda talked me into it. He believes in mental masturbation.'

'A psychologist?'

'A wanker.'

He laughed and leaned back in his chair. 'Personally I think we're getting somewhere.'

'Seems I get nowhere fast, Doc. Never seem to like it much when I get there either.' I had nothing else to say, but Dr Phillip wasn't looking likely to jump in and fill the silence any time soon. I glanced at the clock above his head and saw we had five minutes left. I took his pound of flesh from my pocket and slipped it under the box of tissues.

'Ray?'

My name sounded like it was coming from a hundred miles away right at that moment. There was a tissue in my hand before I realised it, and I was screwing it up tightly between my index finger and thumb. The clock on the wall seemed to be ticking loudly, echoing in my head, like a slow-beating drum.

'Ray?' A million miles away now, that name.

Then I was inside a memory that was loud and bright and real. It was our last summer together – the four of us: Katie Fenshaw and Ray English, my best friend Danny Radleigh and the terrifying wannabe actresses, Vera Franks. Southport pier. Years ago, or maybe yesterday. Word for word, I hear it. Frame for frame, I see it. Katie and I are singing drunkenly at passers-by and Danny has his guitar and is strumming away behind us. Vera is unamused by the whole thing and that only makes us laugh, and laugh loudly, and now we are serenading the sea with a rendition of *Everlasting Love*. Someone tells us to shut up, but we don't even look at them; we just sing more loudly. Standing up on the barriers now, arms outstretched, singing up to the sky. Danny telling us to be careful up there, telling us it isn't safe, warning me not to fall.

'Ray?' Loud now, that name; loud and annoying.

Words came, and formed, and dribbled out of my mouth, and the anger felt like venom. I wasn't there at that moment; I was a million miles away, and five years ago.

'We were at a bus stop when she did it,' I was saying. 'Well, the last time I saw her was at a bus stop. She did it in my house. The kitchen. Four lines, that's all it took. Four lines. Twenty-five words. Three months of flirting to win her heart. Twenty-five words to break mine. She did it all without drawing breath. She was looking at my shoulder as she said it. We were going to have a Caesar salad. I was going to make her one because she'd never had a Caesar salad before.' Still I carried on speaking, the acrid taste of anger burning its way down my throat. 'She probably has by now. She's probably done loads of things by now. She could have done anything. Could be anyone. Perhaps she's dead? That'd solve a few problems, wouldn't it?'

Dr Phillip moved his hands forward and rested them on mine. 'That's us for today. Let us talk about this again at our next session, Ray.' He took torn-up pieces of tissue paper from my hands and dropped them in the bin.

The day of Katie's birthday I spent in bed, the duvet pulled over my head, pretending I wasn't there, as daytime TV soundtracked my misery; a limp burger of gristle with not even a pretence of a pickle. I ignored the phone; I ignored the delivery driver who rang incessantly on the doorbell. I ate something from the fridge I couldn't identify, and drank flat lager. I even cleaned up Danny's plate of mouldy toast. I stared into space, and I stared out of the window, letting the day go as fast as it saw fit.

The shift that night was unbearable. Where was she right at that moment, and what was she doing? I started to think about what I would have done with her for her thirtieth – where would I have taken her? I had no idea. Was she still friends with Vera Franks, and were they together? I immediately hated Danny for not being with Vera any more because then I might have known. Maybe Katie was having a nice night out with the girls. Something innocent like that. That made sense. That was the sort of thing she liked to do. Nothing too wild or crazy; Katie was never like that anyway, milestone birthday or not. The cinema, a restaurant, a quiet little pub in the country with no males anywhere near it except old men drinking real ale and smoking pipes. That was where she was. I could see it. That was what she was doing. Of course it was. She looked happy too, and that was good. Happy with her girls.

But that didn't last.

No, now there was suddenly an endless parade of younger men at the bar too, and I didn't see them coming – taller men, muscular men, witty men. They stank of cheap aftershave and their hair was sculptured. They all looked the same. They were chiselled and perfect and straight out of a catalogue; morons, ape men, predators, nothing going on up top, except the thought of what they would like to go on down below. But still, that was all okay, because Katie was never that shallow. She always needed more than a nice face and a six-pack. But then one turned out to be a singer, and he was in a band and they had a record deal, and now she was talking to him, and there was another one who was actually funny and charming and everyone was laughing. Christ, even Vera Franks was laughing and she never laughed because she was built from granite. Fuck, they were multiplying, and they were swarming around her, these good-looking and interesting men were everywhere, and she couldn't stop smiling or laughing and, fuck me, she was doing that thing with her eyes that she swore she never knew she did, but I knew she did and I found irresistible and I knew that other men would too and…

I gave a single scream on the top floor of Galton Insurance, staring out across the night skyline, and no one heard me.

Perhaps it was all a dream.

I soon developed a routine at work, usually based around my tea breaks. The most important of these was my half-midnight cuppa that I would have on the top floor. I would take a chair from one of the offices (top floor = bosses = best chairs) and sit looking out across the city towards The Shard. What a grand building. London is beautiful at night. Looking at that skyline at night you could get lost standing still, it's so exquisite. I would often lose an hour on shift just staring out of that window with my cup of tea. Sometimes I would read up there; sometimes I would just crank the radio up and sing along, taking a hat stand from time to time and standing in front of the full-length mirror in Galton's office, making like I'd made it.

As it was, that night, I had barely sat before my mobile rang in my pocket, and a mobile number I didn't recognise flashed across the screen. It wasn't Katie's mobile, I knew that instantly. I wondered for a brief moment whether she had changed her number. It was entirely possible. People change their numbers for all sorts of reasons. Perhaps she was getting cold callers?

My heart missed a beat as I answered.

'I hung up on you last time, I'm sorry about that. Even though this means so very little, a girl likes to have manners. How are you, Ray English?'

It took a moment to place her voice.

'Hello? Ray?'

'Anya.' It wasn't a question; I was telling her her name. 'Anya Belmont.'

'Yes. Well done. It's not too late to phone, is it? I'm not trying to make a point, just because you phoned me late last time, just so you know.'

'No. No, of course it isn't too late.' I came back to myself with a jolt and sloshed tea on my boots and the wedding invite from Tim that I had been using as a bookmark in the crappy E. B. Cunningham crime novel I was reading. 'Shit!'

'Caught you at a bad time? I can always call back…'

'No!' I shouted at her, and then dropped the phone into the tea puddle. 'No, don't go, just wait…hang on…'

I think I heard her laughing. It's more than likely. She did seem to enjoy laughing at me. I quickly padded the tea-spill down with the invite and then stood, brushing droplets from my trousers. 'Just spilt some… doesn't matter. How are you, Anya Belmont?'

'I find myself wide awake, Ray English, when I should be asleep. There was nothing on the TV. Thought I'd phone you.'

'Why?'

'I don't know. Do I need a reason?'

'You tell me.'

Silence. The phone line crackled and then she was back: 'I was a bit rude to you last time we spoke. Not that I feel guilty, it's just—'

'You were brought up well enough not to hang up on people, I remember.'

'Quite right, so yes, sorry about that.'

'Don't worry about it.'

'I wasn't.'

'I think, if memory serves, Mrs Belmont, you were going to tell me about yourself, weren't you?'

'Maybe. Who knows? Probably not. Not today, not tonight. That's not a phone call for the middle of the night.'

I held the damp wedding invite up and watched it wilt, droop, and then break in two. 'I got this wedding invite a while back, Mrs Belmont, and I think it mocks me.' I sat back down and started rubbing the toes of my boots against the backs of my trouser legs. 'That's the third one this past year. I didn't even get a plus one this time. What does that say when you don't even get a plus one?'

'It says, "We assume you are single, what with you being socially and romantically inept."'

'No, they don't know me that well. What this invite says is, "We don't really like you, but we feel obliged." I've become an obligation!'

'When is it, this obligation?'

'Third week in August.'

'Well, that doesn't give us long to work on your social etiquette, does it?'

'Oh, I'm not going to it. You've got to be joking.'

'All those bridesmaids, Ray?'

'You trying to set me up?'

'Would I really set myself such impossible goals?'

'Would you?'

'I do like a challenge, Ray. I should have told you that. But perhaps not that much, and besides, surely I don't need to anyway – you have this speed dater that fell for your irrepressible charms, don't you?'

'Ships that pass in the night.'

'You utter tart.'

'Well, we docked for a while. Wasn't so bad.'

'You mess that up too, did you?'

'I don't know. I don't think so.'

The phone line gave another crackle. Anya was talking, but her words were lost. I stood and wandered back out to the lifts and started to make my way back down to the cafeteria to refill my cup of tea.

'What was that?'

'What?'

'You said something and I missed it.'

'I asked why you weren't going to the wedding.'

'I'm not going back there. Not interested.'

'Back there? Back where?'

'Back home. Southport, it's up near—'

'Yes, I know where Southport is, Ray. I don't get a nosebleed when I go north of Oxford. I think I understand now. I wonder, am I right…she will be there? Is that it? That is the reason for your reticence? You can't stand to face dear Katie again. You're scared to meet her. Is that it? Am I right?'

'I shouldn't imagine she will be there. No.'

'Then what's the problem? Apart from your social leprosy, I mean.'

'I don't think I can be bothered to pretend I care. They want us to reform our old college band for the do. Personally I think they can whistle, and try dancing to that instead.'

'That's right, Ray the old troubadour. I remember now.'

'The idea of playing with the band again, that used to have so much romanticism to it. But now it just feels tired. Bride's cousin is a talent scout or something, so that's being dangled in front of us. Just doesn't mean much to me any more.'

'I never would have had you down as a singer.'
'No?'

'Bass player, perhaps. Drummer at a stretch.'

'Guess you don't know me like you think you do.'

'I don't know you at all.'

'Oh you'd be surprised – there's not much going on under the surface. It's me that doesn't know you.'

'No.'

'No.'

'That's all for the good.'

'Worried I might like it?' Instantly I knew I shouldn't have said it. I had crossed a line, shoved my tea-stained boot in my mouth, and made a fool of myself. Another awkward silence, in which Anya Belmont and I seemed to specialise, came down between us. 'Anyway,' I started, trying to push the conversation on, 'yeah, so, sorry…okay…'

'You don't half stutter and prattle when you are embarrassed, Ray.' The temperature in her voice had plummeted. 'Take control of your vocabulary at least, even if you haven't got anything else in hand.'

'I'm sorry…'

'And stop apologising. Why are you apologising?'

'I shouldn't have said what I did.'

'No.'

'I'm sorry.'

'I said stop apologising.'

'Do you want me to go?'

'I phoned you, didn't I? At least let me hang up on you.'

'Woman's prerogative.'

'You've been hanging around with the wrong women.'

'Tell me about it.'

She didn't. She hung up instead.

The Fourth Call

ANYA

'So why did you phone him, this mystery man of yours?'

'I honestly don't know.' Eva could see the lie but she didn't push. She didn't need to. 'And don't call him a mystery man, that makes it sound romantic. I'm married. I don't do romance.'

'I'm sure Len would be delighted to hear that.'

'You know what I mean. It's no mystery. Ray's no mystery, not at all.'

We were sat at our usual table in the café, staring out over the high street, only now Eva was more intent on staring at me as she took gentle sips of her coffee and slow, contemplative chews on a chocolate flapjack. At least talk of Ray had managed to subdue her paranoid ramblings for a short while. She had taken the high-backed wooden chair at the right-hand side of the table, rather than sitting on the old reclaimed school bench where we usually sat, and she looked like a queen on her throne. That in itself was enough to make me feel like I was being interrogated. Knowing Eva, it was surely deliberate.

'So Len knows about this trifling affair, does he?'

'I am not having an affair!' I shouted across at her. Instantly I could feel people turning to stare. I could also feel my face flushing with embarrassment.

'Okay, it's nothing, of course it is,' Eva said casually whilst giving one gawping customer on a nearby table the finger. 'These phone calls to some strange man are nothing. Certainly couldn't be seen in a million different ways, Anya.'

'Shut up, he's just a voice on the phone. He doesn't really exist.'

I gazed down at the hustle and bustle on the street beneath us. A busker was playing the blues, and people were passing him by, hurrying about their business, bound up against a spring shower. A *Big Issue* seller was being unfailingly courteous to everyone who ignored him and two charity supporters, in bright coats and armed with clipboards and rictus grins, were haranguing anyone within spitting distance of their well-rehearsed charm. Everything looked as it always did; yet something felt different, something was slightly askew.

'I talk to my regulars here. What's the difference?' I asked, turning back to face my inquisitor. 'Every day I'm having conversations with strangers, most of them are men too. It's the men that start the conversations here. I know all about Archie Deeks' prostate. Donald Banton got to telling me about that old dear he was thinking of shacking up with before he even considered telling his wife. I even had him wailing on my shoulder one time in the staff room. Talking to people is part of my job. They expect it here. So what's the difference? Why aren't you bringing me to task on that?'

Eva carried on chewing on her flapjack and said nothing; she gave the tiniest of shrugs and then leaned back on her throne, waiting for me to carry on. I turned back to the window and folded my arms on the windowsill, petulantly.

I knew what Eva was thinking, so I stole her chance to say it and make me feel even guiltier: 'And you can forget about Mr Two-Trousers too. It is nothing like that.'

'I already had forgotten him,' she lied. 'Hoped maybe you had too.'

I had, until then. I had scrubbed that sorry little episode from my mind in shame and had hoped never to be reminded of it. I knew what was going through Eva's mind, but she was wrong. It was different. I was different.

His name was really Jake, but we all called him Two-Trousers because that was all he ever seemed to own – in the near two years he was a regular, coming in for his Americano and bagel, almost every day, he was always wearing one of two pairs of jeans; stonewashed denim, or faded black. He was pleasant, didn't say much, and was quite easy on the eye. He was much more of an age with Mig and Nate and Sal than with me, but it was clear to all of them, even if it wasn't to me initially, that he had the hots for me. I got the smiles and the random lines about the weather. The tips went in my jar. It became a bit of a joke for the others, and they delighted in taking the piss and trying to embarrass me. Sometimes they would all part from the service area when he came in and leave me alone, all of them busying themselves with other things.

He never saw it, I don't think, and if he did he didn't seem to mind. Over time though, the joke became less funny, the reality slightly more troublesome.

I never fell for him, despite what others thought, but it was true that his very presence began to flatter me into stupidity, and stupidity started to make me forget who I was. It wasn't fate, it wasn't kismet, no stars aligned, nor did any planets collide; it was merely bad timing. Len and I had been spending too long apart, not that such a thing was rare back then, because even when he was at home we might as well have been apart. He was still commuting to London in those days, so he was up at dawn, home long after dusk, and in bed before midnight. Some weekends he would never come home at all, and even when he did he wouldn't do much more than sleep. Holidays were never really on the cards. Even if he had had the time, Len doesn't really do holidays, jaunts or jollies. Len works. Len has always worked. I can barely get him into a different jumper, let alone a different postal code. Even now he's working in Salisbury I still don't see enough of him. Sometimes he stays awake long enough to watch the soaps and sometimes, since he hit fifty at least and decided to become a hypochondriac, we have been known to take a brisk walk together on a Sunday. As much as I love Len, and despite my actions and all the years we've been together I do still love the stupid sod, he does infuriate me too. I know the feeling is mutual, and thank God it is. That's a better balance than some marriages.

'You were lonely,' Eva said quietly, as if she were reading my mind. 'You still are.'

'No. No, I just wanted him to notice. I needed him to show he cared. I needed him to fight for me.' I rested my chin on my folded arms and sighed into the window. 'Christ, that sounds so childish when you say it out loud.'

'Most mistakes we make do, darling.'

And it was a mistake. It was also the behaviour of a game-playing teenager, and that shames me almost as much. Even when I was a teen I never lowered myself to such actions. There had only been Andrew Moorcock (and what an ironic name that had been) before the bastard Henry Gage, and after that nightmare no one was getting near me, not until Len, that unlikeliest of white knights, came along. Maybe that was the problem: perhaps I hadn't got my stupid mistakes out of the way when I was a teenager; I hadn't got my sugar rush from the pick and mix, as Eva was so fond of saying. Sometimes I look at Mig and Nate, even Sal, and I get jealous of their freedom and the time they've got to get it wrong. But then, they don't have what I have, and they possibly never will.

Who said it had to be perfect? Where was that ever written? People chase an ideal they see in films or read in books, but the truth is no one would be stupid enough to celebrate the truth; there is no money in the grey areas of life. I had someone I loved, and who loved me back. We all make a mess of it from time to time; it is only then you know whether you've got it right. Or, if you prefer, as Eva puts it, 'If you inadvertently catch your partner taking a dump and don't feel utter revulsion next time you are getting it on, then you've got a keeper.'

'I do love Len, Eva,' I said quietly into the air. 'I know what you are thinking, but you're wrong. He is my husband. I've always loved him.'

'I never needed to ask you, Anya. Why did you need to tell me?'

How we even got onto the subject of Ray, I don't remember. We had been discussing Eva. Again. Just as we always seemed to be doing. She had come to me in another morbid panic as she fretted and flapped about her forthcoming promotional tour for her new book. She had been looking drawn and haggard the past few weeks, even more than usual, and I could smell the vodka on her breath when we met. She had played the best friend card whilst we drank our coffee, always a weak spot for me as she well knows, and quietly, gently, she started suggesting that this awful torture that she must endure would be so much better, so very much more bearable, if it were shared with her dearest friend. She hadn't come straight out with it and asked me to go with her, but she was being about as subtle as teenage foreplay.

'You want me to come with you, I get that, but I've got a job.'

'You're the boss, aren't you? Mig can cope here. What is the point of being a boss if you can't take time off whenever you want to?'

'Yeah, whenever *I* want to, that's the key part of that statement, isn't it?'

'Well, what else have you got going on? You certainly weren't planning on going on holiday, were you? I mean, Len is...'

'I know full well what my husband is, thank you.'

Eva was staring into her latte, her lips pulled down, head tilted to the side like a confused puppy. 'You should see it, Anya, you'd understand if you saw it. You'd know why I don't want to go. It's crazy. Obscene. I don't do well around lots of people, you know I don't…and Jim doesn't understand me. You do, though. I need someone with me who understands me. You could ask Len to come. Couldn't you? Yes. Ask him. He could, couldn't he, if he wanted to? Len should come too. That would be good.'

'Len won't come.'

'No. I suppose…' Eva was fiddling with her hands, and seemed to have discovered a nervous twitch. My ball-busting, force-of-nature friend, laid low by the prospect of adulation. It was such a strange equation. A psychiatrist would have a field day with her.

'Hey,' I said, nudging her with a foot. 'Get yourself together. We'll sort something out. Let me have a copy of your dates and I will see when I can get cover. Deal?'

Eva gave a flicker of a smile and nodded, her coffee mug paused in front of her lips. 'I've trapped myself.'

'Yeah, you're trapped under a cash cow. Whoops, how'd that happen?'

'Yes, I know, poor little rich girl. I made my king-sized four-poster bed and now I should just shut up and lie in it?'

'Something like that.'

'I'm a stupid bitch, aren't I?'

'Aye, you are. But you're my stupid bitch. Shut up and drink your coffee.'

Mig, or Mignona (French I think, or maybe just pretentious) had been with me for two years and had proved herself indispensible. Barely nineteen, with more piercings than years on the planet, she was a tough little worker, and had quickly worked her way up to assistant manager. It was a meaningless title really, it purely meant she had a set of keys and I had someone to use when I wanted a day off. Thankfully she was still young enough to believe in titles. She was always friendly, always on time, a stroppy customer never fazed her and, blessedly, she seemed to be happy in her job. I was dreading the day she decided to up and leave me. She'd been talking about art college ever since she first rolled in the door, and now and again looked like she was ready to jump into it, but she hasn't yet. Plus there's Nate, and he might be the saving grace when it comes to keeping her.

I think it had been love at first sight for Mig. I doubt it was for Nate. The idea of Nate being that decisive about anything is ridiculous. Nate is a tall, gangly lad with lanky hair and a beard that reminds me of stuffing hanging out of a sofa cushion; dopey (in body and pastime) and clumsy, he's also the sweetest lad, and that is more than enough to compensate. The two of them are unbearably cute together, though a little less so whenever Mig decides to confide details of their sex life to me. Which she does frequently.

'...He stuck it in up to the knuckle,' she was saying to me in the staff room after I had gone to ask her about covering for me. 'Not the main one, mind you, the one mid-finger. Is that still a knuckle? I suppose the fact it wasn't all the way makes a difference. At least that's something.' Sat opposite me, cross-legged on the sofa, a serious, considered expression on her face like she was contemplating a deep political discussion, she seemed to be chewing the idea over in her mind. I averted my eyes and tried to lose myself in my coffee mug, praying for someone to come in and disturb the conversation. 'Then he wiggled it about a bit.'

A bit of coffee seemed to go down the wrong way and I lapsed into a coughing fit. Mig didn't seem to be aware.

'I had been on top, riding him mercilessly, and had just reached the point of climax. Then there it was – a tickle, a poke, and then a little shove. Completely put me off my stride, and then I broke wind. I don't think he will do it again now, and that's a shame because I don't know how I feel about it yet, you know? I don't know if I liked it. If I'd been ready I could have decided. It might have been nice. Thing that bothers me, though, is I don't know why he did it. Isn't that the sort of thing you discuss first? I mean, I'm all for acting on impulse, sure, anything else is an open ticket as far as we are concerned, there's no drawing of a line…and we've done some truly filthy things.'

'Yes.' *I know. I remember you telling me. Please stop saying these things to me.*

'But that is different, isn't it? It's sacred. I think he should have asked me. We should have talked about it. Do you think we should've talked about it, Anya?'

'Well…I think…maybe…' I spluttered between coughs.

'When he wanted me to stand on his balls in my high heels, we talked about that beforehand. I just don't understand what possessed him to do this without mentioning it first.'

I checked my watch and stood. 'I think we should—'

'Has Len ever…?' She looked up at me and then frowned, before giving a little, dismissive laugh. 'No,' she said simply, and then stood and took the calendar down from the wall. 'So what dates were you thinking of?'

That single 'no' gnawed at me for the rest of the shift. It was ludicrous that it should annoy me so much, but it did. The gnawing became a sore and then that sore began to fester into anger. Of course, it wasn't the act of perversion that was the problem, indeed the very thought of it made me simultaneously want to laugh and also vomit on her; no, it was the fact that she didn't need to make an assumption, because she had certain knowledge. It was the aching predictability of two old people to a pair of young eyes. And, it was the fact that she was right. I was old to her. And she was young. And none of it mattered yet for her.

Watching Mig and Nate touch each other during the rest of that shift – a little brush of the arm, a hand on the small of the back, a flick of the hair – made me hate them. I wanted to take them both aside and tell them that what they had was never going to last. That it didn't actually matter, not really. I was trying to swallow jealousy down like it were bile, and I was choking on their happiness. I could feel another panic attack coming on – the fluttering inside me, the tightness – and I wanted to scream but I suddenly had no voice.

Stupid fool.

I saw limp balloons on my mantelpiece at home, and five measly cards. *Five people sent you a card, one of whom was your husband, and one was from your parents and they have to. So three people really sent you a card. Just three. Three people care enough to send you a birthday card.*

I finished my shift early and left without saying goodbye. There would always be tomorrow to apologise and try again.

I didn't go straight home. I didn't see the point. Walking through the dwindling shoppers and small clusters of tourists, I found myself in the cathedral close, sat on a damp bench, staring gormlessly at some new sculpture that had found its way onto the grounds. *Strangers*, it was called, and it seemed to consist of five different-sized blocks, connected haphazardly to each other in the very vague shape of a person. It meant nothing to me. Like most art in middle-class cities, it was there to be pontificated over rather than enjoyed. Three tourists in red and orange macs were stood around it, eyeing it up, scrutinising it, and then they were shooting it what seemed like a hundred times with cameras. Then they were off, joining a larger group of garish macs, all descending on the cathedral itself. Salisbury was always a popular stop-off for box-ticking tourism.

The smell of wet grass was thick in the air. It was earthy and slightly cloying. A dog bounded along the grass chasing a stick, stopped just beyond the sculpture and took a piss, before returning proudly to its owner, stick in mouth, and with a happy swagger. On the bench to my right an old couple were nibbling on sandwiches and taking delicate sips from a thermos. The old man caught my eye from time to time and smiled. To my left schoolchildren were dotted on and around another bench, eating takeaway pizza, laughing and showing off, and talking loudly about things of no great importance.

My mobile phone was vibrating in my pocket. As I answered, two of the schoolchildren started play-fighting, hitting each other with their games bags. Both of them were kneeling on the wet grass, laughing themselves snotty, and shouting themselves hoarse. The others were laughing too. It sounded like they were bearing witness to the funniest thing in the world. When the world is theirs, perhaps it will be?

'Hey,' I said into the phone. 'How you doing?'

'Are you still at work?' Len asked.

'No. Why?'

'You're at home? Great, then can you have a look in my office and see if there is a black box file on my desk?'

'I'm not at home.'

'Are you on your way home?'

'S'pose. I'll have a look when I get in. Black box file?'

'Black box file, yeah, can you give me a bell on the mobile and let me know if you find it, sweetheart?'

'Sure. Hey, I was thinking, you know, Eva's been asking me to hold her hand on this wretched book tour she's doing. Well, I really think I should, I thought maybe I might take a week of holiday for it, look after her, you know, because if she's left to her own devices…'

'You're good to her. But you also indulge her too much.'

'It's what friends do. I think.'

'Yeah, well, as long as it's a two-way deal.'

'So you want me to say no?'

'Not at all. You could do with a break. If she lets you get one. Yeah, go, it's a good idea.'

'Is it?'

'Sure.'

'I don't have to go.'

'Of course you do. Listen, I've got a meeting with management, I've gotta shoot. Let me know about that folder. Love you.'

'Yeah. Love you too.'

I sat on that damp bench and watched the world go by; the tourists, the children, the couples, the strollers, the joggers, the shoppers and the workers, and none of it meant anything. I watched but I barely saw. The schoolchildren had gone, leaving an empty pizza box and cans of drink on the bench, and now the old couple were leaving too. They both smiled at me as they wandered past my bench, and I smiled back. They stopped where the children had been sat and gathered up the litter and dumped it in a bin about six feet away.

Sorry if I offended you. Did I? the text said. I wondered if he had debated whether to put a kiss on the end of it. Was he that sort of person? I doubted it, but I wanted to ask him. Not that I would. Three days I had had the text and wondered what to do with it. Maybe my silence was speaking volumes, speaking loud enough for even Ray English to hear. It surely was. Though it probably wasn't saying what I wanted it to, and that was the problem. I'd drafted two replies but they both sounded stupid. Simply saying "no" would have been easy enough, but how to say that without sounding curt? I could have put an *x* after it, but that would have been a bad idea. That simple little letter has far too much to say for itself. *No. NO! No, not at all…nope, nah, you're all right, mate, fine, don't worry about it. Didn't offend me a jot.* None of it looked right. None of it sounded right in my head. Better to phone him, clarify the situation and clear the air.

Alone on my bench, a spring drizzle dancing about on the breeze, I scrolled through the phone until I found his name, and pressed dial.

'Why aren't you going to the wedding?' I asked him as soon as he answered. 'I mean, I know your official line, I remember some cryptic rubbish that you gave, but we both know that wasn't true. What's the real reason, Ray?'

'No small talk?' There was relief in his voice, and that made me feel good.

'No, we're past that stage, I think. Go on, why aren't you going?'

'We have stages, do we, you and I?'

'Friends have stages, Ray. Yes. Don't you have any friends?'

'Got a couple.'

'Damn, I've only got one. Can't have someone like you besting me. I will have to sort that out.'

'I only like one of them though, if that's any help?' he said with a chuckle.

'But do they like you?'

'I've never really been sure about that. Am I a lost cause?'

'I think you might be, Ray English, yes. I think I must be too. I will keep you company. We can be two cold fishes together. Don't worry, it's a big pond.'

'I wasn't cold until I met the other fishes, Anya Belmont.'

'You haven't met them yet, you're still swimming in circles.'

'Are we friends, then?' His voice dropped a level, the light playfulness no longer there, and I felt unnerved by it.

'I don't know. What would you say we were?'

'Strangers?'

'But I know so much about you, Ray. How can you be a stranger to me?'

'I know nothing about you though.'

'Why would you want to? I'm not remotely interesting. You, though…far more to talk about where you're concerned. You're much more interesting, Ray.'

'I've already got a counsellor, you know? If that was what you had in mind.'

'Yeah, but there are things you can say to me that you could never contemplate saying to them, aren't there?'

'Likewise.'

'I have nothing I need to say to you, Ray. I don't need a shrink. I don't need to unburden my woes to anyone.'

'Yeah. If you say so.'

Even Ray English could read that lie. Which served only to show me how blatant it must have been. A moment of shivering stupidity shot through me, and I heard myself in my mind opening up to him, wondering how that would have sounded. *Well, now we have discussed the breakdown of your relationship, let's discuss my first marriage, and what it was like watching my husband die, and then let's talk about the fallout from that and how I went and hid under the safety blanket of this dull life I'm living.* Yeah, it sounded pretty bad.

'Why won't you go to the wedding, Ray?'

'So is this how this is going to work: you ask all the questions? That's a little one-sided, that sort of friendship. Not sure I like that.'

'You answer my question and then I will answer one of yours. Can't say fairer than that.'

'Okay.'

'Why won't you go to the wedding, Ray?'

'I don't want to. I've moved on.'

'No you haven't, you've moved away.'

'Same thing.'

'No it isn't.'

'I don't want to go. Why has there got to be a reason? You really do sound like my counsellor, you know? Some things don't necessarily have a reason behind them. Some things just don't need analysing and poking apart. I don't feel like it, I can't be bothered, I can't really afford it, I don't like the guy getting married…no, strike that – I barely remember the guy getting married. I don't want to play with the band again, I don't want to go back home…'

'In case you meet Katie?'

Silence. A cough. It was so easy to land a blow on Ray. He needed to toughen up.

'If you want my advice, Ray—'

'You're being presumptuous again.'

'Only because you're being predictable. I think you should go to the wedding. I also think you should go and search her out.'

'I don't even know if she's still there.'

'Find out. Go find her and get some closure. It's the only way you're going to restart your life. Could be she's not the same girl who's been keeping you up at nights all these years. Could be you might wonder what all the fuss was about.'

'What do you look like?' His voice was quiet, almost a whisper, with a slight crack in it, like a crossed line.

'Why?'

'That's my question to you. What do you look like, Anya?'

'Don't ask me that. You don't need to know.'

'Don't I?'

'No. We're never going to meet, so you don't need to know.'

'Why do you feel the need to tell me that? Did you think I was about to suggest something? Or maybe you're telling yourself that? What makes you think I want to meet you?'

'Just laying some ground rules. One of us needs to, don't you think?'

'Hadn't given it a moment's thought.'

'Lucky you.'

'I do know how it is.'

'I doubt you do, Ray.'

'You've got baggage, I get it.'

'Baggage? And you haven't? You need a concierge!'

'Fair enough. Okay, Anya Belmont, I've got another question for you then, if that last one is a no-go area.'

'Go on then, Ray English.'

'Why did you ask me what I looked like?'

'I didn't.'

'Yes you did, the last time I spoke to you, or the time before…sometime, you said you needed to put a face to the voice. You asked me what I looked like.'

'Did I? Don't remember that,' I lied.

'Is that an admission of fallibility?'

'Not where we are concerned, Ray. You're a social vegetable, whereas I'm merely withering on the vine.'

He liked that; he laughed hard at that. He did have a good sense of humour at least, which was just as well.

'You know, I didn't think I'd hear from you again. I thought perhaps I'd offended you last time we spoke.' Once again his voice dropped a level, and sounded earnest and serious. I didn't like him like that.

'You probably did. It probably doesn't matter.'

'No.'

'None of this matters, does it? That's why it's perfect. You're nothing, Ray. Just a voice. A voice can't mean anything. Also, you're one of life's failures. I like that. It means I can talk to you and none of it matters because you don't matter.'

'Thanks. I also cook.'

Once more we laughed together, and that made me happy. I wondered what the reaction would have been if I had said that to Eva or to Len. I couldn't see either of them taking the joke before the insult. Somehow this stranger I had found did, and that was a wonderful thing.

'You're stuck, Ray. You're in limbo. You've chosen to swim in circles.'

'You make it sound like I enjoy it.'

'You probably do. I'm not saying it's intentional, maybe it's just subconscious, but misery is so much easier than happiness, isn't it? Self-pity requires a lot less than optimism. You think it's a barrier, something to keep you safe from hurt – that's what you tell yourself. But the opposite is true, because the only person that hurts is you. Because no one else cares. Why should they? All it does is keep you locked in a trap you set for yourself.'

There was silence on the other end of the phone. I could almost see his petulant expression, the pursed lips and the raised shoulders. Clearly he was no Paul Newman. Paul Newman would never do that.

'I think I'm not that much different, Ray. At least to a certain degree. I set my own trap, but it was through circumstance, not design. I think that's the difference.'

The silence became a sigh, and then he was back, quieter than before. 'Don't intrigue me, Anya. You're going to make me want to ask questions. You're going to make me want to know about you.'

'Perhaps that's why I needed to speak to you. Because we are both trapped. I don't know. I've asked myself that question a lot but never really got an answer I liked. I found myself dialling you without really knowing why. What does that mean?

'You need to speak to me, do you?'

'Apparently it's good to talk. That's what they say. It makes everything better if you talk. Did you know that? Thought I'd give it a go.'

'Go for it.'

'Don't really want to now.'

'Why not? It doesn't mean anything, Anya. It's just words. I don't mean anything…'

'You're just a voice on the phone.'

'Exactly. It's almost like talking to yourself.'

A final huddle of tourists were leaving the cathedral for the day, moving together in one large, colourful group, back through The Close, past my bench, and then out of the High Street gate, talking loudly and happily. I watched them disappear and then turned back to see a smattering of fat pigeons rummaging around at the bits of pizza crust under the bench on my left.

'I think you should go and find her, Ray. Go and find Katie.'

'That's what you think, is it?'

'If I bothered enough to think about it, that's probably the conclusion I would come to, yes.'

'I think you should tell me what's on your mind.'

'You do?'

'I do.'

'I phoned you, though. I just wanted to feel better about myself.'

'Always happy to help people with self-esteem issues. I do like to try and offer society a use. I need that definition. Makes me sleep better at night. Or not.'

'You've been defined by running away.'

'It's been said.'

'Doesn't work though, does it, Ray?'

'What are you running away from, Anya?'

'You've already asked your question. You don't get to ask another. Maybe next time.'

'Going to be speaking to each other again then, are we?'

'Who knows, Ray?'

I knew. I expect he did too.

The Fifth Call

RAY

'I can't talk now, it's not a good time,' Anya said, instead of hello. She sounded flustered and distracted, and I probably sounded a fool.

'No?'

'No, Ray. What do you want?'

'No. Not a good time for me either,' I said casually, backtracking.

'What do you want, Ray?'

'I was thinking I might go to the wedding after all.' I whispered the words, even though there was no one else in my bedroom. 'You were right,' I added, as if to appease her.

'Well, that's good. Is that it?'

'Just…just wondered if you still felt that was…I don't know…do you feel that…'

'Oh, spit it out! What am I supposed to feel, tell me? Why am I supposed to care?'

'You're not.'

The decision, for my part, felt momentous, making Anya's harsh brush-off all the more hurtful, and that sensation, conversely, only served to make me feel even more stupid than I did already. Mabel and Olive had agreed it was the right thing to do, but I'm not sure they had actually been listening to what I had said. Mabel merely said that she liked weddings and asked if I could take some photos for her. I suspect Olive would have been more receptive if it had been a funeral. Danny had taken my change of mind with what seemed a hard-fought show of begrudging gratitude and we had said no more about it. I felt sure that at least Anya would understand. Maybe she did. Maybe she was trying to tell me something, in her offhand manner. She wouldn't be the first woman to try and tell me something by saying something else. 'It's what they do, women,' Danny told me once. 'It would take a more clued-up man than either you or I could ever aspire to be, to work out what the hell they do it for. It's like the Enigma code. It's a secret language that they alone understand. Top people have spent an age trying to decode it.'

'So by that token, when Katie said that she didn't want to be with me any more, she might have meant…'

'You really are a dickhead, aren't you?'

At the start of the previous shift, going to the wedding had pretty much been the last thing on my mind. Coming in through the door to Mickey P's in the morning to find Danny auditioning singers to replace me may have been the cherry that squashed that particular cupcake, but as ever, it had been my own wayward mind, making logic from the illogical and sense from stupidity, that had started it all.

As with every other shift I began as I meant to go on, and that meant a cup of tea as soon as Morrison had left.

The ground floor of Galton Insurance was essentially, apart from the reception area, one long corridor that wrapped around the base of the building like a coiled snake. There were two conference rooms feeding off it, a cafeteria and a kitchen. A window in the kitchen looked out onto a public car park and beyond to a seedy, sticky-sheets hotel, complete with neon sign. I'd always bring my own teabags as the brand that Galton supplied tasted like you were drinking steamed wood shavings. Maybe that's the way the rich man's world worked. Perhaps you start with shit tea? Say what you like about old father Evans – and I did – but at least Babbidge always had proper teabags. But then, if you want to look at it another way, Evans is now on the scrapheap and Galton is likely teabagging a six-foot Danish lingerie model.

Tea. Lots of answers in tea. And biscuits.

The car park was still at least a quarter full of cars. The odd figure stumbled through the drabness towards their ride home, overworked workers or late-night shoppers. I saw a couple pass by hand in hand and stumble into their car, catching a long kiss before the car's interior light faded out. To one end of the car park a small group of youths were congregated, huddled together over cheap alcohol and even cheaper impulses. Galton had told me that the car park was often a playground for the drinkers and the shaggers, but that as long as they kept away from the building I wasn't to care about them. I was way ahead of him.

I was too tired to care even if it had been in my remit. Tiredness teased me that night, toyed with me, and as I walked the carpet felt like sponge beneath my feet. I would perhaps take an hour or two in one of the offices later and see if the tease went any further. I wasn't holding out much hope, but something seemed different that night. It felt like there was lead in my eyes, and cheap stuffing in my legs. Maybe I would actually sleep. Maybe I would actually be normal again, just for one night.

I decided to break from tradition and move my half-midnight, comfy chair cuppa forward and took the lift up to the tenth floor. (Lift up to the tenth, and then the stairs back down, floor by floor, sweeping the offices and making some half-arsed show of doing the job I was paid for; that was usually the routine.)

The radio was playing some tedious phone-in when I turned it on – tiresome people bleating about politics and getting aroused by their own opinions. I fiddled with the dial but only found more people talking, and then further along the dial, even more still; tired voices, shouts, barks and whispers. So many people with so much to say. I gave it up as a good idea gone south and then decided to go back to reception to get the crappy crime novel I was nearly done with; I had worked out on page ten whodunit, but I was hoping for a twist. That was surely some sort of metaphor.

As I stepped out onto the stairwell, the air conditioning started stirring again, and I stood under the nearest vent and let the secondhand air blast onto my head and into my heavy eyes. It ran its fingers over my face and down my body and probed my ears, aggravating the headache that had been hanging around the base of my skull like a flattened house. I closed my eyes and tilted my head forward to let the air flow down the back of my neck, and then I shivered, the jumper itching against my back as if I were in another man's skin. Tiredness covered me like a thick shroud and then seemed to fall through me. I swayed, I sagged and I yawned. Outside, beyond the walls, far away, someone shouted and someone else responded with a laugh.

I pulled my eyes open with an effort, stepped forward, had just enough time to ask myself why I was taking the long way down instead of the lift, and then tripped on the top step and fell.

I came to in what felt like three pieces, lying on my back on Galton's desk with my trousers around my ankles. I could smell antiseptic and perfume, and the two aromas were dangerously adjoined. A small medical kit lay open on the desk next to my left elbow, bandages and plasters scattered around it. The phone on Galton's desk was ringing, right next to my head, and the tone was insistent and demanding. She had been standing over me for a few minutes, so she said, before I noticed her. In fact I noticed the cup of tea she was holding out before she even registered.

'Hello,' she said. 'Two sugars still? Am I right?'

I grunted, sat up, shook at the concrete planet in my head and gave her the thumbs-up. The phone finally finished its ringing and fell silent. There was the perfume again, hanging over her. She was small and fragile, her face kindly yet hidden under a garish make-up job that was trying to make her look older, harder and cheaper, all focused around lips that promised great pleasure and unbearable pain. It was paint-by-numbers beauty hiding a broken canvas. Her hair, a dark auburn colour, was tied up in a tight ponytail, a small plastic butterfly clipped to the band holding it in place. Her age was a mystery to me; she could have been anything between late teens and late thirties. She spoke with the confidence of youth, yet her voice carried a weary detachment that you would struggle to put with it.

Yet it was definitely her. It was my Katie.

'I've had a go at attending to your…' she pointed down, between my legs, then her finger spun a small circle, 'bumps and bruises. What happened to you?'

I shrugged my shoulders and slugged at the tea. 'I don't know. Fell down.'

'Men do that a lot, don't they?'

I stared at her, no doubt with a look of undiluted dumbness on my face. 'They do.'

'I'm Katie.'

'Why are you telling me? I haven't forgotten.'

She giggled stupidly. Either she was easily amused or I didn't get the joke. Somehow I knew it would be the latter. She crossed to a small filing cabinet just to the side of the open office door, eased herself up onto it and slowly, purposefully, crossed her legs; slender and toned, covered in flesh-coloured tights. She knew what that action did to me. She was working the situation, feeling her way across my shadow. She rolled her right foot around and around; the black stilettos on her feet were new, unspoilt and deadly. I wondered how many men had fallen for her, fallen under her.

'Katie,' I said over the rim of the cup.

'Yeah?'

'Thanks. Thanks for…' I looked around me and then raised the cup to her.

She giggled again, her narrow shoulders bouncing up and down. 'What happened to you? Why'd you fall down?'

I shrugged again, only too aware that I needed to find a new response soon, as even I was tiring of it. But at that moment words were flattened by the truth, the truth sagging under the bent bows of confusion. She didn't seem to care.

'How did you get in?' I asked, now sipping at the tea. Good tea. Not winning any awards, but good enough to dunk a biscuit in. I had no biscuits. I made a mental note to rummage through the kitchen downstairs. Someone had to have biscuits.

She seemed to blush at my question, though it was hard to tell under the slap on her face. She certainly gave me a coy look, raising her shoulders and pulling her arms into her lap. A hand went to a small bag slung over her shoulder. I had only just noticed it. She never wore bags before. This was a new thing for her, just like the skirt and the make-up and the expensive perfume. I know nothing of bags. It was a sort of tan-coloured bag. Shiny. Probably carried a name that carried a price that carried the vain to an empty satisfaction. She pulled out a small ring of keys, which she waggled in front of her face.

'Your predecessor. We were close.'

'I hope he didn't give out keys to the front door to everyone.'

'Oh no, these are to prise open the window in the cafeteria. We worked a system on a dodgy latch. It's easier to come in through the car park. Wouldn't do to be seen. He was such a wonderful man. Did you know him?'

'I don't know. Did I?'

She turned away, politely ignoring my question, and gazed out into the empty corridor. Once more the perfume seemed to come to me as if carried on her breath when she spoke. 'Do you mind me being here? I hope you don't mind. It's just...well...'

'No. I don't mind. Of course I don't mind. You should stay forever.'

The words made her face flash with an unnatural happiness and she turned back to me, beaming. She uncrossed her legs and then moved them apart more than the situation or comfort warranted. She was playing me, working me, gauging her power. I stood and pulled up my trousers before anything else could stand or be pulled.

'So why don't you tell me about yourself?' I said to her, trying not to make a big deal of small talk, not looking at her; focusing instead on a clock on the wall, the hands turning fast anti-clockwise, then turning slowly, then stopping altogether and then disappearing.

When I looked back at her she had crossed her legs again and her head was bowed, her hands playing with each other in her lap; long, painted fingernails which she never had, scratching palms and then tapping tunelessly against cheap gold rings, that she never wore. *Are you real?* I asked someone inside my own mind. She was surely as real as me. Not the greatest of compliments, of course, but she didn't need to know that.

'I think I loved him a little bit,' she said to her shoes, shoes she would never wear. 'Your predecessor. Not in the sense you are probably thinking, certainly not in the end. It was not the flowers and chocolates and live a life on a sunbeam kinda sense of love. This was a friend-love thing. I loved him and I needed him because I needed a friend. But he loved me too much to be my friend. So he couldn't be anything. We had to be strangers.'

What a load of bullshit, I thought. 'I understand,' I said.

'You have friends that love you, right?'

'I don't even have friends that like me.'

'That's sad.' She looked up at me coyly again, raising her eyebrows. 'I should go.' She got up and turned away from me, heading for the door. Once more the perfume came and went like a promise and a taunt. 'Have you got the time?'

'Why do you have to go?'

'Why do I have to stay?'

With that she turned out of the room and left me alone.

Several minutes later, as I lay on my back on the stairwell, dabbing at a hefty cut above my right eye, and a slow trickle of painful tears, her perfume did the same.

DANNY

I hadn't expected much of a response to the adverts; in fact the whole thing had been a last-minute scramble, a shot in the dark. The initial suggestion from Dave had been that I take over from our errant, former vocalist, and we reform Broken English as a threesome for the wedding – Clive would just have to put up with it, either that or I would have to have him Hucknalled into submission. But after a couple of shabby jams after hours at Mickey P's, whatever concessions Clive had been willing to offer soon dried up, and our drummer suggested, as tactfully as an A-bomb, that we get someone else in, preferably a woman, because I was 'a bit shit and a whole lot more ginger'. Domesticity certainly hadn't blunted Clive, despite his wife carrying his balls around in her handbag.

Dave had been up for it from the start, even down to booking out all his holiday entitlement to cover the weeks before the wedding. 'If we are going to do this, we are going to do it right, and that means rehearsals.' He came down from Cheshire and pitched up with his second cousin in Hampstead. It had been a huge surprise to both of us when the call came from Clive's ivory tower somewhere in the wilds of Surrey. We had spent weeks leaving text messages for him and had got no reply. The onus had been on Dave because he heard more from him than I did. For that, you can read – Clive's wife approved of him more than she did of me. Anna Mann had left neither Ray nor I in any doubt as to how she felt about us. Dave had a six-figure income, two kids and a wife who worked in law, and he knew which wine to drink. Ray had Charlie Watts' signature on a vinyl copy of *Goats Head Soup* and I still had five *Star Wars* figures in their original packaging. It was no competition.

When Clive rolled in to that first meet-up, he looked like he had been turned inside out and washed hot. His face had aged, his clothes had aged, and miracle of miracles, even the old victim of cool's hair had aged; our drummer was now rocking more of a Phil Collins than a Paul Weller, though unfortunately it hadn't imbued him with any of Phil's talents with the sticks. But Clive's acid tongue was still there, and marriage seemed to have made it more potent than ever.

'Why's that sodding ball-ache not doing it?' had been Clive's colourful way of asking about Ray's absence. 'Pretentious gobshite. I suppose he thinks he's above it, does he? He always did have delusions of grandeur. The amount of gigs Tim came to back in the day – reckon we can do this for him, don't you?'

'Is he still…' Dave stopped and scrunched his lips up as if he were chewing on the words he was about to say, considering how they tasted. 'A bit mental?'

'He's getting there.'

'Where? Seems he's standing pretty still from what I hear.'

'What?' Clive snapped. 'He's not still hung up on that bloody Kate Fenshaw, is he? Good God! That daft little fuck-nuts needs to find himself a bit of dignity. Never understood that one – he had plenty of girls after him back in the day, so why he gets so hung up on her I don't know. Plain. Funny-shaped. Odd. He only got her singing with us because he had gone gaga, you do know that, don't you? Girl couldn't carry a note to a letterbox. No timing either. Always reckoned her and that psycho drama student you shacked up with were lovers. Vera, wasn't it? Always thought there was something going on there. The pair of them were tighter than a Yorkshireman in a charity shop. What happened with you and her, Danny? She beat you up?'

So it was at every rehearsal. Clive ruled the show. Every now and then Dave and I would catch him on the phone to Anna, squirreled away in the gents' or outside where he thought we wouldn't notice, and we would hear what he had become: 'Yes, dear, of course. Yes, Anna. No, Anna. Thank you. Yes, of course I love you. No, I won't. Yes, I will. Would you mind if...?' Dave and I would smile at each other, count our blessings that it wasn't us, and say nothing. Even Clive deserved his pretence.

We both knew the hidden message behind Clive's suggestion that it be a female that took Ray's place. He had always been lecherous, and it seemed that marriage to the queen of castration had not tempered it. Even at college he had argued against Ray fronting the band, and claimed it was a slight against him. 'It's okay for you lot, you get the audience in your face. Me, I've got a view of the singer's arse the whole time. At least get me someone a bit more pleasing on the eye. No one gives a shit about the singer anyway. It's all about the drumming. Everyone knows that.' Dave and I always liked to think that that was reason Ray developed his famous little bum shimmy. It's always better to think he did it to piss off Clive than to think he actually thought it looked good.

So it was that I made up a few cards and posted them at Mickey's and various shops along the Broadway. We got a steady number of responses, everything from the deluded to the distinctly average. Clive wouldn't even let some in through the door. Tobaccofinger tried to suggest we give his niece a shot, and even brought her along to audition for us. A small, pale, sickly-looking child – who he swore was in her twenties, but who barely even looked in her teens – she was shoved in front of us, bound up in an old lace dress that was every bit as stained as her uncle's index finger, and then started to squeal a rendition of *Frère Jacques* to her feet. It was hideous. 'It's the elevator music on the way down to hell,' I heard Clive whispering behind me.

Come the last day of auditions, we were down to two possibles, and I use that term loosely. We hadn't just scraped the barrel; we had splinters in our fingers. Jodie from Kilburn talked herself out of it that morning by telling Clive she would wrap the mic stand around his head if he didn't stop staring at her legs, and so it was that Heidi from Highgate, the best of a very bad bunch, was asked back to audition again.

We were halfway through *Mustang Sally*, Heidi not quite murdering it, but certainly threatening it with violence, when I noticed Ray had come in and taken a seat next to Tobaccofinger. A huge plaster was over one blackened eye, and there was a small line of stitches on his forehead. Neither was as noticeable as the stupid smile on his face. I called the song to a halt.

'Don't let me stop you,' he said through that wide-angle grin.

'What are you doing here?'

'Having a drink.'

'This early?'

'Been a strange old night, dear. A strange old night.'

'We're in the middle of rehearsing,' Clive barked, shuffling around on his stool and facing across to the bar. 'And who the hell do you think you are, swanning in here like you haven't just pissed on all of us from a great height? You may have binned the band off, Raymond, but some of us still think it's worth fighting for.'

'We haven't played in nearly ten years,' he said with a laugh.

'Well that's neither here, there nor anywhere else, is it?

'What does that mean?'

'Come on, Ray, don't do this…' Dave said, putting his bass down and rolling his shoulders. 'It's great to see you and all, but—'

'I'm not being funny here, but what is all this?' Heidi piped up, hands on hips, lips on pout. 'Do you mind, darling?'

'This is my replacement, is it?'

'*This?*'

'What did you want us to do?' Clive shouted.

'You think we would turn down the chance to play in front of a scout, and not go, just because you didn't want to?' I asked him calmly, trying to diffuse the ticking bomb sat behind the drum kit. 'Tom wants us singing at the wedding. It's a big deal to him. I don't want to let a friend down even if you do.'

'Tim.'

'Whatever.'

'So you are doing it out of loyalty to a friend, then? Not just because you've rediscovered some childish dream of superstardom? That's good to know. In that case, count me in. If you want. Just out of friendly loyalty though, you understand?'

'Look, sweetheart,' Heidi shouted, 'I don't know what all this is, but I don't need you here putting me off. I don't need an audience.'

'You don't need an audience?' Ray looked at me again with that stupid grin of his. 'You'll fit right in.'

'Piss off, Ray,' Clive growled. 'Go crawl back under whatever rock you've been hiding under all these years.'

Ray downed a measure of brandy, winced, and then slid off his stool and stumbled to the door. As he passed Heidi he paused, wide smile meeting pouting lips. 'Sorry they've wasted your time, love.'

'Oh, you think we have, do you?' came the shout from behind the drums.

Ray gave me a sideways glance as he left. 'Yeah.'

And he was right. If he hadn't heard Heidi auditioning I might have been able to make him sweat a bit, but he saw the shambles we were. Not only couldn't I keep the upper hand, I didn't have a leg to stand on. Clive's wrath bristled and blustered but soon blew itself out. The three of us knew there was no real choice.

I heard Leonard Cohen's favourite-uncle baritone rumble even before I reached the front door. Ray's been listening to an awful lot of Leonard these past five years, but never this early in the morning. Everything felt out of synch, and that could only mean trouble. Ray was lying on his bed, feet up, arms behind his head, when I wandered into his bedroom.

'Okay,' I said simply, not wanting to prolong the conversation and the admission of failure. 'You'll have to do it then. No talent in this part of town. What happened to your face?'

He shrugged. 'Nothing. Everything. It doesn't matter.'

'Why'd you change your mind?'

'Because I've had this nagging sensation for five years that someone stole my life, that when we moved away I somehow left it behind without noticing and some little bastard has slipped into it and is living it instead of me. Does that make sense?'

'Not really, no.'

'You see, the thing is, I might not think it's worth getting back. It might be that what I left behind doesn't actually fit me any more anyway. But I don't know, and I have to know.'

'This your shrink talking? Or is this your old women? One of them called while you were on shift. Twice. She was going on about weddings. I think she thinks it's you getting spliced.'

Ray tapped the side of his head. 'This dumb idea is all my own.'

'And what are you going to do if you see her? You even know if she still lives there? Kate?'

'I have no idea.'

'You really thought this through?'

'Not really. Am I doing the right thing?'

'Shit, I don't know, dude, but do something, will you, before life runs out on you and you're the one in the nursing home boring some old Bertha with this story? I can't keep having this same conversation with you.'

'I know.'

'Right, well…okay then. Best I put the kettle on before you change your mind.'

'You know I couldn't give a limp toss into a stiff breeze about a talent scout, don't you? I know you want it back, and all power to you, dear, if you wanna chase that again. But I don't want it.

'I know.'

'You cool with that?'

'Sorry to pop your bubble, love, but it ain't all about you.'

He smiled. I smiled. We shrugged in unison. All words said. I turned from his room, stopped and then moved back. 'I'm not picking you up this time. I don't think that I can do that again. That make me a total shit?'

He laughed again and seemed to brush my question away with a quick shake of the head. 'Course not, you twat. I know you can't, and I'm sorry. I know how good a mate you've been to me. I do. I really do. I know you've tried to help me out, and help me move on, and I know you would do anything for me. I do know that.'

'Good. After all this time I should think so.'

'And I know you will help me find her too.'

'How am I supposed to do that?'

Ray sat up on his bed and stared at me intently. 'Because Vera Franks is bound to know where she is.'

'You can fuck right off, dear. I don't like anyone that much.'

I moved out of his doorway again and left him alone with Leonard, a crazy, knowing grin plastered on his face, as if he had just discovered the meaning of life and the answer to everything. If he had then it would mean the answer lay in Southport. God help us all if he was right about that.

ANYA

'Do you believe in fate?' I asked my oldest friend, already suspecting I knew the answer.

She laughed. 'Good Lord, no, that word is misused too often. That is just a word people tag to their mistakes to try and justify their stupidity.'

I'd woken that morning, as I had every day that week, with a raincloud hanging over me like an 80s perm, and Eva's presence over breakfast hadn't done anything to remove it.

We had arranged to meet at the train station, but she was restless and agitated, awake since dawn, she had told me on vodka breath, and it had been a choice between wandering over to me, or through the city centre like some tramp. She wouldn't eat, barely took a sip of her coffee, and had the appearance of a woman on death row. She gazed out at the wall with huge, pale eyes, muttering things to herself from time to time, jumping at the slightest sound. It would have been laughable if I hadn't been the one indulging the joke. Len was struggling to keep a civil tongue, and made his excuses from the breakfast table. As I poured coffee into me I sat there and let her talk, let her moan and whine, and tell the same stories over and over again. Not ideal for an author.

'Do you still get panic attacks?' she asked me, feeling her pulse. 'How do I know if I'm getting one? I think I might have had one last night.'

'You'd know.'

'How did you stop yours?'

I thought of my fortieth birthday party, the crushing panic and the creeping terror, and the knowledge that I had to run out of the room, the house, even away from myself if I could. It had been my first panic attack in as long as I could remember, and that I had had one again invested me with even more panic, and so the cycle had started all over again. She didn't need to know that. She didn't need to know that since then, I was getting them almost every week.

'They just go,' I told her. 'Don't worry about it.'

'I have to do some radio when we get to Birmingham. Did I tell you? Live radio. I told him, I told St James not to put me on air live, I told him I wouldn't be able to help myself but he wouldn't listen. Why won't he listen to me?'

'Eva…'

'Now what do I do? I'm supposed to mind my Ps and Qs when some cheery, cheesy numbskull starts asking inane, asinine questions? No way I can do that. The man has no idea how hard that is for me. Or worse, he does and he doesn't care. It's probably that. He's simply a heartless man. "So what's your book about?" that's what they will say, in some goofy bloody voice. That's always what they start with, all of them – how utterly dull and predictable. But then of course they don't want an in-depth breakdown of the plot and the structure, this isn't some chin-stroking, middle-class intellectual wank-off on Radio 4 – this is commercial, wacky shirt-wearing, aren't-we-all-having-fun radio, so they want me to summarise in guff, airy soundbites so they can shoehorn my prattle in between adverts for tile shops and songs by Shalamar.'

'Eva, listen—'

'The book may be a whole load of tosh, but the day I write something that can be summed up to the liking of commercial radio is the day I walk away from this. They think just because it's a kids' book that it hasn't any meat to it. No meat? This is the most intricate thing I've ever done. Shit, yeah, but a meaty shit.'

'Perhaps don't use that description?'

'That reminds me...' Eva rummaged in her bag and produced a brand-new copy of her book, offering it to me delicately like it was a dog poo bag. Meaty seemed to be an understatement. It was almost as big as the toaster.

She followed me around the house; to the bathroom, the bedroom, and then hovered over me whilst I finished packing. I was beginning to get cabin fever. In the bedroom she sat at my dressing table, poring over the itinerary I had drawn out for Len, sighing between manic lip-chewing sessions, and then turned her attention back to her book, idly fondling the freshly delivered copy of *The Demons in Dudley*, running a finger along the spine and brushing a palm across the cover. I could, for a moment at least, see pride shining through her carefully convinced gloom.

'You going to sign that for me or just look at it?'

She opened the book and sniffed it. 'Smells cheap.'

'Just sign the damn book, will you?' I took the pen I'd drawn out the itinerary with and tossed it at her.

'What do you want me to write? I can't just sign my name. Not to you. Do you want me to write a message?'

'Write what you want!'

'Tell me what you want me to write.'

'That defeats the purpose, doesn't it?'

Eva leaned back in the chair, rested her feet on her bag and started nibbling on the pen, considering her message. 'I could write something offensive. That would make it unique, though it might lessen the sell-on price. I tell you what, I won't put your name on it, that way it will be worth more. Don't read it though. You mustn't read it.'

'Yeah, sure, wouldn't want to reduce the worth of my investment, would I?'

'Yes, that. Plus it's garbage too.'

'You ridiculous woman.'

I moved out onto the landing and crossed to the bathroom with my wash bag. Len was shaving, the bathroom door pulled to, and he jumped as I entered, no doubt expecting Eva to be standing there. His look said more than enough.

'I know,' I assured him. 'Give her a break. You should get the lock on the door fixed whilst I'm away.'

'Yeah.'

'You've been saying that for two weeks.'

'I'll do it. It's on the list.'

'You going in late today?'

'Have a meeting with Pete at ten.'

'Pete?

'Pete.'

'Do I know Pete?'

'Course you do. Big Pete? He came to your fortieth.'

'Oh, right, that was who that was.'

He waved his razor towards my mobile phone sat on the shelf next to the window. 'You've been buzzing.'

'I wondered where I'd put that.'

'Mig already struggling without you?'

It wasn't Mig. Somehow I knew it wouldn't be. There were two missed calls showing on the screen. His name was next to them, bigger than a measly three letters had a right to be. I sat on the edge of the bath and clutched the phone to me like it was something fragile.

'Mig? Everything okay at the café?'

I watched him shaving, with his delicate, precise strokes of the razor. He always wrapped a towel around his neck like a bib, gently wiping off any stray blobs of cream. Diligent. That was how he was when he shaved. Fussy. When it came to matters of his body he was always overly fastidious. He would already have checked his pulse twice today, examined his balls and applied cream to the rash on his leg. Stress, the doctor had said. Leprosy, Len had convinced himself. I saw a pair of latex gloves balled up in the bin and wondered what else he had been checking. I looked up, over his shoulder and gazed at his reflection in the bathroom mirror, watching those eyes watching me, looking for the roguish twinkle that would forever make me smile. Laughing eyes, my mother said he had. Like he was always having a private joke with himself. Maybe he was once, but surely not now. Len was death-fixated. Death and work. There couldn't be any room between death and work for humour. Or life.

'Sorry?'

'Everything all right with the café?'

'It wasn't Mig.'

'Oh, right.' He wiped some cream from up his nose and then wedged an end of the towel into an ear. 'You sure you don't need a lift to the station?'

I stared at his back as he bent over and washed his face. 'It was some guy.'

'What's that?' Len started towelling down his cheeks, turning to me, standing over me, eyes twinkling.

'On the phone. Some guy has been phoning me.'

'Secret admirer? How exciting.' He playfully flicked the towel against my arm. 'My wife, the heartbreaker.'

'He works in a call centre. He phoned up one day and we just got chatting.'

'Oh yeah? I bet that's riveting. You're too soft with people, sweetheart. I keep telling you.'

'I think he's infatuated with me.' I kept my eyes on his as he slipped his shirt on and checked himself in the mirror. I kept looking, watching, waiting, wondering how far I need take the conversation before he bit. 'He's been calling for months.'

'Well, have you spoken to the police? What about the company he works for? You should phone his company and speak to his boss. There are laws against harassment. Do you want me to have a word with Pete?'

'Who's Pete?'

'Big Pete! He came to your fortieth. We just had this conversation.'

'Why would you speak to him?'

'He's the company lawyer.'

'Don't be daft. I'm a big girl now.'

He leaned over and kissed me on the forehead. 'As long as you're sure.' A tiny blob of missed shaving cream from his earlobe landed on my cheek.

'Of course I'm sure,' I said softly to his back as he strode off down the landing. 'I like it.'

I watched him turn and disappear at the staircase. I felt my eyes grow heavy, my pupils itchy, but I refused the old, familiar salt sting of tears. *Stupid woman. Stop it.* Suddenly I could feel the phone vibrating against my chest like the insistent purr of a cat. *No. No! Whose twisted little joke is this?* Could the son of a bitch see me? How was his timing this bad?

I answered with a growl, and spoke with a snap. 'I can't talk now, it's not a good time.'

'No?' He was smiling. Just from that single word I could tell that he was smiling on the other end of the phone. That only made me angry. He had no right to be smiling. None at all.

'No, Ray. What do you want?'

'No. Not a good time for me either.'

Liar. Grow a pair of balls and stand up to me.

'What do you want, Ray?'

'I was thinking I might go to the wedding.' He whispered it like it was some great secret and we were conspirators. 'You were right.'

'Well, that's good. Is that it?'

'Just...just wondered if you still felt that was...' *Blah, blah, blah.* 'I don't know...' *Blah, blah, blah.* 'Do you feel that—'

'Oh, spit it out, Ray!' I screamed at him. 'What am I supposed to feel, tell me? Why am I supposed to care?'

Eva appeared on the landing, hanging out of my

bedroom door, her house brick of a novel under one arm. 'You talking to me, darling?'

I stood up and kicked the bathroom door shut on my friend.

'You're not,' Ray said simply. 'You're not supposed to care at all.'

'I'm sorry. I'm a…a…' *Bitch?*

'Don't worry about it. I shouldn't have phoned.'

'Sure you should. That's what friends do, isn't it? Why did you change your mind?'

'Oh, I don't know, it doesn't matter. You don't want to know.'

'I asked. I want to know.'

'It might sound pretentious.'

'I promise I won't judge you.'

He laughed. 'Sure about that?'

'No. I might be laughing on the inside.'

'The day of the wedding, August 17th…' He fell silent for a moment, thinking through the right words to use.

August 17th… Something whispered inside my head. Some lead weight inside me seemed to drag at my heart, pulling it down. *August 17th. No. No…*

'I don't know if I believe in fate,' he continued. 'But that is the date I last saw her. That was the date she left me. I know that it doesn't mean anything. Not really. I know that. I know it's stupid. Really. But…oh, shit…just shut me up, Anya.'

I put the lid down on the toilet and sat. 'Shut up, Ray.' The weight released my heart, and just for a moment it seemed to push up through me, into my head, and I wanted to laugh and I wanted to cry. I wanted to scream at him.

'I wanted a definite ending, Anya,' he said, and then paused again. 'Yeah, I think that's right. Well, I didn't want an ending at all. I wanted to marry her, but given the shit end of the stick that was poked in my eye, the best I can get from it is a clean ending. Something conclusive.'

'Closure. Yes.' *You self-absorbed fool.*

'I guess so. Something like you get in books or films. That would be perfect. Something where I get to walk off into the sunset as the hero, or I can deliver some wordless statement, and be dynamic and decisive. Something defining. When I last saw her we were at a bus stop. She asked me for the time. That was the last thing she said to me. When I left her there, I vowed to myself that I wouldn't look around as I walked away. I was trying to make the statement. Plus I knew that if I saw her again whatever was left of me would likely snap off and I'd end up in the gutter, blubbing. But I didn't look back at her. I was true to my word. I'd almost got to the corner of the road, almost made it, but then I tripped on the curb and stubbed my toe. Stumbled against a bin. Then I just ran.'

'Been running ever since.'

'Yes. And now it feels as if I left my life behind, like a coat in a bar, and some other person is wearing it better than me. But I need to know, I need to know if I can still wear it, and if I'd want to even if I could. I'm running out of time to know.'

'No one has a clock on you, Ray.'

'I'm thirty. Everyone I know is getting spliced and reproducing. Changing. Everything is changing.

I don't recognise the people I was at school with any more.'

'You're talking to a forty-year-old, married to a fifty-year-old. Did you want sympathy?'

'Does it get better?'

'You get invited to a few less weddings, certainly. One or two more funerals.'

'I'm sorry, if—'

'Stop apologising to me. And stop thinking you have some great life design that you aren't living up to. Take it from me, no one cares.'

'You're happy?' he asked.

'I'm okay,' I replied.

'Is that enough?' He didn't wait for an answer. I had no answer to give him. 'I want to hate her.'

'I know.'

'I'm so good at hate.'

'Yeah.'

'But I can't. I can't get past the thought that one day she might just phone up. Write to me. Be there on my doorstep. I was going to ask her to marry me, you know? I was going to make her a Caesar salad. Then a beef Wellington, and then I was going to propose during the key lime pie. I was convinced she was going to say yes.'

'Ray…'

'It was going to be perfect. I had it planned for weeks. It was going to be the start of great things. Now there's just this unholy mess. Everything is screwed up and confusing. And I will never understand it unless I go back there. I know that now. I will never get my ending unless I see her. I should do that, shouldn't I?

That's what you said, isn't it? That's what you think I should do. I can do that, can't I, Anya?'

'Why the hell not? We're still young, Ray. We can do whatever we want. Go forth and conquer.'

'You're right.'

'I know.'

'Thank you.'

'Of course, if you find you can't conquer, it's always best to submit with good grace. That'd be a neat and tidy ending, wouldn't it? Like you get in books?'

'Maybe. But this is real life.'

'I guess we are stuck with it.'

'What a sobering thought.'

Eva was sat at my dressing table, still caressing her book, when I wandered back in. 'I've signed it: *To my favourite old bitch*,' she told me proudly. 'How's that?'

'Perfect. Thank you.'

Eva had moved the itinerary from the dressing table to the bed. I spared it a glance when I sat down, though I needn't have; I didn't need to confirm it. I knew as soon as I had heard Ray say the date.

August 17th – Southport, I had written on the itinerary for my husband, next to the address of the bookshop and the address of the hotel.

I wanted to laugh, but I didn't know what was funny.

'Do you believe in fate?' I asked my best friend.

My best friend laughed at me.

The Sixth Call

EVA

She was distracted through Bristol, seemingly in a dream in Gloucester, and by the time the train arrived in Birmingham she was somewhere else entirely. She fondled her phone constantly, staring at it as if she expected it to suddenly come alive. Often she would check her answerphone and her text messages several times in the same hour. When my phone buzzed whilst we were at dinner that evening, she almost jumped out of her chair.

'What?' I asked her.

'Nothing,' she replied quickly.

Which meant something. And something meant him again, the mystery man, I had no doubt. 'You heard from Len?' I asked casually, and she told me she was phoning him that night and that she missed him and wished he were there with us. It was too much information for me to believe it.

That night we talked until three in the morning and we both fell asleep in my room. She phoned no one, as far as I was aware. Mind you, I was too busy tied up in a nightmare to have noticed. It was a doozy. I should never have had the Camembert.

The queue outside the bookshop was immense, and stretched out of sight around the corner. People were five abreast, and they were all dressed up in the most hideous and grotesque of costumes. They weren't characters from my books though, I recognised none of them; a boy was dressed as a dung beetle with the head of a yak, and his mother was dressed as a milkmaid and had two bald heads glued to her chest. Someone else was dressed as a bear; another as a snail, a slime trail smeared behind him. There were zombies all around them, and they were mine, I think; limbs were lopped off and heads were carried under their arms, blood and entrails cluttered the street, and two children were fighting over a spleen. Warlocks guarded the entrance to the bookshop, tall and imposing with giant beards wrapped around their waists.

I walked along the road, past the waiting crowds, and I was stark naked and trying to cover myself with hands that were the size of pinheads, and they all laughed at me as I walked into the bookshop. Inside I was sat on a throne and my legs were in stirrups, and one by one they came to me with other authors' books and pens that were five foot long, and they would throw the books at me whilst their parents signed their names on my old, sagging, very naked skin. One particularly muddy little boy climbed into my lap and tried to breastfeed from me, and he had hands in the shape of pork chops. I woke up screaming just as my tit fell off.

As ever, my agent proved as useful as a VD clinic in a nunnery.

'Why do you make me do it?' I asked him. 'Sitting there having inane conversations with those snotting little bastards, and then pretending to care that some parent has spent weeks fashioning some ridiculous costume for them. When did it become permissible to flaunt that in front of me? I never asked for that. Why do any of them want to meet me anyway? I wrote the book, that's enough. Read the book! You know they only want the damn thing signed so they can flog it. Then they will just move on to another author and leave me high and dry.'

'It's half past five in the morning, Eva.'

'So? Am I supposed to schedule my fears and concerns to fit in with your sleeping patterns? I wasn't aware, I'm so sorry – perhaps I should start sleeping through the day so I only have nightmares when you're awake? Would that be easier for you?'

'Eva, dear—'

'Don't dear me, you're not my dear anything, darling.'

'It was a bad dream, nothing more.'

'Oh really? How nice to have your easy-fit view of the world, Jim. Just a dream, you say? Well, what a silly little tart I must be not to have realised it was simply that and not a portent of imminent doom.'

He said something under his breath, but hid it in a yawn. 'What's the correct answer, Eva? Tell me what I need to say.'

'I wasn't aware I asked you a question.'

'Look, I understand. Really, I do. I know this isn't your forte. I know you're not comfortable with it, but just suck it up and smile sweetly. You can do that, can't you? And as far as your readership goes, trust me, you're worrying unduly. They love you. They worship you, and all that is from just one book. That's something special right there, Eva. Imagine how much they will love you once they have read the new one. There are no more loyal readers than children. Listen, Lydia will be there in the morning, and she understands too. She'll look after you. We all understand.'

What a weak, useless little man. Lydia didn't, on the surface, seem to have much to her either. I've been through three publicists since I've been with Jim St James; quite why they keep leaving I have no idea, but they never seem to stay long. Lydia was a tiny little thing that looked scared of a stiff breeze, and she introduced herself to me over breakfast in the hotel. I was blessedly free of my erstwhile agent until Manchester, where he was to join me at some signing, which he was threatening would be covered by local television, so Lydia was to be my chaperone and bodyguard until then.

Her enthusiasm made me feel sick. She talked through breakfast, barely pausing to nibble at her grapefruit (a health nut too, it would seem; she also carried a purple drink around with her in a flask, and she smelt of plants), and the coming days' plans were laid out before us. Local radio first – she got me on a pre-record per my request, so perhaps she had something about her – then a telephone interview with someone, somewhere that was oh so excited to speak to me, and honoured to be featuring me in their magazine. The first book signings would be in Liverpool, Southport and then Manchester, and then seemingly on and on and on they would stretch until either my hand fell off, or people started twigging that it was all a sham. As the morning wore on, Lydia's words just began to blur into one tedious, grating noise as her platitudes, fake empathy and aching sycophancy became a continual blast of skirt-blowing hot air.

And all the while, my dearest friend said next to nothing to either of us.

Anya's quietness since we had set out was becoming all too evident. Neither Lydia nor I could get more than a few words from her. I was starting to get concerned that perhaps I was driving her a bit nuts, and that maybe she felt I was going on too much about the book and all the promotion. I couldn't believe it was that, because I was sure I wasn't. I know it easily annoys Len – everything I say and do seems to annoy dear Len – but he really doesn't understand what I have to go through. He has never understood the artist's mind. Len needs a good plot in his films and his books; he never sees the grey between the black and the white. We all know the sort. Simpletons.

I love the old rascal but he really has no idea about the insecurities and fickle fortunes of the sort of world I live in. Anya does, as there was a time, before she fell into a marriage to Henry Gage and life as a publican's wife, where she was considering following her dream of becoming an artist. Great she was, at college, very talented, though she would tell you that she never really considered pursuing it. That's merely a convenient lie. She never believed in herself, that was her problem; even though countless others did, so it's a far easier thing to tell yourself. Keep lying long enough and you might not wake up in middle age screaming about where it all went wrong.

Len thinks she indulges me, and maybe she does, but it is a two-way deal. Len will never truly know all that I have done for his wife; nor should he. I don't know what she has told him about Henry Gage, but I know it won't be much. She hasn't even told me much, and I'm her best friend. Len knows that Henry Gage was a bastard and that Anya barely shed a tear when he died. I suspect she told him about the gambling debts, the robbing and the cheating, but I doubt she has told him anything about the day she watched him die. That is a no-go area with Anya. I've asked, many times, and she won't tell me. It's not morbid curiosity, really it isn't – I've asked because I think she wants to tell someone. I think she needs to. I also doubt Len knows about the abortion either. She only ever mentioned that to me in passing, and what with Len packing an empty chamber, I shouldn't think it's much of a dinner conversation for them. I can only imagine what sort of little shit Henry Gage's offspring would have been. I think Anya spared the world there.

Still, none of that matters any more. It was another life and she was a different person. In those years before Len came bumbling along, my girl Anya was a pale imitation of what he married. A cruel man could say I indulged her then. I prefer to call it being a friend. What would Len know anyway? He is probably too busy trying to beat back the Grim Reaper with a stick of Ryvita to have time for friends.

Len has always been middle-aged. That was the joke, even when they married. He is seemingly stuck there, like a stylus on a scratched record. He was lucky to bag himself someone like my Anya, and to his credit, he always knew that, though life with Henry Gage had put a good few years on her so the ten-year age gap that had always bothered her dad wasn't, really, all that wide. Henry Gage had done a number on her far greater than that.

She always said, when she first met Len, that part of the appeal was his age, or rather the fact that her life goals were far more aligned with those of someone older than her. There had been plenty of guys her own age that chatted her up and asked her out, when she finally came back into the game, and why not, because she's a gorgeous girl (if you can get into that boho chic thing), but Anya felt alien to them. She said as much to me after one particularly disastrous date: 'He told me even before we finished the first course that he knew what he wanted to name his children. Now, I've got no issue with that, whatever floats your boat, but what scared me is that I think he was telling me that because he thought it was what I wanted to hear. I'm a thirty-year-old woman, so obviously I'm broody, right? Obviously I'm only looking at men in relation to the strength of their sperm and the suitability of their character to fatherhood. I think if I had told him that I didn't want children he would have shattered.

'Then he takes me to the cinema. Great. But he's booked tickets for the back row. I mean, seriously? The back row! We aren't teenagers. In fact I never even did that when I was a teenager. Okay, so maybe the view is better. I gave him the benefit of the doubt. Maybe the seats are comfier? Nah. His hands were trying to get happy before the trailers had even finished. I don't want to slag him off for that, poor guy, but you know what I kept thinking about? I really wanted to see the film! The idea that some sweaty little mitts were going to try pawing me throughout just really annoyed me. Maybe that's some sort of life milestone, when you'd rather see the film than get groped by your date? If it is then I've got my milestones all back to front and mixed up. My life's all higgledy-piggledy, darling.'

She would never admit it, but I think Anya wanted to be bored. She wanted to feel safe, and who could blame her after her first marriage? That's not to say she doesn't love Len, because she truly does. But perhaps love hadn't been the first thing on the list for her. I don't know. But she had lived a lifetime with Henry Gage, and I suspect that when she was ready to start again, beyond all her talk of life goals, part of her was probably too scared to look for that reckless stupidity of the teenage years she had lost because of him. It was safer to go the other way. Len was easier.

People need to be stupid, though. It's human nature.

ANYA

My friend was a diva; there was no other word to describe her. I had given her the benefit of the doubt for long enough, putting her sniping, her curious peccadillos and her runaway gob down to nerves and to fear. But now it was getting intolerable. Eva was one step away from requesting Lydia go and buy her some M&Ms just so she could demand them to be colour coordinated, and I wanted to slap her.

A single morning with Eva, and Lydia was already looking broken. She sat back and took the onslaught with carefully timed nods and timid little squeaks of agreement, bowing to as many of Eva's ridiculous assertions and demands as simple humanity would allow. She had taken the pale and shaking radio presenter aside that morning, after a somewhat disastrous interview, and apologised profusely, giving the man a gentle hug and offering up suggestions as to which parts of the interview might still be useable. I even heard her explain to him what a 'puffed-up winkybag of worthless wad' was. The girl was thorough if nothing else.

I couldn't see Lydia lasting long at the end of Eva's double-barrelled arsey attitude, and I wasn't sure I would either. I was all too aware that I was already failing in my best friend duties. I had come to look after Eva, to be a shoulder to lean on whilst she was worshipped and adored by strangers, and all I wanted to do, right at that moment, was kiss Lydia for taking her shit so I didn't have to.

Things came to a head in a motorway services, just outside Birmingham. I doubt for the first time.

We were sat in a busy restaurant, in a table by the window, eating plastic food and drinking lukewarm coffee. Eva had made a point of sitting opposite Lydia with her cheese roll, moving seats when the little girl sat with her strange purple drink, so she was directly in her eyeline.

'Can we have it written somewhere that they are not allowed to touch me?' Eva asked Lydia. 'That would make me more comfortable. I think we need to establish some boundaries. I'm not public property and they need to know that.'

Lydia scribbled in a notebook, nodding unconvincingly. 'No touching by the adults, understood. I will see what—'

'Well, I would have taken that as read, wouldn't you? Of course no adults shall touch me, I'm not a prostitute, despite what some of the broadsheets would like to think. No, Lydia, I was referring to their offspring.'

'I don't quite know how that is possible to enforce. You see—'

'Of course it is possible to enforce. If I touched them I would probably end up on a list. So why should they be allowed to touch me? Because they have read a book I have written? How extraordinary an assumption. No, there will be no touching.'

'I will see what—'

'And no photographs either. Can we have someone on the door saying all this to them? Wouldn't that be easier, and make more sense? Can we make them sign something before they can come in?'

I couldn't take any more at that moment. Part of me wanted to laugh, the other to scream, and neither felt like a good idea. She had drained me, and I felt embarrassed for Lydia. Rather than intervening like a good friend should, I decided to run away again instead. I was getting good at that. I needed to get out, to get away, so I finished my coffee and slipped from my seat. Neither of them noticed me leave.

'Hey, Ray, how you doing?'

Phoning him seemed the obvious thing to do, a natural reflex that I didn't question. Those questions would come later that night, and even then I had no answers. He still sounded happy, renewed with the confidence of a decision made, and I envied him that. I walked out past a newsagent, past a dirty-looking coffee shop and a small arcade, and then took a seat on a bench and watched the strangers pass me by. The panic attack I had felt twitching inside me, threatening me ever since I stumbled out of the hotel bed that morning, flickered and died like a starved candle flame. A stoical calm, as evident as the voice in my ear, as artificial as the flashing lights of the arcade, rained through me and seemed to pool around my gut. A fragile sustenance, but all I needed at that moment. And all I got.

A child was sat on a small ride-on elephant opposite me, eagerly bouncing up and down and kicking its plastic trunk with a trainer, whilst his mother fed coins into a slot. A stupid grin on his face. Her mouth a weary slit. The elephant smiling bigger than both, a beaming, toothy happiness under his trunk chipped white, and flecked grey. As the plastic animal rocked back and forth, the boy whooped and wailed in excitement. A simple pleasure, an enormous smile, and just as I had envied Ray, I found myself being jealous, just for a moment, of this child before me.

'You must be leaving for the wedding soon?' I asked Ray.

'End of the week, yeah.'

'You're still going, then? That's good. I'm glad. You should, I think, for what it's worth.'

'Gone too far to back out. No choice now, Anya.'

'You've always got a choice, Ray. Tell me, can I ask you a question?'

'You've never felt the need to ask permission before.'

'It's personal. I don't want to cross a line.'

'We have lines? When did that happen?'

'You ever wanted children, Ray? Have you got any? Ever plan to have any?'

'Where's that question come from?'

'Been on my mind, that's all.'

'Do you?'

'My friend, Eva, she doesn't like children, really she doesn't, and I don't quite understand it. I wonder sometimes if it's an act. Or at least an exaggeration done for my benefit.'

'I don't understand.'

'How do you feel about them? Children. What's your take on them then?'

'I don't really have a feeling either way. I wanted kids with Katie, obviously…'

'Why is that obvious?'

'Well, why wouldn't I?' He sounded genuinely confused at that question. Bless him.

'That's convention speaking though, isn't it? That's sheep talk. Find a girl, get married, have some children, get a dog, holiday in the sun. That's your parents saying that, isn't it? You're not a cliché are you, Ray? That would be so disappointing to find you're a cliché now, after all this.'

'I never looked too far into it. You obviously have.'

'You should do. Having children? Big responsibility. Should be thought about a lot, shouldn't it?'

'You ever thought about it, Anya?'

The child was laughing big, childish, snotty laughs, hugging the elephant around its large head, and then he was gazing up at his mother with eyes that told her this was the best thing in the world. She didn't see, didn't seem to care; something far more interesting on her phone. Laughing eyes found me then, and I smiled at him and gave a thumbs-up.

Always. 'No.'

'Katie and I never got that far. That was a conversation we never got to.'

'Why did you want to have children with her?'

'I don't know.'

'Is it ownership? Like some people view marriage? Is that how you saw it? I knew a man like that once. Get a ring on her, get a child in her, and she's more likely to be yours forever. Is that it?'

He didn't reply to that. Perhaps I'd found the line he didn't seem to think we had. I could hear other noises on the phone: murmured voices, and what sounded like a muffled crash of cymbals.

I talked over his silence; I had learned it was the best way. 'She's not maternal, my friend, not remotely, but it can't just be that. Perhaps it is just for my benefit after all. Perhaps she thinks highlighting her disdain for children will make me feel better.'

'Why would that make you feel better?'

'Though I think it's because she just doesn't understand them. Eva. I think it's just that, really. You get frightened of what you don't understand, don't you?'

'I guess so.'

'Like you and women?' I said casually, a light dance in my voice. That worked, and we were both laughing again. Ray English wasn't so difficult.

'If you say so.' His laughter became a splutter and then a long sigh, one of those sighs that would become a prelude to a shift in conversation, and I wasn't going to let him have it. Not just then. 'Anyway—'

'It's not a crime though, is it? Eva shouldn't be condemned for not caring about children. Each to their own and all that. She does have some good points.'

Does she? Where was I going with that?

'Okay.'

'She's been very good to me. She's been there when I've needed her. Never questioned it, never – she's always been a good friend to me.' I was trying to justify to myself why I was still putting up with her. I was talking myself into not running away. Shit. Was it as obvious to him as it was to me? I kept on talking in the hope that I then wouldn't have to think about it. 'She's my best friend. My oldest friend. My confidante.' (*she's not, though, is she?*) 'And my support. My rock.' (*Hahaha!*) 'She always says she's like my right hand. Does that make sense?'

'Erm...'

I was gabbling. I must have sounded ridiculous. 'You know, like an influence, a guide, a part of who you are. Like a dominant right hand? We all have them, I think. We all have someone like that in our lives. All of us. Even you, Ray. Even you.'

'I do have a mate – he's been good to me. But he's a little bit useless. Much like me. I'm not sure I could elevate him to such an exalted position.'

'You don't consider him a part of who you are?'

'More like the only right-hand left handy.'

That made me laugh, and then he was sighing again. This time I let him have it and waited to see where he went.

'I suppose…'

'What?'

'I suppose there is my granddad Bertie. Well, I mean there was – he was special to me. He was always the person I went to when I needed some guidance or advice. Maybe he was my right hand. Maybe. I don't know. I loved him anyway. He was a good man. A better man than I could ever hope to be.'

His words were suddenly very flat and lifeless. It didn't sound like pity or indulgence, it just sounded like a very sad person. I felt sad too, and then angry; angry with Ray for making me feel sad because that was not his job, that was not why he was there on the end of the phone. That was not why he was in my life.

'Why do you say that?'

'He just was. He was nice. Kind. Friendly. Loving.' I could almost hear the heavy shrug of the shoulders in his words. 'Bertie got life right, twice, even after it threw him the biggest curveball. Even after my Gran died. He didn't sink, he kept afloat, and then he fell in love again.'

'And you won't? Christ, Ray, that's a bit overly dramatic, isn't it?'

'I'm not saying that, no. I will when I can, I'm sure I will, when I can see past the mess, when I can get over…it…'

'Her?'

'Bertie was lucky in a way. Gran died. He had his ending. She had hers. There was no grey area. It was just obvious. Life told him what he had, showed him his hand, and then he knew what he had to work with.'

I said nothing to that, hoping that Ray would somehow hear his words echoing back at him in our silence and realise what he was saying. It took a moment, but he got there. Which was just as well.

'That sounds terrible.'

'It does, Ray.'

'I'm sorry. I didn't mean it to sound so cold.'

'I know. But death isn't always an ending for those left, you know?'

'You sound like you are speaking from experience.'

'Maybe I am.'

'And?'

'And we weren't talking about me, were we? Go on, Ray.'

'I don't know what I'm saying.'

'Yeah, you do. You were about to tell me that if Katie were dead you'd find all this easier, and then I was going to have a go at you for being so selfish and shitty and tell you to pull your act together. There, that's saved us a few minutes.'

'You're good.'

'One of us needs to be.'

'Bertie got it right, you know? Second time, with my Aunty Liz. They were each other's life, and when she…she's still in the nursing home, you see, fading day by day, advanced Alzheimer's, legs and arms and every other damn thing given up the ghost…well, when she went from him, when she stopped recognising him, I think he just gave up on it all. He packed it all in. As if somehow he knew that there was no point. He had made her his life and she had gone. Everyone said he died from a broken heart, and that that was such a romantic thing. Maybe he did, and maybe it was, but he could get away with that because he had lived a life. That's okay when you are in your eighties. Maybe that is how it has to be when you are that old. But how the fuck did I let it happen to me at this age? And why can't I let go of this grubby, tangled mess that I'm clinging on to? How did I make her my life? How did I let everything I had get coloured in by another person? Why did I keep nothing of my own that she couldn't touch? What a total idiot. I don't want to be like this, Anya.'

'I know you don't.'

'I have never wanted to be like this. I want to live my life.'

'I know, Ray.'

'And I don't want to be left behind.'

'You don't want to be left behind in the pond, just another cold fish swimming in circles. I know. Believe me, I do.'

'Speaking from experience again, are you?'

Shut up.

'You're getting better though, Ray. I think you are, anyway. For whatever that is worth coming from a complete stranger. It's comforting to think one of us cold fishes could escape the pond.'

'It's worth a lot, stranger. Thanks.' His words were smiling again. I liked it when he spoke to me like that. It was when he spoke like that that he looked like Paul Newman in my mind.

'I don't think you're beyond redemption, Ray English.'

'Likewise, Anya Belmont.'

'But I do think I'd like to meet this Katie that messed you up so much. I'm intrigued. How did she end it, Ray? Did she do it to your face whilst you were making the Caesar salad? Or when you were at the bus stop? Or was she a coward and did it on the phone? Sent a text message? An email? Perhaps it was a gradual change of Facebook status? *In a relationship. It's complicated. Single.* That would have been a virtual slap around the face if she had done that.'

'Why do you think it would be something so impersonal?'

'Isn't that the way we have all become now, in this advanced society of ours?' Still the woman gazed at her phone whilst her son laughed. Busy, well-practised fingers tapping away, dead eyes, her mouth a flatline. 'Write many letters any more do you, Ray? I know I don't. Speak to people face to face much? Or is your life just lived behind a computer screen and a mobile? Every now and then jumping up from behind your social parapets with a little *Hey, don't forget me!* status, or perhaps, in those all-too-fleeting moments of wilful abandon, a picture of a cat looking cute?'

He liked that. 'Feel like you don't belong?'

'Who'd really want to? My husband always said the more the world advanced and pushed us towards each other, the further away we were actually getting.'

'A man of depth?'

'Not really, he's more fraud than Freud.' Ray chuckled and I cut him off. 'But I do love the old fraud.'

'I wasn't asking you.'

'No.'

'No. Why would I?'

'How did she do it, Ray? Tell me about the Caesar salad.'

'Why?'

'I want to know how much we can salvage from you. I want to know how much she took.'

And so he told me, in long, intricate detail, as if he was an artist describing a painting in front of him on his wall. I listened with half an ear. The child finished his aimless rocking back and forth on the elephant and wanted to go again, but now his mother's free hand reached for him and absently tugged at a sleeve, and the boy slid off into a limp embrace. They were walking away now. Far away. A man was waiting for them at the doors, and he took the boy into a hug. But the boy was looking at me. I was sure of it. Soon they were gone and strangers filled the spaces where they had been.

'...I was going to make her a Caesar salad, because she'd never had one,' he finished.

'You ever find yourself wondering whether she's had one yet?'

Somewhere on the other end of the phone the sound of other voices came again; some were shouting this time, and instead of a cymbal crash there was a drumroll.

'Ray?'

'I'm here. It's okay.'

'Thought I might have crossed a line.'

'We don't have lines,' he said, with an assertiveness I hadn't heard from him before.

'No?'

'There doesn't seem to have been any lines since we started this, no.'

'Started what?' I asked innocently.

'*This.*'

'Oh, *this*. This is a thing, is it?'

'Some sort of thing. Listen, I've got to go.'

'No you don't.'

'I've got a rehearsal, Anya.'

'How's that coming along?'

'You really want to know?'

'No. Tell me, Ray, what are you going to say to Katie when you see her?'

'I don't know.'

'Do you even know that she is still there?'

'No. I don't know anything.'

'Sometimes that's the best way to be, don't you find?'

I returned to the restaurant and was greeted by the gawping, disbelieving face of Lydia, sat at our table, rolling her purple drink container around in her hands nervously. I could hear a commotion to one side of me, the sound of shouting, and was aware of diners' faces all turned in one direction, but it still took me a moment to understand what they were all looking at.

'What is this? What the hell is this?' a woman was screaming. I tried to convince myself that it wasn't Eva, terrified at the thought of what she might be doing now, this unruly charge of mine. I searched for a wilful delusion but came up empty.

People parted around the restaurant counter, those queuing up in a long snake-line to be served backing away with their trays, leaving one poor woman standing alone behind the counter, with nothing but a pair of plastic tongs for protection. I saw my best friend standing there in front of her, heard the ferocious roar coming from her, and then I gazed back helplessly at Lydia, only to see that she was looking at me for answers. I remained rooted to the spot, guilt-infused and hopeless.

'What the hell is this dangly red creation hanging from between my fingers, you tedious little woman? Answer me!' Eva was waving something at the woman behind the counter, holding it high above her head. 'What is it?'

'It's a tomato,' the woman with the tongs said, helpfully.

'That's right, a sodding tomato!'

'And?'

'And what is it doing in my cheese roll?' Eva shrieked.

'You didn't order a tomato?'

'Would I be standing here waving the little bastard above my head if I had ordered it? No, I would be sat at my table consuming the little beggar, wouldn't I?'

'I suppose.'

'You suppose? You mean part of you isn't sure? Part of you actually thinks I'm standing here holding this just for something to do? For annual Fun With Tomato Week? Is that it? Good God, your stupidity violates me. I feel dirty. Do I look like the sort of person who would hold a tomato aloft in a public place without a good reason?'

'No.' The woman was flashing looks to either side of her, waiting for backup. A young man wandered from the kitchens behind her, took one look at the raging woman at the counter, pretended he had forgotten something and then quickly ducked back through the kitchen doors.

'No, that's right!' Eva continued, on a roll about her roll. 'I'm showing you this tomato because I would like you to explain to me how it managed to infiltrate my cheese roll.'

'I'm not exactly sure, madam. Would you like to see the manager?'

'Why would I want to see the manager? Does he do a trick?'

'No, madam.'

'Did he make my cheese roll?'

'No. No, he didn't.'

'No, he didn't, so he wouldn't know how this tomato came to be in my cheese roll, would he?'

'No.'

'He's pretty redundant in this conversation, isn't he?'

'Yes.'

There was sniggering from the customers gathered around her. Others had given up the spectacle, dumped their trays and gone elsewhere. One man by the side of the counter had his phone up, surreptitiously filming the unfolding drama.

I stumbled across to Eva and tugged lightly at her top. 'What the hell are you doing?' I whispered into her neck.

'Don't be a killjoy,' a man behind me said. 'This is hilarious! You give it to her, love!'

Eva didn't even seem to know I was there. 'So it's down to you,' she boomed, swinging the sliced tomato around like a Morris dancer would a hankie. 'You made the damn thing. I asked you for "one cheese roll"; I did not ask you for "one cheese roll with a slice of tomato in," did I? No, no, I didn't. You just didn't give it a moment's thought, did you? You were scooping it in with those crappy bloody tong things, saw the bastard fall into my roll and ignored it.'

I tugged harder at her top and she jerked away, accidently elbowing me backwards into a table, my right hand landing in an old man's bowl of Mulligatawny soup.

'Did you once think, *Oh, I wonder if this lady likes tomato?* or maybe, *Oh, I hope this lady isn't allergic to tomato?* Did you consider what the shock of finding a tomato in my cheese roll might have done to me? Did you? No, of course you didn't. Your ignorance could have killed me. Did you ever consider that? No, you didn't, did you? What do they teach you here? How hard can it be to understand the basic faux pas that you have made? Not only have you endangered a customer's well-being, but you have been blatantly erroneous in your advertising as well by moistening bread that you've confidently described as fresh and crispy. But worse than that, the upturned fly on your steaming turd of a being, you have committed the cardinal sin of the service industry: you have married food together without the customer's permission!'

With a single flick of the wrist, the tomato spun through the air and landed with a delicate, barely audible splat on the woman's apron, before slipping off slowly and landing on the ground at her feet.

Her rage seemingly doused, Eva gave a small, satisfied sigh, turned on her heels and strode back to our table, an embarrassed best friend and the applause of two customers following in her wake, as slowly, blessedly, the stunned silence all around us broke apart, and normality returned; talk of tomato finally replaced by rhubarb.

The Seventh Call

DANNY

Those few days before we left for the wedding had been like old times, and it felt wonderful. Broken English fell into their stride and hit their groove as if the intervening ten years had all been one endless gig, and we had been best friends living within each other's worlds, rather than strangers with little in common except a shared history. We had laughed and played and swapped stories of stupid dreams and, just like the good old days, Ray and Clive still hated each other. We were a band again. If not a band of brothers, then certainly one of second cousins and right then, that was enough.

Mickey had stars in his eyes about the whole thing the moment I had mentioned the supposed talent scout at the wedding, somehow convinced that we were suddenly destined for superstardom, and his infectious enthusiasm started to rub off on me. I would find myself in quiet moments wondering whether this could continue, if the four of us could realistically stay together for a concerted crack at it. It was what we had all wanted when we were young, before life got in the way. Ray might not want it now, at least he would never admit that he did, but maybe the other two still had that dream inside them? Priorities change, circumstances change, lives change, yeah, but sometimes dreams remain regardless, held all the more vital for the heavy weight of life that you inadvertently put on your shoulders. If we got a chance, I don't think even Ray would run from that.

I found myself practising more at home than I had ever done, at least in the last few years, since London had sucked out any last vestige of dreamy possibilities from me. (And how weird that was – shouldn't it have been the other way around? Wasn't London the great place where you went to pursue your dreams, like some vagabond Dick Whittington? When did it change and become the place that kicked your hopes and dreams in the teeth instead?) I even started writing again, something I had convinced myself I was no good at long ago, choosing instead to belt out other people's masterpieces.

That inner voice that constantly reminds you of your stupidity – we all have that, right? Well, mine was shouting at me, screaming at me; a persistent, bleating nag at this point, and it was telling me I was being a fool for even allowing a fleeting thought of success to infiltrate my mind. It masquerades as a safeguard, this voice, a sort of circuit breaker, and we let it. That's how it gets away with it. Well, I reckon it's actually nothing more than an obstacle we let our fear put in the way. It's easier to cave in than climb up. Pessimism is easier than optimism. I read all that once in a psychology book. The author had a shitload of letters after his name, so, you know, he's probably right. Right?

Mickey, bless the dirty old man, took me aside one evening and suggested that Tobaccofinger would make a good manager for us. 'Don't be fooled by image, lad,' he whispered to me outside the gents'. 'He's got some nous, you know? There's more than seems apparent going on up there in the old grey matter. Plus, he kinda freaks people out. They usually think he's a serial killer, so you got the fear factor too. Reckon I can do you a decent deal on the percentage. What do you say, Dan?'

I didn't have the heart to say no to him then, or even tell him that the chance of ever needing a manager was pretty damn slim. Let Mickey believe what he wanted, I figured – the bullshit always sounded better than the truth anyway, and what is the point of playing in a band unless you open yourself up to delusions?

'Good evening, Wembley!' Tobaccofinger had shouted into the microphone as we set up for the gig, his arms out wide in a triumphant gesture, his stained suit tearing slightly at the seams. One old soak at the bar suddenly looked confused, gazing around his surroundings in a panic before heading to the door in a drunken stumble.

We played well that night. Our audience barely broke ten people, but that wasn't really the point. Mickey and Tobaccofinger whooped and cheered and applauded like performing seals, and midway through the set Beth rolled up with a new boyfriend in tow and proved, unsurprisingly, every bit as vocal.

Dave had hired a van for the gear and would be driving Ray and I up. Clive, much to Ray's relief, was making his own way there with Anna. We arranged to meet at Ray's work after his shift and make good an early start but I couldn't sleep that night, wired from the performance, and so took the first tube in, spending the last hour of Ray's shift alongside him.

The view from the top floor of Galton Insurance was incredible. Ray had told me as much before but I hadn't really believed him until I saw it for myself. Watching dawn breaking over the city, stood there next to my oldest friend, I suddenly felt both comforted and insignificant. Ray walked forward and rested his forehead against the window, his right hand gently jangling the keys clipped to his belt, as if he were trying to find a tune in them.

'Once,' Ray started, before stopping and wiping away his breath condensation from the window, and then leaning his head back, 'once, every day for about a week, I would see a woman in that building over there.' He pointed and I stepped forward to follow his finger. 'Always around six or seven, just as the shift was finishing, I saw her. I think she was a cleaner. She must have been, I guess, at that hour. Well, first day I saw her she noticed me staring and she turned to the window and stared back for a bit. She had her hands on her hips, kind of a stern-looking pose, it was, not sexy – as if she had caught me doing something I shouldn't. Then the next morning I see her and she waves at me and blows me a kiss. At least I think she did. Looked like it. The day after that she does a little dance in the window, this silhouette jigging about, arms waving above her head and all that. Then the next day she does it all: waves, blows a kiss, does a little dance and then she pulls her top open and flashes me her breasts. Haven't seen her since then. Still look for her. Haven't seen anyone since then.'

'Okay.'

'Beautiful view, isn't it?'

'It is, mate.'

Ray pulled away from the window and shoved his hands deep into his pockets. 'You looking forward to it?'

'Playing again?'

'Going back?'

'Guess so.'

'You guess so?'

'Well, I guess I haven't given it as much thought as you have. You think too much. Much too much. I don't know…sure, yeah, I'm looking forward to seeing a few people again, I suppose. See the folks. Get a decent meal for a few days. I am looking forward to playing again. Yeah, it'll be cool. You sure you want to stay in a hotel? You know my two will put you up.'

Ray shook his head. 'Fine. I'll be fine.'

'Well, the offer is there. You know my mother likes to feed you.'

He smiled briefly, and then it seemed to fall away. 'Coming to London, Dan – you never regretted it?' Ray turned to face me, his legs apart; his hands now jingling the change in his pockets.

'Where's this coming from?'

'It was supposed to be the start of so much, you and me getting away from home. We were going to kick some ass, make some money and get a ton of sex.'

'We've done okay.'

'No we haven't.'

'So, we weren't destined for greatness then.'

'Shit, that, isn't it?' Ray laughed to himself and then nodded me down a corridor. I followed him into one of the offices where he wandered behind the desk and slumped into the chair. He put his boots on the desk and then picked up one of five framed photos in front of him and showed it to me. A smiling woman, a grinning man and a beaming child stared back at us.

'I always wanted one of these.'

'A family?'

'Doesn't have to be a family, just someone you gave a damn about. I wanted a framed photo on a desk of someone I cared about that I could look at every day and remind myself why I was bothering. You know, I haven't even got a proper photo of Katie and me together.'

'Yeah, because you burned them all.'

That shut him up for a moment. He stared wistfully at the photo in his hands, running a thumb along the cheap frame. 'I've only got that one of all of us at Pleasureland, do you remember that? Awful photo. I've got my eyes closed and Vera looks constipated.'

'Vera always looked constipated.'

'True.' He dumped the photo down on the desk. 'I have got another one. I think. That old camera in my cupboard? The one Mum and Dad bought me? There's a photo on there of her, just one. Took it at The Ruby Lounge when we went to see The Boxers and Augustines...took it 'cos my phone was bust. Remember? Why didn't I take more photos of her? In those five months, why didn't I take more photos? Strange, that, now I think about it.'

'Don't think about it then.'

'Good idea. I think too much anyway. So they say. Right? So let's get pissed and not think about anything. That's the job, I think.' Ray reached down to the bottom drawer of the desk and took out a bottle of Scotch. 'I want to stop off at the home on our way. That okay?'

'How is she?'

He looked at me, unsure what to say. It was always a stupid question: advanced Alzheimer's and extreme old age – what the hell is the point in asking after her? It sounded a little too much like 'she dead yet?' Yet I had to ask, so what do you do? What are the right words to use?

Once more he shrugged. Yet this time that one gesture wasn't enough for him. 'She's such a proud woman. Liz. Always so house-proud she was, always took so much pride in her appearance, and great care in what she projected to the world.'

'Generational thing, that.'

'Yeah. Guess so. Olive mentions it all the time, says it to me like she's talking about a stranger. Which I suppose, in a way, maybe she is. "She was such a proud woman. Proud to a fault, she was. She'd be mortified to see herself now. So would your granddad, Ray. So strong, and so proud, and so full of life. She would just want to die." And she's right. She would. Liz would want it. If she could see herself, if she could smell herself, if she had enough about her any more to realise how people were seeing her. And what do we do about it? We just keep her going, and for what reason? Quality of life? They were each other's life.'

'It's tough, man. Tough situation.'

'Of course, if you are religious, and you believe in heaven, which most of them do in there, naturally

– I mean, you would when you're nearing the end, wouldn't you? Gotta believe in something. Well, if you take the religious angle, then you have to believe that Bertie is up there, sitting on his cloud waiting for her. Probably getting impatient now, knowing him. Probably well annoyed that she's even keeping him waiting in death. Well, if you believe all that, then there's another reason you have to question it all. Down here, she's fading out slowly. No idea who anyone is in those fleeting moments when she opens her eyes. Legs don't work. Body doesn't work. Can't eat by herself. Can't do anything by herself except lie there waiting. Waiting to be free of this bullshit that we are making her go through because of some perceived goodness. Where is the goodness in that? She wants it to end. She wants to be with him. He wants to be with her. We all want them to be together, and yet we are stopping them because we are good and virtuous and kind. But is it kindness, or are we just being selfish?'

'He'd be proud of you, you know, your granddad. That's some role model you've picked there.'

'Yeah.'

'Going in to see Liz as often as you do. Looking after her. I bet you go more than her own family, don't you?'

'She is my family. Why wouldn't I go?' He seemed genuinely perplexed by the question, and I suddenly felt like a massive scumbag. 'I love her.'

'Yeah, I'm sorry. You know I didn't mean anything by that.'

'But she should…well, she needs to…you know…'

'I know, mate.'

'I'm really just looking out for her until she stops keeping him waiting. That's all. He'd want that. He'd want me to do that.' Ray seemed to lose his train of thought for a second, staring off at the framed photos on the table. Then the Scotch bottle was back in his hand and the smile had returned to his face. 'Anyway, I thought we weren't thinking about anything?'

'I think that sounds like a good idea, love.'

Ray poured a healthy measure of Scotch into two mugs and then we both returned to the corridor, the glorious view and our silent shorthand.

'Good evening, Birkdale!' Ray turned away from the microphone and stared back at us with a furrowed brow and pursed lips. 'Doesn't quite have the same ring to it, does it?'

The hotel ballroom was huge and resplendent in virginal whites and sinful reds. The curtains were tied back, letting glorious summer sun through huge arched windows. Tables covered one half of the room; large, circular ones with cream cloth coverings, white rose flower arrangements and long red candles, and three long rectangular ones, moved together at the head of the room. The opposite end of the room was empty save a wide table for presents and a small stage, where we were currently rehearsing. The rest of this side of the ballroom was all dance floor, waxed to a school assembly hall shine.

'Red and white! Red and white!' came the familiar bellowing instructions from the other side of the room. Tim's imminent father-in-law Frank – half-boulder, half-bouncer – had been striding around the room shouting at random people for the last half an hour. A gruff yard dog of a man with stubby, tattooed arms and fists the size of anvils, he barked and yelled, and scratched his balls. His focus of attention was a huge mound of balloons in some netting, hanging from the ceiling above the makeshift dance floor. 'Red and white balloons only!' he kept on shouting. 'I saw a purple one in there earlier. Make sure there are only red and white. It was stipulated when I ordered it.'

Various silent minions were standing on stepladders, reaching into the netting and picking through the balloons carefully, as if each were made of china. Frank stood between them, hands on hips, little box of a head almost sinking into his elephant foreskin of a neck.

'My little princess only wants red and white. If I see any other colours I shall be deducting it from the bill. Ten pounds per balloon of a different colour seems reasonable to me. Now...' With a quick slap of his beefy slabs of hands, he was off again, pacing around the tables. 'Place names!'

'Well,' Dave said quietly to the rest of us on the stage, 'I think I can speak for every man here when I say that our old friend Tim has done well for himself. I can only imagine what the fruit of that man's loins must look like.'

'What would you say to a man like that when you want to marry his daughter?' I asked the others. 'I mean, seriously, what would the opening conversation be?'

Clive piped up from behind his drum kit: 'I bring you gifts of raw steak and the offer of my firstborn son, any chance of a shag off your daughter?'

'He's utterly terrifying.'

'I hear he's so tough he's got the word "arm" tattooed on his mother,' Ray said, taking a seat on an amp and yawning loud enough for the whole room to hear. Ray's yawn was a red rag to this particular bull.

'All rehearsed, are you?' the voice suddenly boomed out. Frank was heading our way, growl growing louder. 'I'm so pleased. I had no idea you were so professional. Oh, hang on a minute – you're not, are you? So in that case I assume you must be talking about the set list or something, that would explain why you are aimlessly standing around nattering, wouldn't it? Far be it for me to impinge on your old school reunion but it is the biggest day of my beloved daughter's life tomorrow – she is getting married, you know? You understand that, don't you? You are the band for that reception, aren't you? We are relying on you to provide the music, are we not? Yes? I'm not much of a music man myself, so you must forgive my ignorance in this matter, but I would have assumed that does require work, doesn't it? Or does it just happen by magic? Have I just imagined that? Perhaps Timothy was mistaken when he asked you? Is that it? Is my future son-in-law mistaken and foolish?'

Ray cleared his throat and then stood slowly.

I seethed his name through gritted teeth, moving to block the insult I knew was marching unheeded towards the simmering mound of manhood with the giant fists, but Dave beat me to it.

Or rather, the neck of his bass guitar did.

RAY

Danny didn't say more than two words to me on the way back to my hotel. I could still feel the swipe of Dave's guitar neck between my legs, my balls screaming their own feedback into my head, but my best friend's silence was somehow worse. Despite the best efforts of Sam Cooke soundtracking the short lift back, Danny remained furious. The two pieces of the torn flyer lay in my lap. He glanced it at once in disgust as he pulled the van into the hotel car park.

'No,' he said as calmly as he could muster, and then nodded me towards the hotel. 'I'm not doing it. See you tomorrow.'

'But you know she never liked me.'

'Well she absolutely bloody hates me! I don't know what you think me being there is going to achieve. She's as liable to land one on you just for having to see me again as anything else. You want to put your head in the lion's mouth, you go right ahead. I'm done with that.'

'You said you would.'

'I didn't say any such thing. *You* said I would. I said you were a fucking idiot. And you are. You really want to find Kate, then there are easier and far less dangerous ways, you know?'

He gave me a knowing look and nodded, more to himself than to me. Danny knew better than anyone how much I had tried to find Katie these last five years. He called it stalking, but being that I never found her, I'm not sure that's fair. I knew she had moved out of the shared house she had been living in. That much I had.

But of course no one was in any hurry to give me her new address. I checked for her on Facebook on the first day of every month. It became a little ritual, but I never found her there. I would Google her. I would Google her friends and her family, but I kept on coming up empty-handed. I searched directory enquiries and just got her old home, and she wasn't listed on the electoral register (I would have to talk to her about that when I found her.) Her parents had moved not long after mine, not to Spain but to Sidcup. So I checked her name against Sidcup and got nothing. I even checked for a death certificate. Just once. I didn't feel comfortable doing that.

'Just what is it that makes you think she would give you her address even if she had it?'

I shrugged. It wasn't like that outcome hadn't occurred to me. But I knew I had to at least try. 'Charm?'

'She's immune, love. And you don't have any anyway.'

'A valid point, dear.'

It had been Clive that had seen the flyer stuck to a noticeboard in the hotel reception; he had taken it down with a riotous laugh and waved it in our faces. I had taken it as a sign. Clearly Danny had taken it as a cue to run away. Big, blood-red font across the flyer announced, in what felt like a threat: *My Love Is An Elephant In Your Trousers: A one-woman play by Vera Franks*. Her stony, pissed-off face glared out from underneath the words.

'Well, we've got to go and see that, haven't we?' Clive had said between the guffaws. 'Reckon it's based on you, Dan?'

Danny had taken it from him, ripped it in half and dumped it in a bin.

'Is that a no?'

I put the pieces of the flyer in my pocket and turned away from the hotel as Danny departed quickly with a screech of tyres. I needed to walk, to breathe some sea air. It was the one thing I truly missed about my hometown. Well, one of two things.

On the drive up, Danny and I had swapped places at the motorway services outside Birmingham and I had spent the second part of the journey in the back of the hire van rattling around with the gear, yet I had it in my mind that I would somehow know instinctively when we had arrived in Southport. I would smell the sea, or I would hear something outside the van that would stir an old memory. Maybe I would recognise a streetlight from the small slit of window I could just make out over the front seats between Danny and Dave's heads. I would know when I was home. I would feel it. It would call to me. As it was, though, when Dave swung the van off Lord Street and into the hotel car park, I had no idea we had arrived until he opened the back doors. My first view of my hometown in five years was of a brick wall and a door, with *Private – No Entry* written on it.

I had looked out at the view from my hotel bedroom window, down onto Lord Street, trying to remember things. Above the buildings I convinced myself I could see the suggestion of the sea. I opened the hotel window, hoping to find the old familiar salty smell on the air, but I couldn't get to it; I couldn't get past all the other smells. It didn't feel like home, not quite. It felt like I was in my own street, but looking out of a different house.

I walked up and down Lord Street, past the war memorial, the Wayfarers Arcade, the market, and all the shops I no longer recognised. It had only been five years since I had last been there but it may as well have been fifty. It was a strange land. I walked down into the Esplanade, and then past Pleasureland and finally I turned onto Mersey Path, and then there I was next to the sea, the world opening up to my right in light blues and greys and greens. Adults strolled past me at half-speed, children in fast-forward, and seagulls hovered, assessed, swooped and retreated. The air was warm, and I felt a tired old salty kiss. It wasn't enough though, none of it was. I shut my eyes and breathed deeply. I tried to fall back into a memory but there was nothing there to hold me. Someone pushed past and told me to get out of the way. Slumping down on a nearby bench, words and pictures tumbled through my mind and fell away, nothing staying, nothing my grabbing hands could hold.

'Stupid bastard,' I murmured at the phone as I scrolled through to her name. 'I like the sea,' I blurted out to Anya as soon as she answered. I didn't catch the break in her voice, the weariness and the tears. Not right then. 'I don't think I ever told you that before. I don't know what that says about a person. What do you think?'

'It doesn't matter what I think.'

'Yes, it does.'

'Why? Why does any of this matter?'

'Does it mean I'm someone eyeing an escape? That I want to be elsewhere? Maybe. I don't know.'

'You don't need an escape. You got the escape. You want back in.'

'But do I?'

She sighed and it reminded me of my mother, the way she always used to answer me with a weary exhale of breath when she had nothing for me but a desire for me to shut up. 'That's why you are here, isn't it?'

'Here?'

'There,' she corrected, quickly.

'Where are you, Anya?'

'Isn't that why you decided to go back home, Ray? To find out whether that life you left behind still fits?'

'Yeah.' There was something about her that sounded off and I couldn't place it. I didn't like the feeling it gave me, the uncertainty. I started talking again, hoping it wouldn't still be there when I stopped. 'I always did like the sea. I always found it comforting when I was a child. So my mother always said, anyway. She knew that if I was ever throwing a wobbly, then all she had to do was take me down to the sea and I would stop almost at once. Kind of looks different now though to how I remember it, but I'm sure it's not. I had it in my head that it was a deep blue colour, but it isn't. It's like dishwater. Is that me doing that? I think it probably is.'

She sighed again, but quieter this time, and she whispered my name softly, as if it were just for her.

'Sorry, have I called at a bad time?'

'Is there ever a good time for you to call?'

'I don't know.'

'No. Me neither.' I could hear noises in the background, traffic and voices, shouting and laughter. It sounded like she was standing by a window. 'Ray…'

'Why is it I always have the feeling you are about to tell me something, yet can never quite get there?'

'I don't know.'

'I think it's because you are. What is it?'

'Stop it, Ray. Just…just stop. Okay?'

'You know you can tell me anything, don't you?'

'I have nothing I want to tell you. You've got me wrong, Ray. You don't know me.'

'Sure. If you say so.'

'I can't do this, Ray.'

'Do what?'

'This, whatever this is. I can't keep speaking to you.'

A seagull swooped down to one side of the bench and landed on a bin. It turned a circle, squawked at me and then flew off. I found myself looking out to the sea again. Looking for something that wasn't there. 'I understand.'

'No you don't.'

'No.'

'Neither do I. Everything is wrong, though. Nothing makes sense at the moment. But this…*this*…it can't happen.'

'Nothing is happening. This is just two friends talking.'

'Yeah,' she said darkly, 'friends.'

'Friends.'

'Two friends talking. Yeah. Words are meaningless, aren't they? My best friend tells me that.'

'She's right.'

'She's an author.'

'She not very good then?' My laugh sounded hollow, and she didn't reciprocate this time. I felt a warm flush of embarrassment creep up my cheeks, and my ears started to tingle. 'This the child-hater you mentioned?'

'She would like you to think that.'

'Makes sense, writers are supposed to be socially deficient, aren't they?'

'Are they?'

'I think I read that somewhere.'

'She never used to be though, but then people change, don't they? That's one of the guaranteed disappointments in life: death, taxes and people letting you down. Lovers, friends – no one ever stays as exactly the same person that you found in the first place. People are supposed to grow, sure, but why do they always have to grow away as well?'

'I haven't changed,' I told her firmly, hopefully.

'No. And you are one person that really should.'

I laughed again at that, assuming it was a joke, but again she didn't join in.

'This girl that broke your heart, whatever the hell she was called…'

'Katie.'

'Yeah, whatever, like I care. She changed, didn't she? She grew away from you. Or outgrew you. She changed. They all do.'

'Some do.'

'They all do. You do know that whoever she is now, Katie, whatever she has become, there is no way she is the same person that you last saw at that bus stop? This rosy-tinted ideal you have, where everything was perfect, you know it's bollocks, don't you? I mean, you aren't that naïve are you, Ray?'

'I didn't think you cared?'

'Care that you don't get hurt all over again? Sure I do.'

'I need to know. I need an ending.'

'You've had it. She ended it. You should have known then. By doing that she stopped it ever being the same again. No matter what happens, you can never get that back. Even if she runs into your arms and tells you that she made a mistake and that she loves you and that she wants to grow old with you, none of that means it will ever be the same again. Because it won't be. You might get lucky and get a few years where you can confidently con yourself, and a man like you doesn't need much help, but some day it will start to change, you'll see. You will wake up and there will be a different person lying next to you, someone that won't fit that ridiculous notion of happiness that you have been carefully constructing. She won't fit any more, and then you will start to resent her, and it will only be when your heart breaks again that you will realise that it wasn't her to blame for it, but you – you and your foolish dreams.'

'You told me to go and find her.'

'No I didn't.'

'Yes, Anya. Yes, you did.'

'Why would you pay any attention to what I say? You don't know me – if you did you would run a mile.'

'Try me.'

'No. You don't know what a mess I've made of everything.'

'Tell me then.'

'No.'

'What is it, Anya? Tell me, what have you got to lose? I'm just a voice on the phone after all. None of this means anything. I've opened myself up to your ridicule and advice. Let me return the favour.'

'You hang on my advice, then you are in more trouble than you realise, Ray.'

'Sounds like we deserve each other.'

'Life is unfair, you don't always get what you deserve.' Her words were breaking; she sounded tired, spent. 'Get on with your life, Ray. Just get on with it. Do it now. Loving someone doesn't make you immortal.' Then the tears came and her words drowned. She started to sigh, but it became a great, racking sob instead. I said her name; again and again I called at her down the phone line and all I could hear were great childish wails. I stood from the bench and then shouted her name. There was another seagull back on the bin, maybe the same one, and it was squawking at me. Squawking her name with me.

'Hello?' I thought instantly that the man's voice was coming from next to me and I spun around, first left and then right, and only then did I realise that the voice was coming from the phone, and I was all alone. 'Who is this, please?'

I hung up quickly, pocketed the phone and then sat down on the bench with a thud. 'Fuck it,' I said to the seagull. The seagull didn't reply.

I stayed there until dusk, until the warm air grew sharper, the salt kisses less inviting, and then I stood on aching legs and turned back the way I'd come, what felt like years ago.

It's fair to say *My Love Is An Elephant In Your Trousers* is not going to be troubling Broadway anytime soon. I doubt it could even trouble Muswell Hill Broadway. I'm certainly no theatre critic, but I think it would be overly generous to call it the biggest pile of indecipherable, pretentious trash that has ever been committed to stage. Vera Franks always did straddle the line of pretension with a sturdy pair of size eight boots, even when she was a drama student; earnest, pompous and angry, she had the holy trinity of shit theatre in aces, and what she lacked in talent she sure as heck made up for in self-belief. And what this play lacked in plot (which seemed to be everything), it made up for in shouting. Vera always was a proficient shouter, and in this play she shouted. A lot. For two hours. Playing in a function room at the back of a pub, a vague smell of perspiration and desperation hanging in the air, this complete ball-wash of gibberish climaxed with Vera (wearing an all-in-one Lycra body stocking over her gangly body throughout), kneeling down in front of something that might have been either a toadstool or a muffin, and thumping a fist against her heart. At each hit the audio of an elephant played from a speaker at the back of the theatre/shithole.

'Be still my beating heart!' she blathered to the three of us in the audience that were awake and had endured it to the bloody end. 'For here I discover love in your animal passion! For once my calling was the never-ending black cosmos where I was destined to burn brightly, on fire, shining in my lonely, naked love for all to see.'

A man in front of me, who seemed to be loving the show for all the wrong reasons, was doubled up in laughter and slapping his thighs. 'What a load of shite,' he breathed between his hysterics.

'I now walk into your warm embrace,' she continued valiantly, against the laughter and the sound of the motion sensor hand-dryer in the gents' that was whirring loudly just beyond the emergency exit, every time someone walked past, 'and together we are planets, aligned in the galaxy, orbiting together for eternity. This is the calling. The calling is your warmth. You have saved me from the cold and I shall never forget.'

With that Vera Franks stretched to her full, tree-like height, took an over-dramatic bow and then scuttled from the stage, one laughing man's vigorous applause and wolf whistles following her out.

The inside of the pub was almost as empty as the auditorium had been when I stepped back out to freedom; a small scattering of old men were staring into their pints, and a barman was idly flicking through TV channels on a big-screen TV. The rest of the clientele seemed to be outside in the beer garden drinking up the last drops of the sweltering summer night. I ordered a much-needed pint and dawdled at the bar. She arrived twenty minutes later, her bag under one arm, and the toadstool/muffin thing under the other. She saw me straight away and stalked her way towards me, like she were eyeing up prey at the waterhole.

'Well, well, look what the cat brought up. Ray English.' She handed her bag and the toadstool/muffin thing to the barman, who took them both in limp hands and then let them drop casually to the floor behind the bar. 'Well, I never thought you'd have the balls to come back here, Ray.'

'Nice to see you too, Vee.'

'Don't call me that. Only friends call me that.'

'Sure, Vera.'

'And of course, where there's one, there's the other.' She glared around the pub, angry little eyes picking a scattershot path between the old men. 'Hiding in the toilets is he? Where is the great Danny Radleigh? Afraid to face me?'

'Danny's not here.'

'Coward.'

'Quite possibly.'

'So to what do I owe the great pleasure of you?' She waved a hand at the barman, and then pointed at the wine bottles. 'I will have a glass of red. He's paying. You and that ginger tosspot are up here for the wedding of the year, I suppose?'

'You know about that?'

'Of course I do. Tamara and I go way back.'

'You'll be there then?'

She took her drink from the barman, downed it in two huge gulps and handed it back for him to refill. 'I'm committed to my art, and I have a matinee as well tomorrow, so, sadly no, I won't.'

'Good.'

'Good?'

'You're committed to your art. That's good, isn't it?'

'Yes, it is.' She was so self-involved she couldn't even see the insult. Good. That was an invite if ever I received one. She took her second glass, and this time the sips were slower and more considered. She was looking me up and down, scrutinising me, smiling beyond the mask, a look of contempt barely concealed. 'Did you ever make it as a rock star?'

'Not quite.'

'Such a shame.'

'I'm pleased you stuck with the acting though, Vera. It helps disprove the idea that a qualification in performing arts is meaningless.'

'Well, when you have a calling you have to answer, Ray. Not something you would know about, I'm sure. Did you see the show?'

'Oh, yeah.'

'And?'

'Very deep.'

'Yes, well I wouldn't expect a one-woman dissection of the myriad vagaries and foolish indulgences of the love of another to mean much to you.' She flicked a strand of hair back, rolled her shoulders and then leaned one long branch of an arm on the bar. 'Never did quite understand the way of the female, did you?'

'You still see her?' I asked as casually as I could, which wasn't casual at all. I sounded more like a policeman taking a witness statement.

'Of course.' She smiled and sipped her wine, those eyes rolling up and down me in disgust. 'I should have guessed.'

I cleared my throat, shrugged and joined her in leaning on the bar, attempting an air of nonchalant indifference. It didn't work. 'Her family have moved, I hear. Did she stay in Southport by any chance?'

'You sad little man. You still haven't moved on, have you?'

'You and her were best mates. Please, Vera.'

'That's really quite tragic, Ray. Honestly it is. So pathetic. She'd be horrified to know she had that much power.'

'Vera…'

'Dear oh dear. I suppose you probably think it's romantic, don't you? The burning fire of true love? A devotion to a celibate life because there can be no love as acute and consuming as that first one?'

'Well, let's not get carried away.'

'I doubt they will write books, Ray.'

'Is she still here, Vera?'

'Why would I possibly tell you that?'

'Because I asked you?'

She finished her wine and delicately placed the glass on the bar. Standing to her full, considerable height, she crossed her arms, rolled back on her heels and fixed me with a withering stare. 'It's really not for me to reintroduce you back into her life is it? She's a friend, a dear friend, and you're nothing to me any more. Or her. In fact, you, as I recall, were quite the bane of her life, weren't you? The lovelorn leech. The ubiquitous drooling headcase. Honestly, Ray, it was quite the surprise to all of us that you never tried to dress up in her clothes and massacre her friends with a toffee hammer.'

Casual indifference wasn't working. I decided to give honesty a try. I knew it was no more likely to yield results, Vera was having far too much fun for that, but it was all I had left. 'I have to see her.'

'Why?'

'I need this to end, Vera.'

'It did end. She dumped you.'

'Is she still in Southport? Tell me that at least.'

'It's a big town, Ray. Think you're just going to bump into her?'

'So she is?'

'She might be.'

'Is she happy?'

'Well, that's not for me to say, is it?'

'C'mon, Vera, just tell me that, will you? You can do that. Is she okay?'

'You mean does she miss you? That's what that question really means, isn't it? Does she still think about you, or is she happy with someone else, living in domestic bliss with a better man, in the suburbs?'

'That's what you need to be happy these days, is it?'

'That's what you want to know though, isn't it? You are really asking if she's having sex with another man. That's what it all boils down to in the end. I'm right, aren't I?'

'You're enjoying this, aren't you?'

'Enjoying seeing you flail around in your desperation? Hardly, Ray.' She gave me a crooked little grin and tilted her head to one side. 'Certainly not much, anyway.' With a ridiculously dramatic flick of her hair, Vera Franks pivoted on her heels and flounced away from me, heading to the toilets.

'Name?' The barman had drawn up next to me and was leaning across the bar, calmly flicking through a battered, old notebook.

'Excuse me?'

'This girl you're looking for, what's her surname?' He didn't look up at me, but seemed to sense my confusion. 'Her address book seems to have fallen out of her bag. There's a thing, wouldn't you say?'

'Some sort of thing.'

'What's her name?'

'Fenshaw. Katie Fenshaw.'

The barman lightly licked his index finger and skipped through the worn, curling pages. A filthy habit, but I wasn't about to pick him up on it. 'You a weirdo?' he asked me, with the casualness I had been lacking.

'Guess so, a little bit, yeah.'

'I understand. Had a woman once myself. Don't trust a man with a woman who hasn't lost at least part of his mind.' He tore a page free of the book, folded it up neatly and then slipped it across the bar. 'Good luck, kid. Hope you find what you're looking for.'

The Missed Call

ANYA

I assumed it was a dream. It couldn't have been real, it didn't make sense, yet the more the face looked down at me as I lay there weeping on the floor, and the more those eyes laughed despite the solemnity, the more I started to believe it. He was wet, semi-naked, bound up in a towel. The stranded tuft of hair on his head was sticking up, the rest wetted back and combed neat.

'Anya? Sweetheart, what is it? Who were you talking to?'

He was holding my phone up, almost as a way of explaining his question. I pushed at his hand and shoved it away before falling against his chest and crying myself dry.

Then it started to piece together; walking into the hotel and being greeted outside my room by a huge bunch of flowers and his happy face, I could remember that right then, and I could remember the flutter in my heart I had felt when I saw him, and it had almost certainly been joy rather than a panic attack. I had asked him what he was doing there and I knew that it had sounded accusing, like he were a burglar rather than my husband. He had just smiled some more and his eyes had carried on laughing, and that had been his explanation.

He gently lifted me up so we were face to face and then he rested his palms softly on my cheeks. 'Hey, what is it?' There was still steam coming from the bathroom from his shower, and the fan in there was whirring loudly. He smelt good. 'Anya?' My eyes fell on the flowers across the room, lying on the bedside table.

'They need to be in a vase. They need water or they will die.'

He smiled. 'Okay.'

'You came here to surprise me.'

He looked at me like I was mad and then smiled some more.

'It was a nice surprise.'

It had been a crazy three days since Eva's outburst over a rogue piece of tomato. When Lydia had taken me aside that evening and told me it had gone viral it took me a while to twig what she meant. Then she showed me. There she was, my best friend, star of a badly filmed video on YouTube, detailing her moment of madness in a motorway services just outside Birmingham. Hundreds of *LOL*s and *LMAO*s and *ROFL*s accompanied the video, and there were even some comments from people who had basic literacy skills too.

Jim St James was apoplectic and again, poor Lydia took the brunt of the rage. The next morning he was waiting for us in the hotel lobby.

'You're her wrangler, you should have had her on a short lead,' he was saying to Lydia as I crossed the lobby to get another coffee. Jim had his hands on his hips, adopting a pose of schoolmaster reprimanding a pupil. 'You've heard what she's like, heaven knows enough people should have warned you, so what were you thinking, Lydia?'

'I'm sorry, Mr St James.' Lydia was playing her part in the teacher/pupil charade by gazing down at her shoes in shame. 'It just happened so quickly, I couldn't stop her.'

'Oh, you couldn't stop her, great. You couldn't stop her, so now I've got to crawl on my hands and knees with my arse in the air asking for a good spanking. Terrific. Thanks. Remind me to see if I can get you a raise. Where is she anyway, in the kitchens breakfasting on raw meat?'

'She's in bed,' I snapped, moving across the lobby and walking between them.

'And you are?' he asked, his nose in the air.

'I'm her friend, and I will thank you for keeping your snidey little comments about her to yourself.'

'So you must be Anya Belmont? Great. Well, Anya Belmont, I don't want or need your thanks, thank you. What I do need is a moment with my author, if that is entirely acceptable to you, of course.'

'She's in bed, I told you.'

I didn't see the point in telling him that she was also in a Valium and vodka-induced netherworld at that precise moment.

'Well, go wake her up, then! She's got humble pie to eat.'

Lydia filled me in on the way back up to Eva's room.

It transpired that during St James' frantic damage limitation exercise, the woman on the receiving end of

Eva's tomato rage had mentioned that she had a son, and that her boy was, rather fortuitously, a huge fan of *Warlocks of Wolverhampton*. Rabid, in fact, was the word she used. 'He won't read anything else. Just that, cover to cover, again and again,' the woman told a grovelling Jim St James over the phone. 'Imagine my shock when I found out who it was shouting and screaming at me. How could I tell my son that, Mr St James? How could I shatter his illusions?'

'So she wants Eva to meet her son?' I asked Lydia as we got into the lift.

'Mr St James suggested that perhaps he would like a signed copy of *Demons*, hand-delivered personally by Eva. Have a photo taken, that sort of thing. We need a shot of Eva and the mother together to dampen this down. She will need to say something to the press too.'

'Too late to get her a hypnotist, you think?' I asked, quite seriously, as I knocked on the bedroom door.

She answered wrapped in her duvet, a face like a melting clown peeking out from a small gap. Her room was dark and stuffy, and stank of urine and armpit. She greeted us with a guttural warble, something close to English, and then sank to her knees and disappeared under the duvet.

'Or an exorcist?' Lydia whispered to me.

I dragged Eva under a cold shower whilst Lydia tidied the room and laid some clothes out for her. Poor Eva had no sense of what was happening but took it all the same, gurgling and mumbling gibberish into the tiled wall of the shower like a baby. Half an hour later and she looked passably human.

'No make-up,' Lydia advised. 'Be good to see the bags under her eyes, we can make like she's been crying. She needs to show contrition.'

'I'm a contradiction, yes,' Eva groaned into my supporting arm as I led her out to the door. 'My life is a contradiction!'

'No, Ms Cunningham,' Lydia started, 'contrition…'

'I'm a hypocrite. I am a fraud!'

Ten minutes and a strong black coffee later, Eva was bundled into the backseat of Jim's car, her head hanging out of the back window like a dog.

'So you understand, do you, Eva? It has been explained to you what we need to do?' Jim was shouting into the rearview mirror, his glare alternating between Eva and me, his words for both of us. 'Someone talk to me, someone put me at ease and tell me she knows what we are doing and what day it is! Speak! Someone say something, show me I'm not talking to myself here! Anyone!'

'We explained to her,' Lydia said calmly from the passenger seat. 'I think she understood.' It was a lie, but as was evident even to me, Jim St James was someone who only processed the words he wanted to hear; anything else was clearly extraneous and discarded. In that respect I couldn't help but realise that he was probably a perfect fit with Eva.

Eva said only one thing during the whole journey. Just before we pulled up and Jim St James went into full-on smarm effect, she turned to me with big, uncomprehending, watering eyes, gently touched my hand and told me she was sorry. I asked her for what. She didn't seem able to be specific.

They were waiting on the doorstep as we arrived: a photographer, the woman from the restaurant, a Mrs Topley – clearly revelling in her role as victim, if the look of smugness was anything to go by – and a small boy, clinging to her leg. Jim greeted them all with a firm, sincere shake of the hand, and I could see him nodding enthusiastically at the photographer, a nicely manicured hand finding his shoulder and lightly squeezing. The laughs were surface sounds, the conversation a light sprinkling of nothingness. Everyone, it seemed, was acting a role in a game that only one small boy wanted to play. And even he didn't seem too arsed at that moment. The utter absurdity of it all stank, and for the first time in months, since this whole stupid carnival around Eva and her book had started for me, I found myself actually feeling sorry for her.

'And here she is!' Jim announced, his arms extended towards the car like he was performing a magic trick. I was leading Eva out by the hand, a mother taking her child to school for the first day. Jim ruffled the small boy's hair. 'This is Eva Cunningham, Charlie. Come and say hello!'

Charlie Topley looked embarrassed and also slightly scared, and hung behind his mother's leg for a moment as his favourite author swayed towards him like she was walking in sponge shoes on the deck of a boat. I could hear the snapping of the camera and feel the heat of the mother's stare, and found myself, much to my disgust, wearing a cheesy, achingly unreal smile. Mrs Topley shoved her son forward towards us.

'Hello,' I said through my stupid grin. 'How are you, Charlie? My name is Anya, and you know who this is of course…'

Eva belched lightly and stumbled against me before I pulled her straight and ran a hand against her back, clutching at her shirt to hold her still. 'Child,' she said to him, 'sorry that I shouted at your tomato…'

I yanked her back and then gently pushed her to her right until she was staring vaguely at Mrs Topley.

'Sorry about your tomato.'

'She really is mortified about her actions, Mrs Topley,' Jim chipped in, a hand finding her shoulder too. 'Eva is so happy to have this chance to apologise to you in person. She's been under a lot of stress recently with the new book, all the promotion – it is no excuse, of course, but I'm sure you can appreciate that it was not the action of someone thinking straight.'

'Perhaps we should all go inside?' the photographer suggested to Mrs Topley, who grunted and then disappeared through the front door. One by one we followed her in, Charlie coming in last with Eva and me.

Jim presented a brand-new copy of *Demons in Dudley* to Charlie as we all stood about awkwardly in the living room, not knowing what to do, and the young boy's face seemed to suddenly explode into life. He grabbed it with thank-yous tumbling out of his mouth and a wobbly smile that seemed to suggest tears weren't a million miles away, and then sank onto the sofa and started to read.

'Thank you,' Mrs Topley said to Jim, and then nodded unconvincingly to Eva, almost as an afterthought. Eva gave a shrug and fought back a yawn. 'You going to sign it?'

'Of course she will, I have a pen,' Lydia said, stepping forward.

'Perhaps a message too...Eva?' Jim narrowed his eyes and nodded to the extended pen. 'You'd be happy to do that, wouldn't you, Eva?'

'Yerrrp,' came the reply.

'Are you happy with your present, Charlie?' Lydia asked.

Charlie nodded manically, his eyes not leaving the page.

'Good.'

We continued to stare at each other in awkward silence, no one quite knowing what was supposed to happen. As it had since time immemorial, the good old English failsafe of the offer of a cup of tea saved us and stirred us back into action, all of us agreeing at once with enthusiastic nods of the head, Lydia and Jim almost walking into each other in their rush to assist Mrs Topley.

'Perhaps you could show Ms Cunningham your bedroom too whilst she is here, Charlie?' Mrs Topley said firmly, suggesting that it wasn't so much an option as it was an inevitability. 'I'm sure she would like that.' She locked eyes with Eva. 'He's quite the fan.'

Eva leant into my face and whispered, 'I shouldn't go to his bedroom, should I? Why does he want me to do that? I shouted at his mother, that's all, it doesn't give him a right to see me naked, does it?'

Tea drunk, all the right words spoken, and the obligatory everyone's-a-friend photos taken, Charlie led me by the hand up the stairs to his room, whilst I led a quickly sobering Eva behind me with my free hand, squeezing it hard every time I sensed she was about to speak. Mrs Topley stayed at the foot of the stairs, her son's protestations about her accompanying them no doubt still stinging her. Her little boy's first flash of the teenage rebellion and mortification at his parents' very being that would soon be commonplace seemed to be a smack around her face, and I couldn't help but feel sorry for her. It didn't last, though. The more those soft little hands gripped mine and those happy eyes gazed up at me, the easier it was to turn sympathy to jealousy. Bollocks to Mrs Topley.

Charlie's room turned out to be a veritable shrine to the parallel-world version of the West Midlands in Eva's books. Walls were covered in articles and drawings, blown-up versions of *Warlock*'s cover from different countries, fan art, interviews, and even his own artwork of the monsters and heroes in the novel. He presented it to us with no small amount of pride, dragging me into the room as Eva languished by the door, her mouth agape.

'Wow, Charlie, this is great!' I said, giving him a small hug. 'Very impressive.'

'I drew this for school,' Charlie chirped, turning me towards a painting above his bed. 'We had to draw a picture of our favourite monster for Mr Salmon's art class last term, and he knew that I loved *Warlocks in Wolverhampton* so much because whenever they let us take a book in to read I always take that, and he said I should paint something from the book. I got an A for it!'

'I should think so, Charlie!' I said, running a hand over his shoulders and stealing another hug.

Eva stepped into the room, turning a shambling circle as her eyes took in the decor; her own creations brought to life around her by the minds of others, colourful and incredible and hideously beautiful. She stopped behind me, almost fell into me, and then sunk onto the bed, staring up at the poster with us. 'Yes,' was all she could bring herself to say for several moments. 'What is it?'

'It's Grand Justice Gong Kelk, of the Warlock Council!' he told her, as if she was stupid and not in fact the person that had actually created him and given him that stupid bloody name in the first place.

'Oh yes. It is. I see it now. Very good.'

'Mr Salmon said he is going to read the book now because I keep going on about it so much.'

'I like Gong the best,' Eva continued, ignoring Mr Salmon's literary intentions. 'He's my favourite character.'

'Mine too,' Charlie breathed across at her in adoration.

'He was based on an ex-boyfriend.'

'Oh?' Charlie was staring at her with saucer eyes that seemed unable to blink.

'My editor suggested Gong was better than Dong, which it was in the first draft, even though I was only trying to be ironic…' The little finger of her right hand suddenly jutted out and started to waggle. I quickly stepped in front of her and cut her off from Charlie.

'Did you draw some of these other pictures too, Charlie?' I asked, pointing to the wall by the door, forcing him to turn away from Eva.

'Some, yes.'

'Why is that in Chinese?' Eva said from behind me, an arm suddenly snaking out from my side, a finger pointing towards some Oriental lettering underneath a piece of printed-out artwork on the wall by the window. The picture seemed to be of the hero Warlock's wife, whose name completely escaped me at that moment. (It was a handy name for Scrabble, that much I remembered, but not a name for instant recall.)

'It's Japanese. That's by IKO9101, he's from Japan.'

'Who is IKO9101?'

'He's on your forum. He does drawings and puts them up and I printed that one out because I liked it so much. He's older than me, though.'

'Forum? I have a forum?'

'Yeah! Loads!' Again Charlie looked at her incredulously, speaking to her like she was the biggest idiot in the world. Out the mouths of babes. 'Tons! I started that one though, so I don't go on the others too much, this is the best one, I think. IKO9101 says that he has got a tattoo on his leg of Gong Kelk, but people keep asking him to post a picture and he doesn't so I think he's lying.'

Eva was once more gazing around at the walls, her eyes opening and closing, stretching wide and squinting almost closed as she would lean in and read things. Once or twice I even saw her lip quiver, twitching at one end like a dog giving a warning growl. There was a smile there somewhere, trying to break through, disregarding every ounce of cynicism that she wore like war paint.

'And people put art up on this forum, do they?'

'Yeah, it's not all that good though. IKO9101 is the best.'

Eva nodded at a laptop open on a little table across from the bed. 'You want to show me this then?'

Charlie eagerly obliged, grabbing up the laptop and throwing himself down on the bed next to her. Her hazy, wet eyes looked up over his head, lingered on me for a brief moment and then returned to Gong Kelk in all his majesty.

'And have you put your pictures on there too, Charlie?' she asked.

'Yeah!'

Eva nodded simply and then let her eyes fall onto the laptop that was now in front of her. 'Good.'

We seemed to leave part of the gathering storm cloud behind us when we left Birmingham, and headed further north to Liverpool. Despite Eva's zombiefied state and Mrs Topley's seeming desire to not let her off without squeezing every last opportunity from the situation (we had ended up staying for tea so Charlie's friends could come over and stare at Eva like we were in some sort of freak show, which may not be so far from the truth), the newspaper piece that emerged the following morning turned out to be far from damning. Possibly this was because the reporter hadn't actually been there in person, or maybe because of my suspicion that Jim had slipped the photographer a few notes.

To try and further quell any lingering fears Eva might have had, Lydia uttered half-baked reassurances over breakfast, like, 'It'll all blow over now,' and 'It'll be something else getting people talking soon, anyway,' and, 'It's tomorrow's chip paper.' She tried hard, Lydia, but she clearly still hadn't learned whom she was working with. Eva simply came back solemnly with, 'People don't eat chips from newspapers any more.'

Eva's demeanour had changed since Birmingham, the fear and panic seemingly washing out of her and leaving behind the wreckage of misery instead. I wasn't sure which version of my friend I preferred. She would sit in silence most of the time, gazing out of the window as we travelled, and answering people in brief grunts or whispers. The vitality and spark seemed to have been sapped from her, and although it made for an easier ride for the rest of us, it worried me. I didn't like seeing her this way.

The book-signing in the centre of Liverpool proved to be more uneventful than any of us could have dared hope for. They came en masse, more than anyone had expected, which perhaps proved the old adage of no publicity being bad publicity. They came in their costumes and clutching their books, and there was wide-eyed excitement, there was fascination and awe and a palpable buzz in the air. Eva sat there in stony acceptance of it all, rigid and pale and ever so slightly blunted by shame, and she signed books and mumbled words, and even had photos taken. Some came with tomatoes, of course. It was funny the first time, slightly tedious by the fifth, and by the time some self-congratulatory wag approached her with a book, bookmarked by a slither, Lydia stepped in for her and moved him out of line. Eva stayed there for two hours, robotically going about her business, and when finally they dwindled away and the bookshop owner was professing his gratitude and shaking our hands, she quietly slipped away and headed out to the car in tears.

We went out for a late lunch and she said very little, and ate even less. We mooched around the shops, moaned about the service in a coffee shop and then took a cab over to Crosby beach, somewhere we had both long wanted to visit so as to see Antony Gormley's wonderful *Another Place* sculptures. Only then did she open up to me.

'I'm always going to be the angry tomato woman, aren't I?' she said glumly, staring out at the figures along the sand, lit magically by a warm summer sunset.

'Oh, don't be ridiculous.'

'You know how it works. It's going to be tomatoes every day now. Tomato juice, tomato ketchup, anything and everything. It will be my catchphrase and epitaph, Anya. What the hell have I done? I write books, I can't compete with that little video.'

'You're an author, a damn good one, and that isn't going to suddenly change. Let people take the piss for a bit, but it will grow old, people will forget and no one will care in the end.'

'I've fucked it all up, haven't I?'

'No, Eva, don't be so stupid.'

She turned to me and grabbed my arm; her eyes were panicked, the pupils enlarged so much that they threatened to swallow any remaining colour. Mascara dribbled down her cheeks, curving to her mouth like some sort of tribal war paint. 'I only ever wanted to write books, you know that, don't you? Just that. That was enough. That's okay, isn't it? I just wanted to tell stories, and I got there, I got to that point and was allowed to do it, and I have no idea how I got away with it, but I carried on taking it even though I knew I probably didn't deserve it, because people were calling me an author and it felt good. I became that person that I wanted to be.'

'You still are. Christ, Eva, don't be so melodramatic.'

'But it won't last, will it? Writing these books, it can't last. Each time I'm starting from nothing and I'm building it all up again, and what if I can't keep on doing that? Every time I stare at that blank screen I convince myself that nothing will come and one day I know it won't, and do you think people will indulge me that? Of course they won't. I write kids' books set in the West Midlands – I haven't written *Catcher in the Rye*, I can't just be enigmatic and disappear from sight. Each time I'm proving myself all over again, and I was a fraud in the first place, do you know how hard that is? Trying not to get found out?'

I felt my right hand twitch, and just for a split second I wanted to slap her. I can take Eva in all her many messed-up forms, but the self-indulgent martyr version has always been too much to bear.

'They'll soon go, these people that trail around after me now – they won't stay, they won't let me get away with it forever. There'll be someone else for them to find, someone who can give them what they want and then they will leave me and I will just be that angry tomato woman. That's all that will stay in the end. The tomato. You know what I mean. Of course you do, it's like you and Len, isn't it? Well, maybe that's what I deserve? Maybe this is penance for stealing a living?'

'Whoa, hold up, what the hell do you mean it's like Len and me? Don't bring my marriage into your delusional ramblings.'

She let my arm go and then waved a dismissive hand in my face and turned to the beach again. Anger bloomed, and this time I didn't try and subdue it. I grabbed Eva by the shoulder and spun her around to face me.

'Explain what you mean by that.'

'Oh, I didn't mean anything. Get over yourself.'

She tried to turn back but I held her there, my grip tightening. 'Eva, you don't get to say that to me without explaining what you mean.' The anger rippled through my chest and I felt an old, familiar tightness, a suffocation that caused a flicker like a blown candle flame in my gut. I felt both cold and hot, my limbs riddled with pins and needles, my breath ragged and difficult. I heard an inner voice trying to tell me it was just another panic attack: *Don't worry yourself, it's just your old affliction, girl, let it be.* But fury always screamed louder than logic. 'Answer me!'

She tried to fight me, just for a moment, but soon gave up and sank into my chest instead, wilting like an old ragdoll. 'You're hurting me, Anya.'

'Deal with it, darling, the real world's cruel like that.' I shoved her back against the barriers to the beach and she yelped. 'Now tell me what you meant.'

'Oh, please, like you don't know.'

I was terrified I did. *There'll be someone else for them to find, someone who can give them what they want and then they will leave me…*

'Indulge me, Eva. See if you're as good at it as I am.'

'Get your hands off me!'

'Are you seriously comparing my marriage to your pathetic paranoia? Tell me you're not doing that, Eva, because that would be lower than even you've ever gone.'

'People move on, people get bored. People change. It's human nature. People are fickle. That's all I'm saying. Now get off…'

'I'm not fickle. That's not what you're saying to me, is it? I know you don't mean that.'

'Sure, like you aren't having thoughts about this mystery man of yours. Like you haven't had your head turned by the idea of something new. Again, Anya. Again! Someone who can give you what you want. Unlike the man you married. Am I so wrong?'

I could feel people watching us, could hear the murmured voices, feel the suffocation of their judgment, but I couldn't stop myself. The slap was hard and cruel, and I could feel my wedding ring strike her cheekbone and graze the skin. Eva seemed to collapse into her shoes, crumpling down to the ground with such a puny willingness I thought for a moment that I had broken her. But then came the sobs, those childish sobs, and a second later she was scrunching herself into a ball, and holding her head in her hands. I shoved my shaking fists deep into my pockets and left her there.

Am I so wrong?

She was. I told myself that all the way back to the hotel. I kept on saying it over and over in my head as I sat alone in the cab ride to Southport. *You're wrong, you're wrong, you don't know me like you think you do. You're wrong.*

By the time I saw Len standing outside my hotel bedroom I had almost convinced myself I was right.

The room stank of sex and the cream that Len puts on his rash. I awoke early with both smells hanging in my nostrils like congealed snot. I saw Len's feet sticking out from under the duvet; he had slept in the multi-coloured socks that I liked. He snored away gently next to me, his stray tuft of hair sticking up like an aerial. He fumbled for me in his sleep as I got out of bed and padded to the window. I peered out behind the curtains and a dazzling summer's day screamed at me, demanding to be noticed. I put the curtains back and sat on the end of the bed next to his multi-coloured feet.

I knew that he would phone.

Even before I looked at the phone I knew that he had.

Somehow Ray English was inevitable. I had switched the phone to divert to answerphone before I went to bed, knowing that his call would come. I needn't have worried though; Len would have slept through it. Len would have slept through Ray standing over him screaming what he wanted to say to me into my face.

One missed call.

I put the phone on the bedside table and showered for what felt like the longest time. Len was still asleep as I dressed, and it was only then that I noticed the time. It was barely past seven. I sat back on the bed fully dressed and stared at the closed curtains and the thin fingers of light that were creeping down the wall underneath the window. I thought about tickling Len's feet or nudging his leg and waking him up. I found myself at the television, fondling the remote control. I thought about turning it on and cranking the volume up, but I didn't do that either. Room service…I debated about whether to call down to see if I could order breakfast for us both. That seemed the best idea, and I even got as far as picking the phone up. But I put the receiver down just as quickly.

I picked up my mobile and left the room.

I walked out along the corridor from our room, past Eva's bedroom, dawdling briefly at her door, hand up ready to knock, before turning away again at the sound of her voice coming through the door. I could hear her chatting away loudly, embroiled in a phone conversation that was managing to elicit laughter from her. I couldn't begin to imagine who had worked that miracle.

I turned a corner and then took a seat on the top of the long staircase down to the lobby. A couple of women in fancy dresses walked past me as I stared down at my phone. At the base of the stairs a squat, hairy man in a morning suit was waving at them and tapping his watch.

I took a long breath and then let it out slowly and then called up my answerphone.

'Hey,' he said.

'Hey yourself, Ray English,' I said to no one.

'I know I shouldn't phone. I know what you said. I suppose it's just as well I got your machine. I hoped I would. I didn't want to wake you up.'

'Get to the point.'

'Pardon?' An older woman in a giant hat like a pink flying saucer sweet was next to me at the top of the stairs, standing over me, her billowing skirt flapping around my face. She smelt like she had bathed in perfume and looked like a child had put her face on with a roller brush.

'Sorry, I wasn't talking to you. I was talking to myself.'

She descended the stairs and muttered something under her breath. I watched her until she reached the bottom, just in case she tripped. Ray was continuing to blather in my ear and, aware that I was missing what he was saying, I ended the message and then replayed it again from the start.

'Hey. I know I shouldn't phone. I know what you said. I suppose it's just as well I got your machine. I hoped I would. I didn't want to wake you up. I couldn't not phone though, could I? Are you okay? It's just… well…' He stopped and then laughed to himself. 'I'm blathering again, aren't I? I do that, don't I? This is usually when I apologise, right? Well, sorry about that, Anya. Are you laughing at me right now? I wonder. I hope you are.'

I was smiling. I couldn't find anything funny in his goodbye.

'I do understand why you don't want to speak to me,' he continued, his voice dropping briefly to his overly earnest tone that I didn't care for. He's better when he's laughing. 'I mean, I know why you don't want me to phone – yeah, that's what I mean, after all why wouldn't you want to speak to me? A man as charming, erudite and witty as I? Please! My joie de vivre is infectious, my charming phone patter makes women go weak at the knees. But I get it, right? I do. And don't worry about it. Not that you probably are. In fact, I'm sure you're not. It's just...well, I guess what I mean is I feel a bit short-changed. No, that's the wrong phrase to use. Sorry. Not that. You don't owe me anything. I guess I feel a bit disappointed. Maybe that's what I mean. I wanted to know your story. I wanted to know you. And I think there is part of you that wanted to tell me, needed to, even, because silence is a disease and I think you know that. I think you needed to tell me something, if not everything. I would have taken something. Anything. But like I say, you owe me nothing. But just know that I mean it, please...I wanted to know you. I wanted to be your friend. But maybe we still are. I consider you a friend. We can still be friends as strangers, can't we? Tim considers me a friend and I haven't seen him in more years than I can remember. Maybe when I get married I will search you out and invite you. Or maybe we will just swim past each other in the pond one day without knowing it. And for what it's worth, in case you wondered, I've always had it in my mind that you look like a young Joanne Woodward. That's how I've always seen you. I wonder if you do?'

He disappeared briefly and then retuned to me with a timid little cough. 'I've got her address, Anya. Katie. I know where she is and I'm going after my ending. And...and you know what? I don't think it matters if it isn't an ending like you get in films, or in books – it just matters that it's an ending. It's always mattered. I think you've shown me that.' He chuckled to himself and then sighed. 'If you ever want a change of career you should consider becoming a counsellor. Though having said that, who knows, perhaps you are anyway? Thanks, Anya.'

I ended the message and then called him back straight away.

No way was he getting to have the last word.

RAY

I must have slept for about an hour. Not a bad return these days. When I awoke I was holding my mobile phone in one hand, the torn piece of the notebook in the other; I was flat on my back, staring at the ceiling, and still fully dressed. I kept saying the details of the address over and over in my head. After all these years she was now just a few roads away from me. Somehow it didn't seem real. I felt nervous and yet excited, my hands were sweaty, my skin prickled with goosebumps. It was stupid, but it was what it was.

By the time I had showered and clipped my ear and nose hair (toenails too, and how's that for ridiculous optimism?) it was five o'clock. I reasoned it would probably be acceptable to be there anytime after eight. If it was acceptable at all. I could then make the wedding at eleven. Three hours would be long enough to be with her; I could always go back later or she could even come to the wedding with me. She might like to see us play again, and she might even want to sing backing vocals, just for old times' sake? Old times' sake means more as you get older, obviously, and now that she had a zero in her age, perhaps she was starting to re-examine her life, and was prone to reminisce and look at the past wistfully, with a sunny daub of nostalgia?

Yes, that was all bollocks, I know. But what the fuck do you want from me? Of course I knew that none of those eventualities would actually happen. I was a fool, but not yet an idiot. But at that moment I didn't allow that to occupy my mind. If it had I would never have left the hotel room, I never would have put one foot in front of the other, and I would never have got my ending.

I took an hour to dress and do my hair. Nothing looked right. Everything I tried on made me feel awkward and stupid, and nothing seemed to fit correctly. I had to try and look like I had made an effort, yet not look like it was an effort. I laid different combinations of clothes out on my bed, picking each up, putting each down, swapping them around and sniffing them to double-check they were clean enough.

By the time I was settled on the right outfit a blazing summer sun was blasting through the window, throwing a wide rectangle of light across the wall above the bed. I crossed to the window and pulled it open. The air was static and felt fuzzy and thick, and I still couldn't smell the sea.

Even outside the hotel I couldn't smell it. There were people out and about already on Lord Street despite the early hour. Traffic trundled past; bodies ambled and strolled, soaking up the loving hug from the sun.

Families were heading to the sea, old people were heading nowhere fast, and a young girl was outside a coffee shop, putting out a sign with a yawn and a scratch of her head. She smiled at me as I caught her yawning, and I gave her one back, and then we were early morning conspirators. I liked that. I followed her inside.

I don't often drink coffee, I don't even really like it; it's not exactly the insomniac's greatest ally, but right then I needed something to blow away the cobwebs of doubt, any artificial shove to keep me on track. I took a cappuccino and sat by the window, flitting nervous glances between my watch and the street outside, like I was waiting for an interview. The coffee shop girl was wiping down the table behind me and I caught her reflection in the window. She was throwing glances my way, I was sure of it. I considered turning around on my seat to catch her, curious as to what she might say or do if I did. I think she probably would have only smiled again, and who the heck knows what that would have meant?

Katie was obviously doing okay for herself. I remembered her road from my old paper round, it was where the bastards who never tipped lived; a large, wide square with a communal garden in the centre, made up of large, mostly detached houses, some three storeys, some with converted basements – a veritable middle-class wealth wave. Danny and I used to take the piss out of any kids at school that lived there, mocking them for their families' money. Looking back I'm not quite sure why we did that. Jealousy, I guess. Being back there, I wasn't sure I understood the joke any more.

I moved around the square the wrong way round, instantly picking out her house from between two slender willow trees. I crossed the road and wandered through a small, newly painted metal gate, into the communal garden, making sure I kept her house in my sightline at all times, and took a seat on a bench. Flowerbeds were either side of me, presented in colourful, precise symmetry alongside a patch of grass that seemed to have been cut with nail clippers. Even the bench was clean, newly varnished and devoid of any wear and tear. My initial fear of being conspicuous was now overpowering. I must have stood out like a sore thumb, and I could sense the twitching curtains, and the faces at the windows. To one side of the gardens a Stepford wife was leading three little Stepford children into a large people carrier, handing each little carbon-copy kid a lunch box as they stepped up. She threw me a mistrusting glare as she clambered into the front seat, and those piercing eyes didn't leave me until the car was past the garden and out of sight.

The very idea that Katie's first view of me in five years could be of me sitting there, the object of suspicion, suddenly seemed unthinkable and it was enough to get me moving again. *Don't think about it*, I told myself. *Just do it*, Danny said from somewhere. I kept her house in my view and didn't falter and didn't stop, and before I knew it I was there at her garden gate, staring up at a giant, three-storey house with a trestle around the door frame holding pink and red and white flowers. There was even a welcome mat. I couldn't have been more out of place. I also realised I didn't have the first idea what to say or do.

I had assumed it would come to me. Some spark of inspiration, some witty, yet casual quip or cheery greeting would blunder forth when I saw her and every word that followed would be automatic and easy, just like it always had been. But standing there, I was empty.

'Yeah?' a man's voice said rather curtly to one side of me. 'What you want there?' I turned to see an elderly man standing in the front garden leaning on a spade. 'You a cold caller? We don't do that here, sorry lad.'

'Hello,' I said rather blandly.

'What you selling? Got to say, at my age, chances are I got enough of it or never needed it in the first place. You understand?'

'I'm not selling anything.'

'Sure you're not.'

'I'm not.'

'Then you must be on the rob, only other reason I can think that you're looking at my house.'

'Your house? I thought...this is number forty-two?'

'It is, lad.'

'I was looking for Katie Fenshaw. Is she...she lives here, doesn't she?'

'Fenshaw, you say? You're about five months too late there, lad. Moved out. My son bought this place. Him and his missus and me.'

'Oh.' It was all I could think to say. Standing there at this stranger's front gate, dressed up in my best, I suddenly felt like I had been squashed from a great height, the pent-up tension and excitement inside me dribbling out onto the well-maintained pavement.

'Got an address somewhere. Only moved other side of town. You want it, or you going to stand there like an ornament? You gonna do that I might just shove a fishing rod in your hands and stick you in me flowerbed.'

He ushered me into the garden and led me around the side of his house. I thanked him at least three times but I'm not sure he heard me.

'I make you a deal: I give you the address and you take this box of shit over there. Been sat in the shed since we moved in. Was told someone would pick it up, but they never have. Don't have the heart to throw it out – load of tat and all, but meant something to somebody at one time.' He led me into a small shed along the side of the house, filled with the predictable garden junk and man tat and, sat on a table by the door, a small cardboard box. He shoved it along the table towards me and then wandered off. 'Got the address in the kitchen somewhere, hold up.'

I stepped forward tentatively and then reached out and delicately pulled back one of the flaps of the box. Soggy with damp and age-worn, the flap came off in my hand and took a curved slice from the side of the box with it, making some of the meagre contents spew out onto the floor. I was down on my knees, sifting through bits of old jewellery, some books and tatty t-shirts, when the old man came back. He dumped a carrier bag next to me.

'Figured it'd be better in that anyway. You got it all?' He ripped open the rest of the box and exposed some more books and several CDs. He flicked through the jewel cases in his hands and gave a dismissive shake of the head. 'Given up trying to understand you kids, like another language to me.' He held out one of the CDs to me. 'Seriously? You listen to this crap as well? Dumb name for a band if you ask me.'

A CD cover with Katie's face on, a cover I remembered making myself like it was only yesterday, stared back at me and when I stood and gently took it from him, my heart seemed to stay behind on the floor.

'Yeah,' I said as I added the CD to the rest of the neglected memories in the crumpled Sainsbury's carrier bag, 'but they did used to be called Climax, so I guess someone had some forethought. Right?'

The contents of that bag told me all I needed to know; as well as the CD I found the copy of *Tales of Ordinary Madness* that I had inscribed with a message and given her and told her she'd love. There were no creases along the spine, no signs at all of it being read, and it was such a miserable sight. But despite the message emanating from the pitiful contents of that Sainsbury's bag I still found myself stumbling and bumbling along streets I had once known so well, heading towards the new address I had been given for her. It must have been something more than merely being a glutton for punishment. I had considered that perhaps once I had seen the house I might feel differently, that maybe that would be enough to sign off my stupidity and close this battered old door.

But it wasn't. None of it was enough. I kept on walking, I kept on pushing, and by the time I found myself standing opposite this new house, in a blessedly far less salubrious part of town, leaning like a drunk against a bin and poring my heavy eyes over every inch of brickwork and window and roof, trying to find an answer or a clue or something that would satisfy me, my breath caught in my chest and I found myself wheezing and coughing as if I had just run a race. I fell to a squat and then shuffled down behind the bin, petrified that she might have seen me, and stayed there until I was sure it were a panic attack and not death. There would have been some sort of vile irony to that I suppose, dying next to a bin opposite the house of the person you loved, holding a bag of things they threw out. Perhaps a poet would get a kick out of that. Everyone else would probably just have laughed.

I only stayed in that position for ten minutes, but it felt so much longer. At one point I had convinced myself that I would never be able to move again. What if she had seen me? What if she had caught me leaning against the bin like a wino, done a double-take of surprise and was still there in the window now, waiting to confirm what she saw? She would see me standing from behind a bin, carrying a bunched-up carrier bag, and she would either laugh at me or she would pity me, and neither of those things would I be able to bear. But what else could I do? Had it been later in the day, or a different season, I could have sat it out and escaped under the cover of darkness. I did consider emptying the bag and then putting it on my head and making a dash for it, but then I would have to have dumped her things and I couldn't do that, plus I wouldn't have been able to see where I was going very well and would likely trip over the pavement and fall, and doing that once in a lifetime in her presence was more than enough.

In the end escape came in the form of Anya Belmont, a saviour I had never been expecting. *Ray, dear oh dear, Ray, you are a sorry state, aren't you?* As soon as I heard her voice in my head, my right hand went instinctively to my trouser pocket to feel for my phone, but instead it found nothing. With a sudden stab of panic I realised my phone was still back in the hotel. I was naked. *You should go and find her, that's what I think. Go and get some closure.* Even in my head her words came through a small laugh. Anya was always laughing at me. *You've been defined by running away.* Had she actually been laughing at me, or with me? I was sure that whenever she laughed at me it was more a sign of recognition than anything else. *You've come this far, Ray. Are you seriously going to run away yet again? When will you stop running away?* They were my words in her voice. I had asked myself time and again why Anya had taken it upon herself to care. If she did actually care, that was, and I wasn't just reading into her things that weren't there. All the advice, and the picking apart of my relationship, the harsh, sometimes cruel truths that she hit me with – why did she do that? *Get it done, Ray. Get your ending.* Why did she want me free? My friends were rarely that kind, so why would a stranger be?

You haven't got any friends, another voice kindly reminded me.

Easier to talk to a stranger though, isn't it? Anya said again. *There are things you can tell me that you can't tell anyone else.* Was it merely the kindness of a stranger? Did she see herself in me?

You still run around with that misguided belief in your head that people actually care. They don't, Ray. This is meaningless. This isn't important. You're reading too much into people – you are quite prone to that, aren't you?

'Of course you are, you stupid bastard,' I suddenly blurted out loud, scaring away a pigeon that had been rummaging around next to my shoes.

I turned sharply and stood quickly, and then slammed my right kneecap into the bin. Paranoia and embarrassment fuelling me to dangerous levels, I hobbled out of my hiding place as fast as I could and then moved back across the street, back the way I had come, and then at the edge of the road I stopped and turned around.

'Fucksakefucksakefucksake,' I hissed under my breath as I limped pathetically towards her house. This time I didn't pause for meaningless debate. I turned across the neighbouring driveway, cut directly across their garden and then hopped over the garden wall, and then there I was at the side of her house. 'Okay,' I whispered to myself.

There was a door along the side, propped open by a broom. Outside a rickety pasting table was set up and paintbrushes lay soaking in a bucket. I wandered in that direction and slowly peered inside. 'Hello?' I whispered, before coughing and saying it again, just a fraction louder.

I was looking into a kitchen in the process of being decorated. Cardboard boxes lay scattered about on the floor and on the work surfaces, filled with tins and cans and packets. An old lino floor had been ripped up, and three carefully placed mats acted as stepping-stones over the ragged underneath. I tapped gently on the door and then found myself pushing past the broom and standing on the doorstep.

'Hello?' it was barely more than a squeak. The bag handle was wound so tightly around the fingers of my right hand that the tips were losing their colour. Pulling them free, I switched hands and stepped onto the first mat. 'Katie?'

I thought I could hear voices further on in the house. I knocked again, this time on the glass in the door, and then stepped onto the next mat. The fridge held photos and postcards and magnetic letters, and in the centre a childish painting of what seemed to be a giant and a dwarf. I couldn't see her on any of the photos. But I recognised her mother in one. She had always liked me.

Next to the fridge an archway led through to a long hallway. Tucked to one side of the archway were a higgledy-piggledy mound of shoes – boots and wellies and trainers, and a battered pair of grey Converse trainers, size six at a guess, lay on top of them all. I smiled to myself and was about to move on when I noticed another pair of shoes drying upside down on a radiator just on the other side of the archway. They were a tiny pair of trainers; miniscule, diddy, almost comical.

'Hello.'

I spun around to meet the voice coming from the open doorway at the start of the corridor, the carrier bag swinging up, and Katie's discarded tat hitting me in the side of the head.

'Fucking hell!' I said to the small boy standing there. Thankfully he giggled at that and bounced back into the room. I could hear a noise further along the corridor; a voice, just one, someone talking, and then a slender shadow crested the wall at the far end of the corridor before dropping away. I followed the boy into the room.

'Sorry…I'm…I shouldn't have said that…'

More giggling erupted from him. Seemingly it was people's default setting on first encountering me.

'I'm…my name is Ray.'

'My name is Max,' he told me, jumping up into an armchair that swallowed him up.

'Hello, Max.' I stumbled into the room, the bag hitting my sore knee with every other step, and then fell into an identical armchair directly opposite him. It didn't seem real; nothing did, it was only the stupid bag in my hand that kept me from believing it was all a dream. Max was staring at me with what seemed an overly keen curiosity, and for a brief moment he steepled chubby fingers under his chin, before balling his hands into fists and idly beating the sides of the chair.

'What's wrong with your face?' he asked me. 'Are you sad?'

'Yeah, I am.'

'Why?'

'Sometimes it's not fun being a grown-up.'

His chubby little feet were now joining his chubby little hands in attacking the armchair.

'How old are you, Max?'

'I'm five this year!'

'Yeah?' I swallowed the number back like it was bile. I didn't need to do the maths. One plus one seemed to equal three, and that equation was more than enough for me to work out at that point.

'Are you a friend of Daddy?'

That little shit? Whoever that little worm is he is no friend of mine. I'd like to smash his stupid face through the back of his head.

'No.'

'Are you a friend of Mummy? She's on the phone, she will be back in a bit.'

I leaned forward and held the bag up for him. 'I was just dropping this off, just some things that Mummy left at your old house. Will you make sure she gets it when she is off the phone?'

He jumped down from the armchair and grabbed the bag, rifling through it and deciding it all bored him and discarding it on the floor, before I had even leaned back on the chair. 'Okay.'

I felt detached from what was happening, watching it from across the room, somehow numb to any feeling or thought. Revulsion and anger came and went like a bad smell passing under my nose. Nothing stayed. *Nothing* stayed. I had played this moment over in my head so many times that I had been convinced of my response to any outcome. I had planned for every emotion except this one, whatever this one was called. I had kept expecting to react to the situation somehow. I had told myself that at any moment I would likely burst out crying, or piss myself, or shiver and break down, or puke on her new carpet. I vividly remembered a time several years ago where I saw an old woman being mugged in town, and I just froze on the other side of the street, watching it happen as people ran across to help or chased down the attacker. This poor woman was picked up off the ground with a weeping cut across her forehead and she looked horrific. I was just stuck to the ground, watching it like a dickhead. That voice in my head, always so garrulous and demanding of me, was shouting, and screaming, and ordering me to do something and to feel something, telling me in a thousand disconnected words that any emotion would be preferable to this gawping, inactive nothingness. Yet that was all I had then, and it seemed it was all I had there in Katie's living room too, this wonderful, nameless emotion.

As Max climbed back up onto the armchair and resumed his feet-and-hands assault on the arms and seat, I found myself idly scanning the room. Freshly decorated, it seemed: the walls were a dull eggshell colour, and mostly bare along with it. She had been a hoarder when I knew her, but now she seemed to be going for the minimalist effect. There was just one picture hanging up; a framed print of Edward Hopper's *New York Movie*; my favourite painting, my favourite artist. She still had a part of me then, and that knowledge didn't quite feel as good as I would have once assumed. Right then it felt like a cheek, a rudeness and a theft. The bookshelves had hardly any books on them, and had become a home to framed photos and vases of flowers instead. On the middle shelf, there were some cards proudly presented front and centre; engagement cards, big, and bland and floral, everything my Katie wasn't. I felt heaviness in my chest like indigestion, and then gave a little burp and savoured the relief. *Relief…*

Could it be relief?

Max seemed to enjoy the burp.

'You look funny,' he told me, with a child's glorious inability to see offence in words.

'Thanks, mate.' I heard her laughter coming down the hallway, a little echo of a memory that died before it reached the open door. 'Does Mummy still sing?'

A comically scrunched-up face told me he had no idea what I was talking about.

'I thought someone told me she used to be a singer? Did I get that wrong?'

'She sings in the shower sometimes and Daddy laughs at her because she's so baaaddd. I sing! I sing at school and I play the recorder!'

'Yeah, you a good singer? Is that what you want to do when you are grown up?'

'No, I want to take pictures. You see that picture there?' He was pointing at the bookshelves and the framed photos. I nodded, giving them no more than a token flick of the eyes. 'I took that, and Mummy and Daddy say that is the best picture of them ever. I'm going to get my own camera for Christmas!'

'Yeah? That would be great, wouldn't it? I used to like taking photos but I wasn't very good – not as good as you, anyway. I had a friend that I used to take photos of all the time. She was great. She was really pretty but she never really liked having her photo taken because she was shy, but she let me. I used to take photos on an old film camera that my parents gave me. It's an old, old thing. You'd laugh if you saw it. I don't use it any more, but it's still got a photo of her on it. Just one. I never used the rest of the film up or got it developed.'

Another scrunched-up face of confusion greeted that. 'Why?'

Bless you that you have no idea. 'Don't grow up too quickly, mate.'

'You're weird.'

'I know.' I pulled myself wearily to my feet, every inch the old man the boy was making me feel. 'I gotta go. Good to meet you, Max.'

'Yeah.'

'Be nice to your mummy, won't you?'

He nodded obediently and kicked the armchair once more. I limped slowly out of the room, back into the corridor and the muffled sound of her voice. 'Hey, Max, ask you a question?' I turned back and leaned against the door.

Max gave another elaborate nod of the head.

'Have you ever had a Caesar salad? Does Mummy ever make you that?'

'Salad? Yuck!' He scrunched up his nose and shook his head, as if trying to rid himself of the very notion of such a disgusting idea. 'No, she hates salad!'

I gave Max the thumbs-up and then turned away so as not to have to explain the smile on my face. I limped back into the kitchen, through the side door, and then out of his and his mother's lives forever.

At the end of the drive I puked in her flowerbed.

Should have kept the carrier bag.

The Last Call

DANNY

The phone kept ringing and ringing, and then his answerphone would finally kick in. I had already left three messages and sent two texts, so on the fourth attempt I just hung up. Catching Dave's enquiring glance as we sat at the back of the church, I just feebly shook my head. Next to Dave, Clive seemed to be growing redder, his lips pursed, his arms folded tightly across his chest. I checked my watch instinctively, though quite what knowing the time would do to explain Ray's whereabouts I wasn't sure. I had half-expected to see him outside the church as we all filed out, but as Tim and Tamara took the adoration (and Tim took a huge mouthful of confetti, launched aggressively by an over-emotional father-in-law) and then stood for the photos, and made small talk with distant relatives, I saw no sign of him. I tipped Dave the nod and we headed off, leaving Clive to come to the boil alongside his wife. (She'd not even acknowledged me when she rolled up, and still had all the charm of herpes.)

As Dave drove us back the short distance to the hotel, I tried him once again, and once more was met by the disinterested tone of his answer machine message. 'Ray, where the hell are you?' I shouted. 'Just…just…fuck!' I hung up, exasperated.

'Think he's done a runner?' Dave asked with a yawn. Dave certainly didn't seem overly concerned about our singer's disappearance, though Dave was never really concerned about anything much. Like most bass players, Dave lived in his own little high-orbiting world, rarely getting vexed or excited about anything much, and only ever displaying signs of animation when arguing the toss between *Under Pressure* or *Guns of Brixton* as the greatest bass line of all time (it's actually *What's Going On*, but let's not digress). How our Dave ever managed to reproduce is one of life's greatest and most unfathomable mysteries. I doubt his kids are the second coming, so he must have, at the very least, got excited twice. Which likely means he finally convinced his wife to dress up as Suzi Quatro.

'No.'

'I wouldn't put it past him,' Dave continued. 'Always was overly emotional and full of dramatic gestures. Being back here…well, from what you've said…'

'He wouldn't.'

'I think he would. Wouldn't he?'

Yeah. Ray probably would do a runner. The thought had occurred to me last night when he told me that he had somehow managed to get Kate's address from Vera. I had assumed, naively perhaps, that he would have the decency to wait until after the wedding before bumbling down memory lane but then, where Kate Fenshaw was concerned, nothing Ray did made much sense. If he had been to see her, and had actually found her, then chances are those old, scabby wounds that he has allowed to fester for so long would have been opened up again, and he would have reverted to form and run away. Where to was anyone's guess. I felt an overwhelming disgust in that moment. But it was disgust for my own selfish thoughts and my inability to care more for his well-being than for our gig at the reception.

'Put your foot down,' I told Dave as I dialled Ray one last time.

'In this traffic?'

I looked up and saw we were stuck in a long line of crawling vehicles; cars and buses all packed with people baking out under the blazing summer sun. Instantly the sight brought back so many old memories – hazy summers that seemed to stretch into endless days under a perfect sunshine, the crowded streets full of families and excitable children, sounds and smells and smiles, the town being swallowed up by bodies, and traffic and noise, and then Ray and me and Kate and Vera, all strolling along the road, stupid and happy, and young enough not to have a care in the world.

'Stop the van,' I told him, pocketing the phone.

'Huh?'

'Dave, stop the van!'

'We are stopped. We're in a traffic jam.'

I swung open the passenger door and slipped down onto the road, quickly dodging between two parked cars before jumping up onto the pavement and nearly bowling into an a couple of passers-by. I turned towards Ray's hotel, started to run and then stopped.

Back in the van Dave was calling my name and asking me where I was going. Good question. I had a choice to make. Ray's hotel on Lord Street was one way; the hotel where the reception was being held the other. And yet it was likely Ray would be in neither. But I had nothing else. I turned one way, and then the other, and then back again. Five minutes later, sweating and out of breath, I arrived at Tim and Tamara's hotel, hoping that I had made the right choice.

The two hotel staff standing outside the open door to the ballroom, exchanging disapproving glances with each other, suggested I had.

The out-of-tune singing blasting out from inside only confirmed it.

There he was, sat amongst a carpet of red and white balloons, an empty bottle of champagne in his hand, wobbling happily back and forth, that stupid wide-angle grin back on his gob. The singing ceased as soon as he saw me, and then he was smiling even broader and brighter. He hiccupped loudly and dramatically and then flung his arms wide to greet me. As I stepped into the ballroom he tried to stand, but got his arse no more than a foot off the ground before falling back onto the balloons and laughing uncontrollably.

'All right, love?'

'Hello, dear. Lovely to see you. Fancy a glass of...' He realised then that the bottle was empty, and launched it across the room. I turned behind me at the sound of the shattering bottle and saw one of the hotel staff peel away from the room, her phone to her ear. I held my hands to the one that remained and gave the universal gesture of "don't worry, I got this", though she seemed as unconvinced as me about that.

'What the hell are you doing, Ray?'

He beckoned me closer and then leaned across, cupped a hand to his mouth and whispered on breath that could strip wallpaper, 'I've done it. I've done it. I've got my ending.' He jabbed a thumb up into my face, swayed and then tumbled into me.

'That's good, Ray, lovely,' I told him as if he were five years old. 'Maybe this isn't the best place for you to be telling me this. Let's get you—'

'I didn't feel anything,' he said into my cheek. 'I thought I would but I didn't, except, actually I think I did, but it wasn't what…I think…I…I have no idea what I'm talking about.'

'Yep. Okay. Let's get you sobered up.'

'I think it was relief. I think I felt relief.'

'Good. Let's go, Ray.'

'She's a mother, did you know that? She's a mother!'

'Right, okay.'

'How can she be a mother? When I knew her she didn't even know how to boil an egg.'

'People change, Ray.' I wrapped my arms under his armpits and yanked him clumsily to his feet. 'Most people.'

He leant into me, his feet slipping backwards along the varnished dance floor. I pulled my arms up and hoisted him until we were face-to-face, eye-to-eye.

'I don't need you to pick me up, dear. I can stand on my own two feet by myself, you know?'

'No you can't.'

Once more his feet started to slide back along the dance floor and his face slithered down onto my chest. 'No, you're probably right,' he mumbled into my shirt.

'What the bleeding hell is all this?' A familiar voice suddenly boomed out from the doorway behind us. 'What have you two shitting bastards done?' His shadow seemed to fall across us as he approached, his words slowly morphing into an animalistic growl.

Ray straightened himself against me at the sound of Frank's voice, his hands gripping my shirt, his feet doing a shambling shuffle on the floor. He patted my chest and then stepped to one side. 'I got this, dear.'

I turned and watched Ray swagger drunkenly up to the ape in a morning suit, stopping just short of him and proffering a clumsy bow. 'Good afternoon.'

'What the hell have you done? What have you fucking pair of bollocks done to my ballroom?' Frank's face was growing purple, as purple as the one rogue balloon that had landed at his feet. His giant hands started clenching into fists that seemed as big as Ray's head. His angry little eyes were fixed on the floor, following the gentle bob of the balloons as they skittered and bounced around Ray's unsure steps.

Ray hiccupped again. 'Relax, Big Daddy, it's all good, I'm with the band.'

'You fix this. You fix this now!' One fat hand uncurled as a finger pointed down at the floor. 'You fix this before my princess comes.'

'Oh, lighten up, you fucking constipated baboon!'

The words struck big, fearsome father-in-law Frank harder than his fists could ever have done, and for a split second the hairy mound of muscles seemed to sway on the spot, every bit as drunkenly as Ray was doing. But then, as my oldest friend jumped up and came down on a balloon, slipped off it instead of popping it, and went face first into the wedding present table, the hairy halfwit suddenly came alive in all his primate rage, and descended on Ray with a ferocious roar.

'Well done, love,' I said to Ray's legs, still sticking up out of the large pile of rubbish where Frank had crudely deposited him. I crossed between two wheelie bins and relieved myself as he mumbled something into the rancid bin bags, his legs swaying from side to side as he tried in vain to right himself.

The alleyway behind the hotel kitchens smelt of fish and piss and vomit. The piss was mine, the vomit Ray's, but the fish was a mystery. The fishy pong seemed to be coming from the very air around us rather than the bins, working its way into our clothing and hair and irritating our nostrils. Ray had it worse, though. I turned back to find him upright on the rubbish pile, a banana skin on top of his head and a smear of that mysterious, unidentifiable bin juice across his forehead. He dabbed puke-tinged fingers at a steadily fattening lip and a puffy, darkening eye as sobriety punched through and anchored him down to this reality.

'Shit,' was all he said for several minutes, and pretty much all he needed to say. He looked up at me with apologetic eyes, but couldn't quite bring himself to articulate it in words. Plucking the banana skin off his head, he tried smoothing down greasy hair that was now sticking up in two places like devil horns. He shuffled up delicately and then sat on one hefty bin bag, and I moved over and joined him, taking a seat on a small stack of three upturned beer crates.

'So, I assume this is why you don't go out much?' I asked, after a couple more minutes of silence.

'You should go back in,' he told me, via the floor, rubbing a palm against the filth on his head. 'You're probably gonna have to sing in my place. I wouldn't imagine that they would want…'

'No, I wouldn't imagine so, Ray.'

He stared down at his shoes. 'Oops.'

He looked impossibly pathetic in that moment, and my resolve not to care began to weaken. The little shit. 'You saw her then?' I asked with a weary sigh, steeling myself for the expected onslaught of Kate Fenshaw-tinged blathering, my best friend's well-worn routine.

'Yep,' was all he said in reply, and the predictable shrug that followed made him wince.

'And?'

Ray looked back to the ground, running his fingers into a muscle in his shoulder. 'That walking, talking yak's bollock has done me good.'

'And you stink,' I reminded him.

'Thanks, dear.' He smelt a shirtsleeve and his face screwed up again, this time in disgust. 'I need to get back to my hotel. I'll see you later.'

'Think I'm going to leave you like this?'

'Why wouldn't you?'

'Why would I?'

He motioned back over his shoulder, back to the hotel and towards the sound of loud, happy voices coming from the ballroom.

'They can wait. We've got time,' I told him firmly, stealing a furtive glance at my watch when he looked away, just to make sure. 'I'm not leaving you like this.'

'I'm fine. Honestly, I am.'

'Yeah, I believe you are. But that is a new experience for me, you understand, I'm a little unsure how to deal with it.'

He laughed and then winced again, and grabbed his shoulder. He kicked out at me playfully with one grubby shoe, walloping me on the leg.

'What the hell you laughing at, love?'

His laugh had made his nose run, a gloopy slither of snot now hanging from a nostril like a bell rope. This in turn just made him laugh louder and more manically.

'Seriously, what you laughing at?'

All he could do in that moment was shrug again, but this shrug made him wail in pain, grab his injured shoulder with both hands and then lose his balance and fall back amongst the bin bags.

The pavements were as busy as the roads, a heavy congestion of meandering bodies scuttling nowhere in particular with all the speed of the cars edging slowly forward on the road. We drew looks from everyone that passed us, or at least Ray did, people greeting this bloodied and bruised, stinking mess of a man with furrowed brows, curious eyes and whispered jokes as they recoiled from the sight of him. He didn't seem to notice, and if he did he certainly didn't seem to care. At the very least the rank odour he carried over him like a slipped halo made a path open up for us as we walked.

We made his hotel in no time, and despite his continued protestations and orders for me to go back to the reception, I saw him back to his room.

'I'm okay, you know?' he told me again, in the doorway to his bathroom, much as he had told me repeatedly on the way up to the room.

'I know,' I assured him, just as I had done each time he had told me before.

He lingered in the bathroom doorway for a second. 'Thanks,' he whispered, and then turned away as if embarrassed.

I was sat on the edge of his bed when he returned, a towel wrapped around his head, his face a flushed pink, scrubbed clean.

'Seriously, you need to get back to the wedding. Clive will probably have combusted by now. Wouldn't want to miss that.' He picked up his mobile phone from the bedside table and seemed to do a double-take. 'Eight missed calls? Well, aren't I popular?'

'Not so much, six of them will be from me.'

As he called up the answer machine, he waved a hand in my face, shooing me away. 'Will you please piss off back to the reception? I don't want that on my conscience as well. Give me a call when you're finished, and then we...'

The pink suddenly drained from his cheeks, his mouth open, caught on a silent word, his eyes widening, watering, as his arm flopped back to his side and slapped against his leg.

'What?' I asked.

Instantly he ended the call and shoved the phone deep into his pocket.

'What? Ray, what is it?'

'Huh?'

'What's happened? Who was that?' I stood and grabbed him by the arm. Those big, watering eyes found me, and then widened even further, as if they were surprised to see me there. 'What is it, Ray?'

'Liz,' he said simply, pulling away from me, just as the trickle from his eyes became a stream. 'That was Abigail, from the home. Liz…she…'

'Oh.'

'Shit.'

'Yeah.'

'Liz got her ending.' He swayed there for a moment like he was still drunk, and then his mouth twitched, and seemed to be considering a smile. His face was a contradiction. He looked winded, broken, exhausted and fit to drop. Yet he also looked, just for a second, happy. Before I could think of anything to say he suddenly lunged for me and flung his arms around my shoulders, pulling me into a massive bear hug. When he released me, we stood staring at each other blankly, neither sure what to do, an awkward silence blooming around us like a bad smell.

'You all right?' I asked him, and almost cringed at the sound of the words. Another ridiculous thing to say, of course, ranking up there in the pantheon of dumb questions alongside every time I had asked after Liz's well-being, this past year. Still, what else do you say? Does it matter, so long as you say something? Right then I could have recited a shopping list to him and it would have been preferable to standing there mute and gawping and useless. At least it would have been for me. 'Silence is a disease,' Ray's granddad Bertie used to say. Reckon he might have had that right.

As it was, we held the silence back by batting some single-syllable swearing at each other. That seemed to do the trick. I think Bertie would have approved.

We both headed south along Lord Street, me, back to Tim and Tamara's hotel, and Ray to the beach. I asked him again if he were okay, and this time he simply called me a twat. It was a far more believable and comforting response that a yes. We weaved carelessly in and around the bodies on the pavement, walking off the kerb occasionally to get around the more stubborn meanderers. As we continued picking a path through the summer Saturday shoppers we were suddenly met by a large cluster of tourists blocking our path; young and excitable and bound up in rucksacks and smiles, the group were taking it in turns to have photos taken in a red telephone box. The sight was as bizarre to me as the pavement congestion was irritating. Then my arm was grabbed and I was being dragged towards them.

'You take?' a young boy was asking, sticking his camera in my face and then waving a hand at the others. One by one the group were converging on this old, beautiful and utterly useless thing and grinning at me. 'You take, please?' he asked again. I glanced back and saw that Ray was languishing a good twenty yards back from me, dawdling, talking into his phone, clearly in no rush to catch up. 'Yes?' the boy asked again, forcing the camera into my hands.

'Yeah,' I told him and then stepped back along the pavement. The group started hugging each other, some of them sticking fingers up over their nearest friend's heads like rabbit ears while others stuck their arms in the air as if in mock-triumph, and the boy who gave me the camera crouched front and centre before them all. I was aware of the people on the pavement slowing either side of the phone box, and then stopping completely to let me take the picture.

As I took a final step back I stumbled into a woman who was walking past from the other direction, the only person in that moment not offering to stop her business and indulge these strangers. I liked her for that.

She told me I stank of fish.

EVA

The text message said simply: *Meet for coffee?*, but she had put a small *x* at the end of it and I took that to be her attempt at some sort of half-arsed apology. That little letter changed the whole text. If there hadn't been one, or if it had been an *X* instead of an *x*, then I think I would have declined. Instead I texted back and said yes, and then she texted back with the suggestion of where to go and I replied and said that sounded fine. Then she sent another text and suggested we go for a coffee right away because Len had turned up and she wanted to spend time with him but he would be busy for the next hour or so, and I texted back and reminded her that we were a mere three rooms away from each other and that this was both childish and a waste of money.

A minute later there was a knock on the door.

'Hey,' she said in response to my rather curt nod.

'Hey yourself.'

She stepped into the room and flung her arms around me, and that broke me instantly. For a good minute then my oldest friend and I fell into apologies and hugs and tears. A porter passed the room and gave us a sly little smirk through the open bedroom door until I proffered him a raised index finger and pricked his idle, perverted fantasy.

'Need to talk,' Anya said in a happy, snotty blub.

'Don't really have anything to say.'

'Don't worry about it, I will do all the talking.'

There was some sort of commotion in the ballroom across the other side of the reception area as we left the hotel; shouts and threats and a crowd of gawping people watching, but we slipped on by without sparing it more than a glance. Anya wrapped an arm around me and pulled me into her as we walked out into a blistering summer's day. Never the most tactile of girls, my Anya, I was a little unnerved by it, but didn't want to pull her up on it – touchy-feely was far more preferable to the feeling of enmity the last time I saw her. We said nothing as we walked, Anya slowly breaking her touch and then moving slightly in front of me, leading the way. She looked back just once on the way to the coffee shop, just as I was absently touching the cut on my cheek made by her wedding ring, and she looked away again instantly, quickening her pace ever so slightly.

The coffee shop was a kooky, independent place, smaller than Anya's own but also replete with the same sort of reclaimed benches and chairs and overstuffed near-to-breaking couches. Laid-back, comfortable and full of heart, it was like being back home again. Though I did consider pointing out to Anya the two separate toilets they had at the back of the building. Perhaps I would, I thought, after I had found out what she had to say.

The young girl behind the counter was stifling a yawn as we approached, and then seemed to back off us slightly as Anya ordered. She set about the drinks with a speed and care bordering on superhuman, and she was unfailingly polite, almost suspiciously so. And then the truth was there for us both as she stared at me from the corner of her eye, and gave me a nod that was nearer to a bow. Anya gave me a nudge as she slipped a few coins in the tip jar. Notoriety, it would seem, might have some benefits after all. Things were looking up.

'Where's Len?' I asked, more to break the silence than anything else, as we took a table by the front of the coffee shop.

'He was on the phone to the office when I left him.'

'Oh. No surprise, I suppose. At least he came though.'

'Yeah. That was nice.'

She looked awful, pale and drawn, her eyes not even seeming to catch the sun that was pouring in through the window, and I thought I saw her hands shaking slightly as she turned her coffee cup in front of her. Anya looked like she had seen a ghost.

'Henry Gage?' I asked her bluntly.

She stared at me, surprise bringing her eyes alive for a fleeting moment. 'Why'd you say that?'

'I can't think of anyone else that would suck the colour out of you.'

She dropped her eyes to her coffee cup and then those shaking hands pushed across the table and covered my own, squeezing them gently.

'I'm sorry,' she whispered.

'You said. Don't worry about it. And, you know… me too.'

'I haven't been much of a support to you this week have I?'

'Likewise, darling. Anya…where has this all come from? That man is ancient history, it's been so long. Why now?'

'I dunno.'

'All that…him…you know you really don't have to tell me anything, if you don't want to. You haven't got to say anything about it. Ever.'

'I do though, that's been my mistake all these years. Silence is a disease.'

'Bit dramatic, isn't it?'

That made her smile and slap my hands playfully. 'It did sound better coming from someone else, have to admit that.'

'Go on then.' I sipped at my coffee and tried to sound indifferent to it all, which I most certainly was not. 'What do you need to tell me?'

She tried to brush that question away with another pat of the hands. 'Yeah, okay, in a minute. What about you though?' Her eyes went to the cut on my cheek. 'Are you, you know…? I'm sorry that…'

'Am I okay? Is that what you're asking?'

'Yeah, sorry.'

'Stop apologising. And yeah, I'm okay.'

It was only a half-lie, and I considered how much to tell her of it. I wondered if she would find the idea that had come to me last night funny or insulting. St James would probably have called it an epiphany, or something equally grand and fancy. Truth was it was an escape, that was all, a fallback and a plan B. That was the phrase Charlie Topley had used on the phone, and I think he was right. We all needed a plan B.

'Mummy said something to me when I was young,' he had said to me.

'You are young,' I reminded him.

'No! Don't be silly! When I was really young and stupid and I wanted to be an astronaut, she told me that that was fine and all that but that I should think if there was anything else I wanted to do too because not many people get to be astronauts, and they needed to take lots of exams and do lots of training and it might not be all that much fun anyway. She said it didn't matter yet but that I would probably change my mind about it. I said I wouldn't. She said I would. Then the next year I wanted to be a vet. She said that was good and that that should be my plan B, and that it was okay too if I had a plan C and plan D and—'

'Yes, I get the point,' I shouted, exasperated by his prattle and his inability to draw breath, 'but I'm not sure what that has to do with me.'

'Don't shout at me!' he shouted back. 'I'm a child, you're not allowed. I think you're frightened to have a plan B because you think no one will love you any more, and that's just stupid because you are a good writer.'

'I am, yes, but you don't understand…'

'I used to be frightened of things too. I used to think that my toys all spoke together at night when I was asleep, and that one day they would climb into my bed and kill me. But they never did.'

'Yes, but with all due respect, that's just downright weird and stupid, isn't it?'

'How do you know?'

'Look, Charlie, I didn't phone you because I was frightened…'

'Did you know your Twitter page has got loads more followers since you shouted at Mummy? You're nearly at two-hundred-thousand now!'

'I don't have a Twitter page.'

'Oh, well you do now.'

'What are you saying?'

'That you shouldn't be frightened, because people like you, and people think you're funny.'

'That isn't a measure of success, Charlie, that's a freak show. You know, like when you go to the zoo and you all stand there watching the animals, and you see that there are always more people at the monkey cages because they are more likely to do something stupid or show their bums and throw things at each other?'

'You're funny.'

'No I'm not.'

'Loads of people think you are, though. It's like that silly man on the television that was in that rubbish programme…'

'Can you narrow that down a bit?'

'Mummy reads his books. He's written loads, every Christmas there's a new book that he has written and he has said himself on TV that it's silly because he's only ever read one book and that was a *Beano* annual, and I laugh at Mummy for reading them because he's an idiot and thick and I tell her that she should read proper books by proper writers, and I don't understand why there are so many books by him and why they are always in bookshop windows and he's always on the TV talking about them, and she tells me she buys them because he's on the TV and he makes her laugh because he's so silly.'

'Sometimes dogs eat their own poo.'

'Erghh!' came his response to that. 'I don't understand.'

I didn't try and explain that to him. The boy seemed clued-up enough to understand that one day. Plus, my mind was already elsewhere. He was right about the Twitter page; I had never seen anything like it. I checked it five times that night and saw the followers rise by ten thousand.

'Nothing to do with me,' St James told me when I phoned him. 'Though I've been imploring you to start one for months. Do you want me to try and get this one taken down?'

'Why? I'm already a monkey in a cage, I've already thrown my shit at a wall, so I may as well seize my chance and start doing some tricks for my audience.'

'Erm, okay…'

'I need to talk about a plan B.'

'What?

'It's my cage, not yours. I'm the monkey and you're the zookeeper. Never forget that.'

'Forget it? I don't understand it. Look, it's half four in the morning, I will talk about this later, Eva.'

'You haven't got to say anything, I will do all the talking. You just have to try and harness stupidity. I'm sure it won't be a stretch.'

Anya was looking at me quizzically, working me out. 'What are you smiling at? Something I said?'

I hadn't been aware I was smiling. I certainly couldn't feel it. 'Something you said, yeah, something like that.'

'Care to share?'

'I'm going to write your story,' I blurted out, 'you and your mystery man. How'd you feel about that?'

For several moments her expression didn't change. Her hands found mine and her fingers dug gently into my skin, and then her eyes flashed as bright as I had seen them in years, though just for a second.

'Why the heck would you do that?'

'Why the heck wouldn't I? Happen to think it's a story worth telling.'

'It isn't a story. There is no story.'

'Course there is.'

'Where's your character arc, your narrative, your exciting incident in the first ten pages? What's your hook?'

'Boy meets girl. Girl meets boy. Old as the hills, darling. There are no original stories any more, anyway. It's all just about how well you dilute your plagiarism.'

'Girl doesn't meet boy though. Girl talks to boy on phone. Then life carries on again as normal. Nothing happens. Not exactly a thrilling page-turner, is it?'

'The story is in the unsaid.'

'Well, of course that makes much more sense. I really don't see why you'd waste your time. Besides, you've not exactly been supportive of the reality.'

'Every work of fantasy needs someone speaking the truth.'

Anya slumped back in her chair and chewed on her lips, tasting the idea. 'Not sure how I feel about that.'

'Don't feel anything. I will change the names. No one will know it's you.'

'And just how much of this little story are you planning on telling?'

'Create enough lies to make a good story, hold enough truth back so as not to get sued. I think that's how it usually works.'

The young girl appeared at our side and bobbed up and down as her hands hovered near our coffee cups. 'Can I get you another?' she asked tentatively, and I waved a hand at the empty cups and ordered the same again.

'She's scared of you,' Anya said as the girl scuttled away.

'Yes. Wonderful, isn't it?'

'Nothing great in being scared, darling.'

And so our conversation found its way back to the beginning again, and the spectre of Henry Gage appeared before us.

'He's dead. No reason to be scared of him any more, Anya. If you are.'

'Him? No. And I never was. Not really. He never hurt me. Not in that way. You know that. I never had reason to be scared of him. Though sometimes disappointment is even worse than fear.'

The girl returned with our drinks and Anya nodded her thanks. Once again my dearest friend turned her coffee cup around in her hands and stared into it as if expecting to see something brought to life there. Seconds became minutes and those minutes seemed to stretch forever, and then finally Anya spoke, first into her cup and then towards me, unblinking, controlled, the colour returning to her cheeks with every word spoken, every broken memory shed.

'I killed him. Like I killed his child.' Anya released a long breath that didn't seem to want to stop, but when finally it did, she sat forward in her seat and gripped her hands together as if in prayer.

'No you didn't.'

'Yes. Yes, I did. I could have saved him. I'm sure of it. I could have saved him from his debts and his problems and I could have stopped them hurting him. And I could have saved him when I came home that night and found him with the…' She stumbled, her control faltering as she opened her hands and ran an index finger across her right wrist. 'He was covered in blood, slumped down in the cellar in the corner like some great bag of rubbish. You know, it would have been better if they had done it to him themselves, these thugs that he owed money to. Better for me because I could have understood that. It would have been their fault and not mine, and that would have made more sense. Maybe they would have done it eventually had he not taken the matter into his own hands? We knew it was them who trashed the beer garden and put the pub windows through the week before. They were squeezing him on all sides, I know he got phone calls and threats and I know people turned up at the pub. They didn't do anything, they just stood there by the door or at the bar, threatening him with their silence. Of course he couldn't go to the police, not with everything that he had been up to, so he was trapped.

'Then the day before I found him in the cellar, I found a bag in our closet, tucked down the bottom, almost out of sight, and it's full of his clothes and a few possessions. He was going to do a runner, Eva. He was going to leave me. He was going to leave me there alone with his debts and his enemies and the thought of that made me want to kill him myself. After everything I had put up with from him, all the times I had stood by him and told myself I loved him, that he could just run away that easily disgusted me. The birthday card he had given me was still up behind the bar. We hadn't even gone out for the birthday meal yet that he'd promised, and yet he was going to run out on me.'

Anya slugged at the coffee, gripping the cup tightly as if it was thinking of leaving her too.

'That night I didn't sleep, I was waiting for him to slip out of bed any time and grab the bag and run out the door, and I needed to be awake to confront him in the act, because then he wouldn't be able to lie and cover it up and bullshit me like he was so good at doing. But he didn't, he slept straight through, and the next morning he acted as if everything was normal. It was a busy day, the pub was packed, but he was happy running the bar by himself and he told me to go out and take the day off because it had just been my birthday, and I deserved to relax. We argued about that, but not properly, not like we usually did. I believed him in the end. I had no reason to think otherwise. If he were going to leave me there would have been no need for the act. If he were going to do it he would have done it in the night like the coward he was. So, yes, I left him there alone, joyful and smiling and acting like he was the happiest man in the world.'

She finished her coffee in two huge gulps, but kept her grip on the cup. She turned from me and looked out at the people passing on the pavement outside, languid and slow under the glorious sun.

'You probably shouldn't put this in your book, Eva.' This time it was me that took her hands in mine. 'Or if you do, at least write it so it all makes sense. Okay?'

I nodded and squeezed her hands. She shuffled back around in her seat and pulled her hands free.

'When I saw him, sat there in the gloom in that cellar, I don't think I felt anything. Not at the start, at least. It sort of seemed...I don't know, inevitable? I think maybe subconsciously I had been preparing to see him like that for as long as we were married. It would have been so much easier if he had hit me, or mistreated me, or even cheated on me. Perhaps I should have had some foresight and seen what he would become and where he would lead us, but then maybe I did and maybe I refused to acknowledge it. Maybe. I don't know. I've spent years asking myself a hundred questions I can't answer, or don't want to answer, and now it's all one great mess and jumble, blunted by time. But what I do know is that I could have saved him, even then. He was looking at me. I could see the whites of his eyes in the gloom and he was looking at the steps as I came down them. I know he was. But I didn't scream or cry or run to the phone. I just did nothing. I just froze to the spot and stood there gawping at him pathetically, uselessly, and then suddenly I was shouting accusations at him, asking him, there and then, why he was going to leave me. "How could you think about running out on me?" I shouted at him. Then, "Why didn't you? What stopped you?" Over and over I asked that as the blood dribbled out of him and those eye-whites kept on staring at me.

'I don't know how long I stood there, how long it was before I ran back upstairs to the phone. But it was too long. It was my fault he died. It was my fault for not seeing the man he was becoming, and then my fault for feeling nothing when he finally became that man. It was my fault for being selfish and my fault for caring only about me, and it was my fault for being weak enough to break because a man was going to leave me.'

I stood and moved around to her side, taking a seat next to her and then holding her hand under the table. Her face betrayed no emotion, almost as if it hadn't decided the right way to feel. I wrapped my fingers around her own and stared off out into the café with her.

'The next week was when I found out I was pregnant,' she told the air in front of us. 'Seems I wasn't done making mistakes. A month later I killed that too.' Anya picked up her coffee cup and stared into it, seemingly surprised that it was empty. 'I never cared that Henry died. I thought I would eventually, but I never did. Not really. I only ever cared that I didn't know how he could leave me. I have always thought I would feel the same indifference about his child. Never quite got there on that, and I know I have to. Maybe one day.'

The front door to the café clattered open and a line of people filed in, chatting and joking. Across the other side of the café a large group of young people were leaving, gathering up their rucksacks and their coats and then piling out en masse, shouting and laughing as they fell back out into their summer.

Anya's limp fingers closed around mine. 'Do you want another coffee?' she asked me quietly.

'No.'

'Okay.'

'Why now, Anya? Why did you have to tell me this now, and why have you told me and not Len?'

'I'm working my way up to telling him. I thought perhaps you'd be a more receptive preview audience.'

'Len loves you. Len won't think badly of you.'

'Maybe not for this. No.'

'What else were you thinking of telling him?'

'I don't know. But it's good to talk, isn't it? That's what they say. It's good to get things off your chest, secrets and hopes and mistakes and dreams. People need to do that. People need to talk. Silence is a disease.'

'And who told you that?'

'Some stranger.'

'Easy to make grand statements and offer great words of wisdom when you are a stranger.'

'Yeah. Can we go? I want to see my husband.'

'I'm surprised you didn't tell your stranger what you have just told me.'

'I did. Or at least, I told his answer machine. He always did want to know something about me.'

I downed the dregs of my coffee and then playfully pinched her fingers before standing. 'Next time start with what your favourite colour is.'

Outside the café we fell in alongside the crawl of human life. We walked close together, our arms brushing each other, as we headed north, back to the hotel. We had got no more than a few yards when Anya's phone began to ring. We came to a stop at the side of the street as Anya stared at the screen on her mobile.

'Probably a cold caller.'

The phone rang off, but then started to ring again as soon as it was back in her pocket.

'I better answer it.'

'Yeah.'

'I'll catch you up.'

Down the street the young crowd with the rucksacks that had not long since left the café were bundled up around a red telephone box, taking photos. Some poor ginger-haired bloke with a nice arse had been railroaded into taking a group picture for them. People were pausing for them, slowing down their life for a split second so as to indulge their stupidity. Stupid people. I left Anya standing by the side of the road and walked towards them.

'Hey!' Anya suddenly called to me, her hand over the phone. 'If you do this story, I mean if you really think you want to write about it...'

'Yeah?'

'What sort of ending are you going to give me?'

RAY & ANYA

The sun was high in the sky and yet the heat, as immense as it was that day, was not stifling, it was freeing. They made their separate ways down the street, he walking south, she walking north, both heading towards the curious sight of a red telephone box, something so familiar to both, yet somehow an alien object too, which to the crowd of tourists gathered around it seemed to produce a sense of wonderment.

They stopped and started, their walks meandering and slow. They said little, and yet said so much. They would pull up by the pavement sometimes, walk a bit more; then turn around and wander back, neither appearing too keen to lose themselves in the throng of people flowing past them.

'Hello, Anya,' he said.

'Hello, Ray. I didn't expect to hear from you again.'

'Yes, I wasn't sure I should phone.'

'Just a phone call, Ray.'

'Just words, Anya.'

'Go on then.'

'You first, Anya.'

'Oh no, you phoned me, Ray. Very much you first, I think.'

They laughed at that. So much laughter there was between them. They laughed at things that were meant for them alone, things no one else would understand. They had a shorthand.

'Just phoning to see how you are,' he told her, somewhat unconvincingly.

'Really?'

'Sure.'

'I'm getting there.'

'You too? Looks like we have something in common. From such sturdy foundations do worlds collide.'

'Did you get your ending, Ray?'

'I did, yes.'

'That's good. I'm glad. I think you will be okay, Ray. For what that's worth. I think you'll get there. In truth I think there's only really one thing left you need to work on.'

'Oh?'

They both heard a small beep on the phone line. Then it came again, impatient and demanding.

'I think one of us has a call waiting, is that you or me?'

'Can't think who would be phoning me.'

'Not thinking of running out on me, are you?'

'Could I do that?'

'You probably should.'

'I know.' He smiled to himself and wandered off the pavement, standing in the gutter as he spoke to her, gazing up the street, shielding his eyes from the sun with his free hand. 'Wow!'

'What?'

'I can't remember the last time I saw a red telephone box. I wasn't sure anywhere had them any more. When did they become a novelty?'

She had only taken a further two steps forward before he said that, and now she could barely move at all. She joined him in the gutter, staring off down the street at the gathered people around the phone box. She stole furtive glances, mere flicks of the eye behind her, then across the road, searching him out, but not wanting to see him. She looked to her feet, then up to the sky.

'Are you still there?' he asked her.

'Yes,' she told him. 'I'm here. But I shouldn't be, Ray. I should go.'

'Not thinking of hanging up on me, are you?'

'I was actually, yes.'

Both heard sadness in each other's laugh then. He was walking again now, heading south slowly, moving out onto the pavement and becoming just another faceless body, passing on by.

'Before you go,' he started, 'if you have to go that is, then do me a favour before you do, okay?'

'If I can.' She started walking too, slow and steady, almost as if she were learning the art all over again. She stepped into a small gap in the passing strangers, and disappeared. 'What is it?'

'You said just now that there was one thing left that I had to work on. Just one more thing to learn before this cold little fish escapes the pond. What is it, Anya?'

They passed at the phone box, she heading north, he south, lost in the crowd on the pavement, swelled by the sudden influx of happy tourists now leaving the phone box to stand alone once more; empty, unused, a curious memory in a world that had moved on and left it.

'Timing, Ray,' Anya said without a trace of the laughter they so often shared together. 'We've really got to work on your timing.'